D0062688

Hot Property

SUSAN JOHNSON

BERKLEY SENSATION, NEW YORK

THE BERKLEY PUBLISHING GROUP
Published by the Penguin Group
Penguin Group (USA) Inc.
375 Hudson Street, New York, New York 10014, USA
Penguin Group (Canada), 90 Eglinton Avenue East, Suite 700, Toronto, Ontario M4P 2Y3, Canada
(a division of Pearson Penguin Canada Inc.)
Penguin Books Ltd., 80 Strand, London WC2R 0RL, England
Penguin Group Ireland, 25 St. Stephen's Green, Dublin 2, Ireland (a division of Penguin Books Ltd.)
Penguin Group (Australia), 250 Camberwell Road, Camberwell, Victoria 3124, Australia
(a division of Pearson Australia Group Pty. Ltd.)
Penguin Books India Pvt. Ltd., 11 Community Centre, Panchsheel Park, New Delhi—110 017, India
Penguin Group (NZ), 67 Apollo Drive, Rosedale, North Shore 0632, New Zealand
(a division of Pearson New Zealand Ltd.)
Penguin Books (South Africa) (Pty.) Ltd., 24 Sturdee Avenue, Rosebank, Johannesburg 2196,
South Africa

Penguin Books Ltd., Registered Offices: 80 Strand, London WC2R 0RL, England

This book is an original publication of The Berkley Publishing Group.

Copyright © 2008 by Susan Johnson
Text design by Kristin del Rosario

First edition: August 2008

Library of Congress Cataloging-in-Publication Data

Johnson, Susan, 1939–
    Hot property / Susan Johnson.— 1st ed.
        p.   cm.
    ISBN 978-0-425-22173-0 (trade pbk.)
    1. Women journalists—Fiction.   2. Intelligence officers—Fiction.   I. Title.
    PS3560.O386458H68   2008
    813'.54—dc22   2008010702

PRINTED IN THE UNITED STATES OF AMERICA

10 9 8 7 6 5 4 3 2 1

One

 "Ask him AGAIN where the goddamn Serb paras are! Don't *look* at me like that! That's a fucking ORDER!!"

"He doesn't know anything! How many times do I have to tell you—he's just a farmer! Give it up you SICK SON OF A BITCH!!"

The two men shouting at each other had been on opposite sides of the interrogation issue from the moment they'd met three months ago. Harry Miller thought you could beat the truth out of people, and after the defeats at the Marine barracks in Lebanon and then again at Mogadishu, he was the first one to point out the military annex to the Balkan peace accord. "We have the *authority*," he would remind anyone daring to question his brutality, "to use deadly force if necessary to carry out our responsibilities." For Harry that meant coming down like a ton of bricks on anyone who got in his way.

As a civilian interpreter, Nick Mirovic hadn't signed on to watch someone beat the hell out of people. Not only did he disapprove of torture on principle, too many of Harry's interrogations ended badly—like with dead bodies and no information. Pretty much like now if he couldn't blast through Harry's one-track psycho mentality. "Isn't the point to get information? Let up a little, dammit. This poor guy is choking on his own blood . . . *Oh fuck*." Nick shut his eyes and inhaled deeply. Opening his eyes a second later, he said bitterly, "I hope you got your rocks off, you murderous motherfucker. You killed another one." Then he hauled off and slugged Harry Miller so hard, he heard Harry's jaw crack before he dropped to the basement floor like the sack of shit he was. Standing over the unconscious man, fists clenched and breathing hard, Nick was so filled with loathing for the CIA agent that if two Pfc grunts hadn't been upstairs guarding the building, he would have put a couple of 9mm rounds into Harry's worthless head.

Instead, he knelt by the farmer's bloodied, broken body, gently closed his eyes, and murmured a totally inadequate prayer. Frustrated and pissed, the dank smell of the basement closing in around him, he felt as though he was sinking into a bottomless pit of depravity. He'd been caught up in Harry's cold-blooded cycle of violence too long. He hardly knew himself anymore. Although one thing he *did* know—he was going to hell for his part in these off-the-record operations.

He always came awake with a start as he found himself plunging into the flames of hell. Dripping with sweat, yet chilled to the bone, he'd try to shake off the horror of those months in Kosovo.

Then he'd reach for the bottle he kept by his bed or think about calling Lucy, who liked to fuck, not talk. After a few stiff shots to blur the most corrosive of his memories, he'd usually pass on the Lucy idea, though, because even with Lucy there was bound to be complications somewhere down the road. He'd generally flick on the TV instead and watch whatever dreck was on until the sun came up the next morning.

The rising sun had become his salvation.

There were times when he'd just sit in the dark on the porch watching the horizon like a besieged trooper in some western movie waiting for the cavalry to come riding over the hill. As the first rays of the morning sun rose above the lake and hit his retinas he'd feel his muscles relax and he'd know he'd made it through another bad night.

A lot of years had passed since that NATO peacekeeping mission in Kosovo, and his nightmares were less frequent. But they weren't completely gone. He could have used pharmaceuticals for his post-traumatic stress disorder, but he didn't like what they did to his head. For better or worse, he preferred living in the real world. Although some days it was definitely not for the better.

Two

This is the reason I rented this place, Zoe Chandler thought, walking barefoot down her sandy driveway to the mailbox on the narrow dirt road that serviced the cabins on the lake.

Peace and quiet.

No neighbors in sight.

Total seclusion.

Okay—so she'd also rented the cabin because she'd always been fond of the old Skubic place *and* it was only two miles to Ely and one of the best baristas she'd ever run across. When one had a serious caffeine habit, that distance factor trumped lesser issues like say, *pretty much everything else*.

She smiled at the beauty of the sunny landscape before her, at the memory of Janie's super triple espresso that morning, at the thought of Joe's call from Trieste last night that had filled in another piece of the puzzle. She was feeling smugly self-satisfied. This was the perfect spot to finish her book. She was far away from the usual interruptions of her life in the city, and if she didn't get her ass sued by one of the major art collectors in the world as a result of her research—really, life couldn't get much better.

Or maybe it could. Was that gorgeous man wearing cargo shorts and nothing else taking his mail out of the mailbox next to hers for *real* or was she hallucinating? Lengthening her stride, she quickly closed the distance between them. Not that she was necessarily on the make, but seriously, someone who looked like he could press three hundred pounds without breaking a sweat was at least worth a polite hello.

"Morning," she said, approaching the rickety stand that supported the two old mailboxes, thinking "tall, dark, and handsome" didn't begin to do him justice.

Nick Mirovic stopped flipping through his mail and looked up. "Mornin'."

While his response wasn't what you'd call friendly, it wasn't exactly hostile. "I just moved in a couple weeks ago," Zoe said, figuring what did she have to lose. "Are you vacationing here, too?"

He'd been half turning to leave and swung back. "Nope, live here," he said in a gruff tone clearly meant to deter further conversation.

As he'd swivelled back, Zoe noticed a ragged scar that ran from under his armpit to his waist. For someone who was known for her nosiness, who made a living investigating things people didn't want investigated, a scar like that screamed for an explanation. Was it a hunting accident? Everyone up here hunted. But before she could conjure up a tactful query, he was walking away.

Not that the view from behind wasn't worth watching. Broad, muscled shoulders, long, lean torso, slim hips, strong legs, and either a nice tan or a natural swarthiness. Whoever her neighbor was—he was *real* easy on the eyes.

Nick had heard the Skubic place had been rented for the summer, but enough acreage separated their cabins that he'd not seen the new occupant before. Nice green eyes, nice blonde hair, and nice everything else, too. Not that he was interested. In fact, the last thing he was looking for was company. He liked his hermitage. He actually needed it, and if he ever was in the mood for something more, there was always Lucy. She and her husband played around. They had one of those modern marriages. But hey, it worked for them and occasionally for him.

It might be a good idea to pick up his mail after dark; that way he'd avoid anymore questions.

Although his new neighbor did have damned nice legs, her little pink shorts barely covering the essentials. Big-city girl, he'd say, from the look of her. The locals didn't wear shorts like that. And they didn't much go for bikini waxes either.

Three

Later that day, Zoe drove into town to get her afternoon caffeine fix.

Janie Sims, owner of the Front Porch Coffee Company, was reading a magazine at a table near the window. This wasn't a busy time of day, not to mention the week before Memorial Day was pre-tourist season. Looking up as Zoe walked in, she flipped back a lock of black hair from her eyes. "Cute shorts."

"Thanks. It's too hot today for jeans."

Janie slapped her magazine shut. "The usual?"

"Please."

Coming to her feet with a graceful spring—the result of hours of yoga and considerable caffeine—Janie walked toward the counter. "How's the book coming?"

"Good. Very good, in fact. I might actually be finished with the first draft by the middle of next month." Janie was one of those people you felt you knew after five minutes. Genuinely friendly, nonjudgmental, and not to be discounted—the Holy Grail of gossip for the entire town. "I met my neighbor this morning." Zoe's pale brows lifted into perfect arcs. "He's definitely movie star material."

"You must mean Nick. He's to lust after, isn't he? Not that he goes out much. He's kind of a hermit. If I was a little younger"—Janie grinned—"I might think about giving him a shot."

Janie was a well-preserved late forties, divorced, her kids grown and out of the house. "The older woman–younger man thing is alive and well, Janie," Zoe said with a smile. "Go for it."

Janie's gaze narrowed faintly. "Actually, it's probably more about timing than age." She smiled. "Mitch has decided to get possessive."

No matter Zoe had only been in town two weeks, it was impossible to miss Mitch Janisek. First, he was in Janie's place a whole lot, and second, he had to be six feet six if he was an inch, three hundred pounds, and definitely younger than Janie. "Sounds like you're set. No sense rocking the boat."

"That's what I was thinking. Want me to put in the sugar?"

"Sure. So tell me about this Nick. Is he like a Unibomber kind of hermit or a pipe-smoking, sherry-drinking recluse who reads Keats?"

"Neither. He's just been keeping to himself since he came back."

"Came back from where?"

"Dunno. Europe I heard, then some military hospital or military something or other, and a marriage that went bad somewhere along the way. He's not exactly dishing out details."

"A military hospital; that explains that really long scar."

"Could be. He didn't have it when he left town."

"He must have been in the army."

"God, no, not Nick. He's not a joiner. His work with whatever this military stuff was—like I say, he's not giving up much—had to do with his linguistic background. He taught Slavic languages in a college somewhere out east. Then last winter when old Frank Mirovic was dying, he came back to take care of his grandpa and stayed on after Frank died. He's working on making himself a canoe. I hear it's his therapy of choice."

"So there *is* something wrong with him."

"Not that I know of. He just likes to be alone. Could be his divorce—it was nasty, apparently. Although there's nothing particularly strange about liking to be alone up here. We have lots of people who live by themselves in the bush."

Zoe had been raised partly in the Cities, but her grandparents had had a vacation cabin in the area she'd visited as a child. It had been sold long ago, but she understood the penchant for solitude that was a way of life in the North Woods. "I don't have to worry about some screwball living next door, then."

"Nah. Nick's as normal as anyone. Hunts, fishes, camps—you know, does guy things."

"That's reassuring. I'd hate to think of all that gorgeousness going to waste."

"Don't get your hopes up, darlin'. He's locked up pretty tight—except for Lucy Chenko, who pays him a visit from time to time. Otherwise, no one's been able to get near him."

"Who's Lucy Chenko and what does *she* have that interests him?"

"No-strings availability, I'd say. Lucy's our local Paris Hilton. Came from money, married money, and she and her husband, Donnie, like to sleep around."

"So this Nick doesn't like his solitude sex-free."

"Nope. Although, believe me, a guy like him could have it twenty-four seven if he wanted it. He comes in here for an espresso once in awhile." She grinned. "He's not addicted like you. Anyway, he politely brushes off all the females who hit on him. Real nicely, mind you. He's not an ass. There you go, sweetie," Janie said, sliding the triple espresso with ice toward Zoe. "That should crank you up."

"Thanks." Zoe handed Janie a few bills and picked up her coffee. "See you tomorrow."

Her cell phone rang as she reached her car. Flipping it open, she said, "Hey, I thought you were flying back today."

"Forget about that. I've got big news, babe. Listen to this."

Zoe's researcher-slash-investigator, Joe Strickland, began to explain how he'd made contact with one of the men who had actually been involved in the illegal excavation of the Roman site on the Adriatic. Suddenly, any thoughts about neighbors, gorgeous or not, available or not, screwball or not, became irrelevant.

Four

Nick looked up as the door of his grandfather's workshop opened. Taking the brass tacks out of his mouth, he smiled. "You're early."

"My composition class was cancelled. You must have started at the crack of dawn. The planking's almost finished."

"Yeah. I couldn't sleep. You can do the rest of the straight ones if you want. I'll work on the wedge-shaped pieces." Chris Smith was a young Ojibway who'd started hanging out in the shop, wanting to learn how to build a canoe. It hadn't taken long to get used to having him around. Chris had a quietness about him that was soothing.

Or maybe it was that Chris reminded him of himself. Nick had started out as a gofer for his grandpa, learning the craft little by little, doing the easy stuff first, graduating to more difficult tasks, eventually building his first canoe from start to finish when he was seventeen. He was still using that canoe. Nothing tracked as well even in three-foot waves or glided through the water as smoothly or paddled as easily. If he needed religion, that was it—him alone on a lake somewhere in that old canoe.

Picking up the hammer with the curved handle Frank had designed to get into corners, Chris shot a look at Nick. "Your new neighbor in her Porsche convertible turned into her driveway just ahead of me. She's definitely sweet—so's her ride. Where's she from?"

"Don't know."

Chris grinned. "Someone like that—it might pay to find out."

"She's all yours."

"As if I want to piss off Dee Dee. Besides, the lady's too big-city for me."

"And not eighteen either," Nick said, drily.

"Okay, that, too. Although you know what they say about older women."

"To anyone but you, she's not an older woman."

"At least you noticed." Chris couldn't understand why Nick didn't take advantage of all the women who were after him.

"She's hard not to notice."

"So invite her over for a drink."

"If only I was looking for female company."

"You're crazy not to—oops—sorry, but you know what I mean."

Chris always treaded lightly when it came to Nick's reclusive lifestyle. "Yeah, kid, I know what you mean. Look, maybe

I'll invite her over sometime," he added to assuage Chris's embarrassment. "You and Dee Dee come over, too."

"How about Saturday? We're not doing anything."

Nick smiled at Chris's youthful enthusiasm. "I'll let you know." Not that he had any intention of inviting the blonde next door over for a drink. As if he needed more problems in his life; for all he knew she was married anyway. Yeah, right—practiced at noticing details, he'd seen that she'd worn neither a wedding nor engagement ring. And she had come on to him—not overtly, but she would have kept talking if he had. "What say we break early and see how the fishing is in the north bay?" Nick suggested, wanting to change the subject, not wanting to think about the good-looking blonde next door.

"Sounds like a plan."

"Let's try those old Forselius lures. We had good luck with them last time." Back on safe ground, Nick wiped the glue off his hands with a turpentine rag. "Five bucks says I catch the first bass."

Chris grinned. "No way."

While the men in Frank's workshop had been discussing her, Zoe had been busy composing an e-mail to her source in the Tutela Patrimonio Culturale (TPC), the arm of the carabinieri charged with protecting Italy's cultural heritage. She was hoping to corroborate some of Joe's new findings. Roberto Fiorilli was willing to exchange information with her in a mutual quid pro quo so long as she didn't publish anything that might jeopardize the TPC's ongoing operations.

In the case of the book she was currently working on, he was more than willing to cooperate since the major American collection she was investigating consisted almost exclusively of looted artifacts from Italy. Museums could be persuaded to return illicit objects in exchange for long-term loans of equal rarity. In the case of an individual collector, however, the Italian government couldn't offer anything more to the collector than the satisfaction that he'd acted ethically in returning the items.

As if that was a good argument for people who had a reputation for dubious purchases in the art market. Like the billionaire couple she was investigating, for instance.

Zoe sent Roberto a list of the items Joe's intelligence had unearthed. At least a dozen pieces from the Adriatic site matched ones in the Willerby collection.

She always felt a real thrill of elation at times like this, when a trail of assumptions and deductions finally brought conclusive results.

Not that she could do her work without Joe. He was her man on the ground who could disappear into a crowd without anyone recalling him. Joe was middle-size, middle-weight, of indeterminate age with a face as malleable as rubber. That he'd started out as an actor off-Broadway was a definite advantage in his line of work.

Zoe's disadvantage was that people remembered her. A tall blonde didn't melt into a crowd with the same anonymity. On the other hand, she knew the gallery scene inside out, not to mention her previous exposés of the underbelly of the art market were advantageous. She had a multitude of contacts in the art world: with law enforcement, for instance, if she needed entrée into custom manifests or IRS documents, or with private collectors, who were an incestuous, jealous lot. She was often the recipient of sniping comments apropos of a rival's new acquisition that may or may not have a legitimate provenance.

Closing her e-mail with thanks and best wishes to Roberto on the birth of his first child, she hit the Send key and sat back with a contented smile.

Really, this investigation was falling into place without a hitch.

Maybe she'd been doing this so long now that she'd finally gotten the hang of it. Or maybe Joe had just lucked out in Trieste.

She quickly crossed her fingers, just in case. She never willingly pissed off Lady Luck. Call her irrational, but those childhood impulses were tough to break.

Five

At the same time Zoe was congratulating herself on her smoothly running research effort, a woman with enough diamonds on her fingers to illuminate Times Square at midnight was tapping her bloodred nails on the arm of a white brocade sofa. Seated beside her was an elderly man who appeared to be perfectly composed. Opposite the couple dressed in casual elegance was an attorney from a prominent New York law firm nervously perched on the edge of an azure silk settee. He looked out of place in the Hamptons in his pinstripes and polished wing tips. But then visitors often did in this world of wealth and privilege.

Or perhaps he appeared out of his element for other reasons.

In contrast to the summer sun sparkling off the ocean outside, the mood in the lavish drawing room was decidedly unsunny.

"You aren't required to return any of your collection," the attorney reiterated, smiling in an attempt to mitigate the obvious displeasure of his client's trophy wife. "The Italian government can't do more than ask. They have no leverage. None at all."

"We understand all of that, George," the woman snapped, waving her be-ringed fingers in a dismissive gesture. "We're not novices in this field." Her voice rose in anger. "We have the largest collection of ancient artifacts in the world for heaven's sake!"

"What Gwyneth means," the elderly man interposed, reaching over to place his hand on his wife's in either affection or deterrence, "is that we don't wish to be the object of scandal. As you know, Zoe Chandler is investigating this matter. As you also know, since you defended Letitia Rankle, Miss Chandler's last book embarrassed Bothwell's immeasurably. If not for her, the world would have been ignorant of those behind-the-scenes machinations at the auction house. I need not tell you how much we abhor the thought of being the subject of scrutiny. I expect you to do something to stop this probe. Is that clear?" He spoke with the authority that a ten-billion-dollar fortune conferred.

"Yes, of course." George Harmon hesitated. Dare he ask what the parameters might be in terms of stopping Zoe Chandler?

Bill Willerby had not amassed his wealth without a formidable intellect. "Pay any price. I'm sure she has one." He smiled tightly. "Certainly, the sum Miss Chandler realizes from a book like this is manageable."

"For my part, I wouldn't give her a dime!" his wife heatedly countered, tossing her head in a little dramatic gesture that flaunted her black tresses as well as her umbrage. "That Chandler bitch is nothing but a scandalmonger! It's time someone informs her in no uncertain terms that her meddling is unwelcome!"

Bill Willerby held his attorney's gaze for a telling moment. "Why don't we begin politely." Turning to his wife, he touched her flushed cheek. "George will take care of everything, darling. Don't worry your little head another minute."

Gwyneth Willerby, who had once been the celebrated face of Estée Lauder, pursed her lips in a sultry pout. "If you're sure she won't say terrible things about us."

"I'm sure." The CEO of numerous international corporations glanced at his attorney. "Tell her you're sure, George."

"Yes, absolutely, Mrs. Willerby. You needn't worry."

"Thank you for coming out." Bill Willerby nodded at his attorney. "Keep us posted."

Rising from his chair, George Harmon took his dismissal with good grace. The Willerby account was not only worth the journey to the Hamptons, but worth a certain degree of subservience. "I'll let you know as soon as I make contact with Miss Chandler."

"With all speed if you will," Bill Willerby gruffly noted.

"Yes, of course."

"I don't wish for this—er—matter to be left hanging."

"I understand." Since the large drawing room had been designed to display a number of their classical sculptures, Willerby's meaning was plain. Nevertheless, George Harmon swallowed hard as he exited the sumptuous room. Zoe Chandler was known for her dogged investigative skills. She might very well be a woman of principle—an old-fashioned concept in his estimation, but one not to be underestimated.

She could present problems.

He grimaced, understanding his plans to spend the weekend sailing were ruined.

It wouldn't be wise to delegate responsibility for this matter to a subordinate.

He would have to deal with Miss Chandler himself.

Six

Two days later, Nick was eating breakfast and reading the paper, the morning TV news playing softly in the background. At the sound of the name Harry Miller, his gaze shot up, his full attention suddenly focused on the small TV sitting on top of the fridge. *"This is breaking news from the White House. We'll give more details on the short list for CIA director as they reach us."*

Reaching for the remote, Nick began flipping through channels, hoping to hear more information on the possible appointment of the man who most likely had a hand in his near-death experience in Kosovo. *If* Harry was picked for CIA director that meant congressional hearings, and *that* meant Harry would be covering his tracks any way he could. So much for his current life of relative peace and quiet.

Not finding anything more about the CIA directorship on

the other channels, Nick pushed away from the table, came to his feet, and moved toward his office. Alan Levaro kept up with the Washington rumor mill. If Harry was about to become a problem, he'd know it.

Turning on his computer, Nick quickly pulled up his e-mail and scrolled past the inevitable spam that got through no matter how much security was in place. He wasn't expecting much correspondence; very few people had his e-mail address. Oh, crap—there it was . . . just when he'd thought he was home free. Clicking on Alan's acronym, *snafu,* he opened the encrypted message based on the Croatian alphabet, a language they both spoke. Nick swiftly translated: *Watch your back, buddy. Harry's gonna be cleaning up his resume if his name is put forward for CIA director. I'm in Vegas.* Which didn't actually mean he was in Vegas. Alan, an ex-CIA agent, didn't even trust encryptions. "Vegas" meant he was holed up at his place near Vancouver. Sending a brief reply, Nick thanked Alan for the heads-up, and asked him to keep him current on Harry's progress toward big-time status. Then, shutting down his computer, Nick leaned back in his chair and swore a blue streak.

He should have squared the scales of justice with Harry years ago. Not that being laid up in the hospital for sixteen months after that *incident* with friendly fire on his last day in Kosovo hadn't forestalled his more lethal instincts. But still, he could have offed Harry that day in that basement outside Pristina. The world would have been a better place—not to mention, *his* life wouldn't be at risk now.

Nick knew too much about Harry Miller's penchant for torture. And while it might not have mattered before—after all, CIA covert activities were not white-glove affairs—if distasteful details about torture were to emerge in a congressional hearing, it wouldn't be good for either Harry's or America's image.

On the other hand, maybe there was no need to get all bent out of shape right now. Harry was just *on* the short list for CIA director. He might not make the cut. If he did, though, Harry was sure to look him up. Nick knew too much about all those *accidental* deaths in Kosovo.

Calm down; take it easy. Nothing's a done deal yet. Time enough to sharpen his survival skills. Right now, after checking his man traps, he was going to head out on the lake. Being alone on the water always helped to clear his mind; the solitude made it easier for him to put things into perspective. For instance, he probably shouldn't do anything rash.

Although, if Harry came after him—well, then, that was another matter. Killing him would be justifiable self-defense. Nick smiled faintly at the prospect. Finally, he might have payback for being dragged into Harry's circle of hell. A further bonus would be the satisfaction of settling the score for all his fucked-up years since Kosovo.

After finding all his trip wires intact, Nick walked toward the dock, his thoughts focused on how to best counter or neutralize Harry. Not that getting out of Dodge might not be a temporary alternative. If Harry sent out hit men, he'd prefer they come to him somewhere less populated.

A few moments later as Nick entered his boathouse to pick up his canoe paddles, he heard his neighbor's voice echoing crystal clear across the stretch of water separating their docks.

"Who the *hell* do you think you are coming out here and *threatening* me!"

That was definitely a pissed-off tone. The answering male voice was less clear; it was low, controlled, mildly insistent with that don't-fuck-with-me false courtesy he'd heard many times before. From intelligence agents.

His adrenaline kicked in big-time, his pulse picked up speed, and quickly moving to the other side of the boathouse, he stopped at the door that faced Skubic's dock. Silently easing it open a crack, he surveyed the scene on the neighboring dock.

"Go back from wherever you came from and leave me alone! *Go*, dammit!"

"Be sensible. We can talk about it, come to some agreement," the shorter of the two overdressed men said.

No way those guys are tourists in those sport coats, slacks, and shiny leather shoes, Nick thought, his paranoia spiking. *Law enforcement*, he decided, *or CIA*. They had the look.

The tall blonde was standing with her back to the water, facing the men with the same bold assertion as her uncompromising statements. That courageous posture only added to Nick's unease. Most women would be intimidated by two good-sized men who apparently had threatened her. Not her, though. She looked about ready to fling her coffee cup at them.

"I'm telling you my answer won't change—not tomorrow, or the next day, or *ever*! There's no agreement to come to! Now get the hell out or I'll call the sheriff!"

One of the men took a step toward her and Nick saw the woman draw in a deep breath. But she stood her ground. Either she didn't scare easily or she was seriously naive. A third possibility leaped into Nick's mind: Could Harry have staged this event? *Is the gorgeous blonde a plant*, he cynically wondered?

Was this a setup?

She couldn't have seen him enter his boathouse from the opposite dock, but it didn't matter. *She* was visible from his cabin and her voice was loud enough to carry up the hill to his place.

Harry could have arranged this little scene—having the beautiful blonde move in next door in order to get close to him. Harry had to have known that he was being considered for CIA director. After all, he'd spent his entire career kissing ass and covering up his mistakes for exactly this moment.

Unfortunately, Nick could confirm a number of those mistakes in bloody detail—including the one that nearly killed him the day he'd left Harry's employ. On that last mission for NATO, he and his driver had been en route to Macedonia to deliver instructions to an observer team in the mountains. The shoulder-fired missile that had struck the Hummer, killed his driver, and tore him to shreds was American. There was never any doubt in Nick's mind who had ordered the hit.

So bottom line, he wasn't going to get involved in the scene next door.

Unless the lady was seriously threatened.

And even then, he'd debate his options.

Since Kosovo, he'd developed a healthy cynicism when it came to trusting anyone and anything. And that was especially true today with the news about Harry Miller.

The two well-dressed men abruptly turned and walked

away, and Nick exhaled a sigh of relief. He supposed it would have been neighborly to go over and see if the lady was okay. In another lifetime, he might have.

Instead, he waited until she walked up the stairs to her cabin and disappeared inside.

Closing the door, he moved to pick up his paddles and exited the boathouse on the opposite side. Walking down the dock, he stepped into his canoe, loosened the moorings, and pushed away from the dock.

As he paddled out to the middle of the lake, he contemplated his vulnerabilities and risks.

Harry had contacts who would dispose of anyone for a price.

Not that he was the only person on Harry's enemy's list.

But he was up there, he figured, after threatening to expose Harry for his ruthless, cold-blooded killings during the Kosovo operations. The day he'd left for the Macedonian assignment, he'd told Harry he was done with interrogations; he hadn't signed on for that kind of shit. He'd told Harry he could shove it all up his ass and anyone else's clear up the line who didn't like him bailing. And if they had any questions about why he was leaving, he'd be glad to explain.

First approached by the CIA because of his linguistic skills the previous year, he'd reluctantly agreed to help out the NATO effort. He'd dutifully performed his job, not begrudging the long, tedious hours listening to intercepts and translating for the intelligence agencies. But he'd never agreed to team up with an executioner. So *Sayonara*, he'd said to Harry that day in Kosovo. *I hope you rot in hell.*

Christ, the lake was peaceful in the morning.

It almost made one forget the brutality of people like Harry.

Almost . . .

Slipping his paddle under the center thwart, he leaned back on the mahogany gunwales he'd cut, boiled, varnished, and screwed into place all those years ago before he'd become a cynic. When he'd still thought the world was full of hope.

When his body hadn't been held together with steel pins.

When he wasn't always looking over his shoulder.

Shit.

So he'd run into bad luck, bad karma—whatever—it wasn't going away.

Now then, if Harry made a move on him, how exactly would he kill him?

Seven

"Where have you been? I've been trying to reach you for over an hour." It was a rhetorical question; Joe didn't get a chance to answer. "You won't *believe* who came to buy me off," Zoe indignantly rapped out.

"Let me guess," Joe said, a smile in his voice. "Does the last name begin with a *W*?"

"Can you freaking *believe* it?"

"Darling, don't be so naive. Why wouldn't they try to buy you off? You're about to screw up their lives and more to the point, screw with their precious collection."

"I told them no, of course."

"They'll be back with a better offer. Willerby can buy off God."

"I don't want to be bought off."

"I know. But people like Willerby think everyone has their

price. Seriously, though, he's not above other means if money doesn't work. I wonder if you should get out of there."

"*Jesus*, Joe! Don't say things like that! This isn't a movie. This is me you're talking to. You're not suggesting that Bill Willerby might actually harm me, are you?"

"It's a possibility. Men like him don't make the kind of money he's made by playing nice. He travels with bodyguards for a reason."

"Jeez, now you tell me."

"So would you have given up your book project if I'd told you before?" Joe asked, drily.

"Okay, okay. So maybe I'll get a bodyguard, too. Christ, how do you do something like that? Look one up in the Yellow Pages?"

"You won't find any agencies in that little burg you're in. It might be wise to go back to the Twin Cities. You'll find security agencies there. Although with this Iraq stuff going on and the big money in the Middle East, the security firms are struggling to fill their ranks."

"Actually," Zoe murmured, "I might have someone *here* who would fit the bill."

"Then go for it. I don't want to alarm you, but it wouldn't hurt to be cautious, at least until your publisher has your manuscript. Willerby could be notified at that point and then he'd have to deal with bigger fry than you. If there's really some dude up there who could watch your back, hire him. Otherwise, you'd better head back home."

"You're sounding way too ominous, Joe."

"You know how many objects in Willerby's collection are

pirated. Even more than we thought. The guy has a lot to lose. *Do not* take any chances."

Zoe softly sighed. "Remind me to stay away from billionaires next time I take on a project."

"You blew me off when I mentioned it, babe, if you recall. Is this where I say, 'I told you so'?"

"You're right—you're right. I was wrong. But not to worry, I'll deal with it. This guy next door looks like he could stop a Mack truck. I'll talk to him."

Zoe's audacity always amazed Joe; she wasn't easily intimidated. Maybe it had to do with being raised in the Amazon by parents who were studying indigenous tribal cultures. She'd learned to cope with unusual situations. "Let me know whether you stay there or head back home," Joe said. "And I'd suggest moving quickly on this. If Willerby sent out two representatives from New York, right now they're back in their hotel room asking him for further instructions."

"Cripes," Zoe muttered. "And I was looking forward to a peaceful summer at the lake."

"Then maybe you should think about some other line of work."

"If I was looking for sarcasm, sweetie, I'd call my ex, who by the way just married his third wife."

"There'll be more," Joe bluntly noted. "It doesn't matter I hope."

"God no . . . Max is ancient history."

"Then first things first. Get yourself some defense or pack up and drive back to the Cities. Consider this my professional opinion."

His stern tone of voice was not to be ignored. "Yes, sir, right away, sir."

"Cute. Now go do it—talk to your Mack truck. Call me back and let me know if he said yes or no."

Eight

Having come up with contingency plans in what passed for his therapist's office out on the lake, Nick was nearing his dock when he heard the sound of the alarm going off behind his cabin. Driving his paddle deep into the water for a surge of speed, he gave Harry points for not wasting any time. The instant his canoe slid alongside the cedar pilings of the dock, he jumped out, secured the craft with a quick knot on the mooring ring, then ran full out toward the noise.

The entire perimeter of his cabin was booby-trapped—a skill he'd picked up in the Balkans, where walking into a village was a tricky affair. Everyone had had to stay alert for that hair-thin wire attached to a grenade behind a door, or a stack of strategically placed debris blocking a path, or a thousand other traps that could be devised by the human mind. After having searched the seventeenth village, the team he'd been with had become textbook proficient. There wasn't a crawl space or attic or barn loft that hadn't offered up a quick trip to the grave for the unwary. He still couldn't enter his house without automatically ticking off his safety list.

He saw her before she saw him. But then that was the point.

She must have come through the woods because she'd stopped just west of his cabin when the alarm had gone off. She didn't have that deer-in-the-headlights look he'd expected—which was not reassuring.

But time enough to brand her as Harry's proxy when he had all the facts.

Or—realistically if he was dealing with Harry—*some* of the facts.

Slipping his combat knife back into its sheath, he silently circled around, approached her from behind, and disengaged the trip wire to the alarm.

She spun around as the blaring stopped. "How did I set off your car alarm from here?"

Her gaze was direct: not assertive, just straight and unswerving, as though someone had taught her to look people in the eye. "That damned thing goes off at the weirdest times," he said with a polite smile. He'd deliberately chosen a sound that wouldn't cause undue comment, although no one had set off his alarm before. "Most people come down the driveway," he added, watching her closely for her answer.

"I took the lazy person's way. Sorry."

No blink, no twitch. Nothing. "Not a problem," he said. "What can I do for you?"

His voice was flat; he so obviously didn't want to know what he could do for her that Zoe blushed. "I probably shouldn't have come." Her lashes drifted downward in embarrassment for a millisecond before she met his gaze once again and, taking a breath, said in a spilling-the-beans rush, "Actually, I have a problem I thought you might be able to help me with."

His first irreverent thought was, if it was about sex he was onboard. She was wearing green shorts today, not pink, but they were just as sexy. "I'm not much of a problem solver," he murmured, not about to fall for the world's oldest lure, no matter how tempting. Although, he had to admit, he preferred seeing *her* rather than one of Harry's gorillas.

"I understand. Janie said you like your privacy—"

"She did, did she? What else did she say?"

His unexpected smile—the first real smile she'd seen from him—encouraged her. She quickly plunged on. "Knowing I'd rented the Skubic place, Janie mentioned you were my neighbor. She spoke of you in the most exemplary way," Zoe tactfully added.

"She must be a good liar," he said, looking amused. "Now, tell me what you want. I'll listen at least."

That didn't sound like a man willing to help her. "I wish I could say I'd come over for a cup of sugar, but it's more complicated."

"Isn't everything," he drawled.

It was as though he had his drawbridge up permanently. Not only his words—his body language was also defensive. Even his T-shirt, emblazoned with the cartoon image of Yosemite Sam, literally read, "BACK OFF." But he was indeed brawny and large, and in her present predicament, she needed that sizeable power. Along with that lethal-looking knife hanging from his belt. "It's sort of a long story," she murmured, glancing toward his cabin.

He should have said, "Come in, sit down, tell me," but he didn't because Harry might have sent her. "I've got plenty of time," he said instead.

"Would you mind if we sat over there?" Zoe pointed at a yellow metal glider set under some birch trees.

He hesitated for a fraction of a second, his first reaction negative. But then he thought, *What the hell—even if she is some fucking black belt, I should be able to take her.* "Sure, why not." He waved her forward.

Sitting down a moment later, she gave herself a push and smiled up at him. "I haven't swung on a glider since I was a kid."

"Be my guest." He stood a short distance away, his expression shuttered.

"You're pretty off-putting, you know."

"Years of practice."

"Why?"

His gaze turned cool. "I didn't ask you to come over."

"Forgive me. I'm way out of line. I'm really sorry."

Having translated for more interrogations than he'd ever wished to, he had a pretty good sense of when someone was lying. That was fucking genuine. Against his better judgment, against all the rules of personal engagement he'd adhered to for the past few years, he heard himself say, "I should apologize for my rudeness. I don't have much company; I'm afraid it shows. Tell me about your complicated problem."

"Are you going to keep standing there?"

"I don't have to, I guess." He sat down beside her, but he carefully maintained his distance.

He smells delicious, she thought, the combination of pine woods and peppermint bizarre on a man so intensely male. "Nice cologne," she said because she couldn't help herself. "You smell of peppermint."

You smell of fresh sheets and apple blossoms, he thought. "I carry them in my pocket." He tapped the pocket of his cargo shorts. "Want one?"

"Not right now." She smiled faintly. "You know—a man who eats peppermints can't be too dangerous."

His dark gaze was assessing. "Who said I was dangerous?"

"No one. You just look like you could deal with trouble— you know . . . you're so big and strong and intense."

Her answer was casual enough, but maybe she was good at what she did. *Enough small talk*, he decided. "I have to ask you something," he pointedly interjected, his voice taking on an edge. "Where are you from?"

"I live out East now, but mostly I was raised in the Amazon. My grandparents had a cabin near White Fish dam, though; I spent my summers in Ely." She grinned. "Does that pass muster?"

"Not exactly," he said, clipped and cool. "Give me your story on the men on your dock. I'd appreciate the truth if that's possible."

Her eyes widened. "You saw them there? Believe me, I'd be more than happy to tell you the truth. In fact, I came over to tell you about them and ask for your help."

He didn't answer. He just nodded, his dark gaze basilisk.

"You're a suspicious man," she murmured, suddenly not entirely sure Janie's benign view of Nick Mirovic was applicable. As he scowled at her, she was becoming less sure by the second that she'd made the right decision in coming over.

"I have reason to be."

His gruff statement sent an unwanted chill up her spine. His size and strength suddenly took on an ominous quality. "I may have made a mistake coming over. My problems are really none of your concern," she murmured. She leaned forward slightly as though to rise.

Putting his arm out, he checked her movement. "Stay," he mildly said. "I won't bite." Her fingers had been laced tightly in her lap, her knuckles still white from the pressure. Either she was a great actress or genuinely frightened. Going with his gut, he offered her a warm smile. "Look, if I can't help you, I know everyone in town. Maybe I could suggest someone else. I have my own problems right now, so I'm probably more on edge than usual."

A smile like his could effectively thaw the Arctic ice cap. Her apprehension instantly melted away. "Maybe Lucy Chenko could help you out," she quipped.

He did a quick double take.

"Sorry, I couldn't resist," she said with a grin. "You know gossip in small towns. I hear she's your release valve."

He gave her a considering look from under his lashes. "For the record—not just mine."

"I'm not in the least judgmental."

"I'm relieved," he drawled. "Are we done with this sub-ject?"

"Absolutely. I apologize for even mentioning it, but you looked so approachable suddenly, I guess I lost my head."

Talk about smiles that made one approachable. He found himself wondering whether she was into sex with strangers. A new phenomenon for him of late—that feeling of instant lust. But there was something about this long-legged blonde that rang all his bells. Then again, he wasn't sixteen, nor was this a particularly good time to strike up a new friendship, with Harry possibly breathing down his neck. Dragging himself back to reality, he said briskly, "Tell me what's up. Maybe I can help solve your problem."

Zoe explained about her book, Joe's recent discoveries, and the two men who had accosted her on her dock. "According to Joe, Bill Willerby isn't above ruthless tactics with his collection in jeopardy. Joe suggested it might be prudent to find myself a bodyguard. Since I'd prefer staying at the lake until I finish my book, I thought of you. I was hoping you wouldn't mind being my security detail for a few weeks. I'd be happy to pay whatever you'd like."

Man—that was one plausible story line, and if he wasn't thinking about losing himself in the Canadian wilderness until this mess with Harry was resolved, he might have been willing to play along with her—true story or not. He could have had some really fine sex—at least for the duration.

On the other hand, his outpost in Ontario would be a hel-luva lot more peaceful without her. Sure, he wouldn't have the sex, but then again, he wouldn't have to go without sleep wondering if she was going to slit his throat at night. "Like I said," he murmured, "I've got some issues of my own that are likely to take me farther north into the bush for a while. Maybe my cousin, Tony, could help you out. He's a pretty big guy, too."

Her eyes lit up. "How far up north?"

"Pretty far." No way was he going to tell her where.

"What do you think of me going with you?" she impetuously asked, sitting up a little straighter and holding his gaze, her voice animated. "I wouldn't be in your way for long. My manuscript should be in good shape in the not too distant future and Joe says once I send it to my publisher, Willerby won't be able to pressure me."

"Sorry. You don't know me. I don't know you. This is a private trip."

"I promise not to bother you at all," she said in a rush, a note of pleading in her voice. "I know how to live rough. I'd bring my own supplies. You wouldn't even know I was around."

Now *that* was highly unlikely. Although, he had to admit, it was damned tempting to bring her along. "Tempting, but no," he murmured, pretty sure even great sex wouldn't compensate for a knife in his back.

"*Please, pretty please . . .*" Suddenly, the perfect solution to her problems had materialized. Far, far up north was an excellent escape destination. Having been raised in the Amazon, the wilds, whether north or south, didn't matter to her. "Come *on*," she begged, lightly touching his arm. "I'd be *ever* so grateful. Really, *really* grateful."

His carnal impulses were translating that gratitude into

lurid possibilities. Not to mention, the tactile sensation of her fingertips on his skin was seriously revving up his lust. Which made sound decision making difficult. But if there was ever a time when clear thinking was required, when intemperate desire was patently inadvisable, when even considering her lying beneath him and begging for sex was supremely wrong—*this* was the time. "There's no electricity up there," he said in deterrence. But even as he spoke, he knew he should have said, unequivocally, *no*.

And he also knew why he hadn't.

"I'll bring extra batteries for my laptop."

He had a generator so she wouldn't actually need extra batteries, but having reined in his lust, he didn't mention it. "It could be dangerous. Seriously, there might be some people after me as well as you."

"Then, it's *perfect*! Don't you see—we could *help* each other. I can shoot a gun, whether for food or for—whatever," she said, so matter-of-factly the hairs on the back of his neck came to attention.

"I'm not sure I care to trust you with a gun."

Her emerald green eyes flared wide. "You think I'm involved with the people after you."

Involved—there was a tame word for Harry's motives. More important, why wasn't she concerned that he might have people after him? "I don't know if you're involved or not," he bluntly replied. "And I don't care to find out."

"I'm telling you, you're wrong. Ask me anything! Really—anything!" She spread her arms wide. "My life is an open book."

It might have been her gesture that was his undoing. Her breasts rose high with the sweeping motion, the fabric of her white T-shirt strained across the ripe plumpness of her breasts, highlighting her taut nipples. Then again, it might have been her appearance of artlessness that overrode his scruples. What if she was for real? "Let me think about it," he said.

"I don't have a whole lot of time." A faint urgency underlay her words. "Joe said Willerby's men are probably phoning him for more instructions even now."

He hesitated, his capacity for trust badly compromised.

"I don't think I can handle those men alone. If I could, I wouldn't press you. And if you didn't strike me as a man I could trust—I wouldn't ask." It was as though she suddenly *knew* with certainty that he was ubercompetent. "Maybe it's Karma that we're both in a pickle." She smiled. "What do you think?"

He thought describing his position in Harry's crosshairs as being in a *pickle* was the understatement of the century. He also understood that he was attracted to her on some level that could very well be Karma, because it sure as hell wasn't business as usual. "Look," he said, ignoring the little voice inside his head screaming, *Don't be stupid!* "I can at least offer you a short-term solution. We can go over to your place, pack up what you need, and bring it over here. Then, I'll check with some of my contacts before deciding for sure what *I'm* going to do. In the meantime, you'll be safe. I can guarantee you that."

"Because of your alarm," she said, waving toward the woods where she'd tripped the wire.

Because he was ready to shoot anyone who came too close.

But rather than frighten her, he said, "Yeah. I'm pretty well protected. It's a long story. I won't bore you with the details."

She smiled, feeling comforted and strangely content considering both the circumstances and their brief acquaintance. "If you let me go up north with you, you could tell me the details then. We'd have plenty of time."

Now there was temptation. Her alone with him at his outpost camp.

Steady. Keep cool. This was about survival, not sex.

"Why don't we get your stuff first. We'll see about the next step later." Coming to his feet, he held out his hand.

"Thanks," she said, placing her hand in his. "I feel safer already."

As his hand closed around hers and he pulled her to her feet, he felt something else entirely. Something he hadn't felt in a very long time. Maybe that's when he suspected he'd be taking her with him whether it was prudent or not.

And if she was Harry's girl, he might not get much sleep, but he'd have a helluva good time while he was discovering the truth.

Nine

Nick stood sentry outside while Zoe packed. He checked the lakeshore, the driveway, surveyed the woods separating their places, then went through the drill again. He was on his third patrol of the Skubic property when she came back out, loaded down with two large duffle bags and a backpack.

"These are sort of heavy," she said, as he met her and took the duffle bags from her. "Most of it's research notes I need."

He did a quick bicep curl with both duffle bags. "Hefty notes." *Or maybe lots of ammo*, his less trusting psyche reflected. She'd changed into slacks, a long-sleeved T-shirt, and moccasins, like she was going somewhere.

"My manuscript is in there, too," she explained, keeping up

with him as he started walking. "I also packed some boots just in case."

In case of what? Funny how the phrase *combat boots* suddenly leaped into his mind. Maybe having her in his house wasn't going to be such a good idea after all.

"I really can't thank you enough. Your letting me stay with you is a real relief," she said. "And if I've brought too much stuff, just let me know. I could probably get rid of some of my clothes. I do need my research notes though."

His libido instantly picked up on that getting-rid-of-her clothes line. Not a big surprise. "Don't worry. I've got plenty of room," he replied, when a sensible man would have said something about her finding someone else for security detail.

"Oh, good, because I really tried to pack only the *bare* minimum." She smiled. "After all those years in the Amazon, living an unadorned life isn't a problem."

Jeez. One suggestive phrase after another—*bare minimum*, *unadorned life*—it really got him thinking. Which meant he'd better get a grip on his libido or he was gonna be suckered in by the oldest trick in the book. Maybe he'd better tell whatever her name was—Christ, he didn't even know her name, which just went to show how some really fine T&A could fuck with your head. Anyway, he *should* tell her this wasn't going to work out, that she'd be better off hiring a bodyguard in the Cities.

Just as he was opting for abstinence in the face of some serious carnal temptation, she took a couple little happy-as-a-lark skipping steps, her boobs bounced in what could only be characterized as a highly erotic fashion, and his libido shoved risk factors clear out of the picture. *So what's the big deal if she stays the night*, his fast-talking libido whispered. *You can give her the bad news in the morning*.

"I feel ever so good now," she said flashing him a dazzling smile. "And considering Joe's alarmist warnings, that's no small feat. I'm really in your debt."

"No problem." And she looked way better than good—like a thousand times better. Which probably meant he'd gone without sex too long. Realistically, what guy wouldn't be thinking about fucking her with those luscious boobs bouncing along only inches away?

"You know what seems amazing? All my apprehension is gone. Like the creeps Willerby sent out don't matter—or at least not very much." She shot him a look. "That must be why people have bodyguards."

"I'm no bodyguard."

But he was smiling, so she wasn't afraid to say, "I feel safe with you, so whatever—it's working."

"You were just out of your element when those two stooges accosted you. It was natural for you to be apprehensive."

The casualness of his answer gave her the impression he was *not* out of his element when it came to danger. For an indecisive moment Zoe questioned her naivete in putting herself in his care. A second later, she recalled how Janie had called Nick Mirovic normal and nice, and consoled by that description, she said, "I suppose you're right. Although, I never thought something like this could ever happen to me."

He gave her a brows-lifted glance. "You mess with big-time crooks, you're bound to run into trouble."

"So I discovered."

Christ, if she's that simple, maybe Harry didn't sent her. "Surely you at least must have *considered* the Willerbys might take issue with your exposé."

"Reporters write exposés every day. I'm just investigating another illicit scheme. It's nothing personal."

"In my experience, powerful people feel that laws were made for somebody else. And believe me, when they're crossed, it's *always* personal."

His voice had taken on such a sharp edge, she felt another moment of doubt. Maybe she'd misread Willerby's lawyers. Maybe she didn't really need a bodyguard after all. "Joe might be wrong," she said, knowing even as she spoke that she was grasping at straws. "Willerby's errand boys might be traveling back to New York even now."

"Could be." And world peace could be just around the corner. "Look," Nick gently said, "there's no sense doing shoulda, coulda, woulda. We'll take a breather tonight, and come up with some plan of action in the morning. Okay?" He felt like he was talking to some kid who wanted to know there really was a Santa Claus.

Zoe blew out a breath and smiled. "Sounds like a plan." Then, running her fingers down his arm, she whispered, "Thanks."

Her light, grazing touch flipped on all his sexual receptors, images of kids and Santa Claus instantly dispelled and in their place an explicit vision of a naked, long-legged blonde lying in his bed. "Watch where you put your feet when we get to those birches ahead," he quickly declared, struggling to keep his mind on more pertinent issues. "Follow in my tracks to be safe."

Probably neither one of them was safe there unless he could keep his libido in check.

Ten

After they entered his house, Nick set down the duffle bags in the entry hall. "Don't freak," he said, "but I have to check out your gear."

"Not a problem."

He waved her to a bench set against a wall. It had several pairs of boots neatly lined up beneath and had once been painted blue—the much worn surface offering only hints of the original color.

Nick's distrust helped ease her reservations about him; they were both a little jumpy, she decided. Sitting down, she leaned back against one of the numerous jackets hanging from hooks on the wall above her. "You obviously hunt." She glanced up at the antlers lining the walls of the pine-paneled entry.

"Sometimes," he said, kneeling down and unzipping a bag. "My grandpa hunted. They're mostly his." He began lifting out items one after another, stacking them in neat piles—papers, books, clothes. Thankfully, not a round of ammo in sight.

Jeez he was gorgeous to look at—all male, honed to the inch, his powerful shoulders, arms, leg muscles flexing with the smooth fluidity of a finely tuned machine. Seriously tempted to reach out and touch those steel-hard muscles, Zoe suppressed the impulse and slid her hands under her legs instead. This was *not* the time to be thinking of turn-ons. Her luggage was currently being searched for God knows what, Willerby was possibly after her skin, and Nick Mirovic, no matter how movie star handsome, was not just another a pretty face.

"I need your backpack, too."

Startled by the sound of his voice, she looked up to meet his dark, enigmatic gaze. Apparently, this wasn't the first time he'd asked for her backpack. "Sorry, I zoned out." Long enough for him to have gone through her second duffle bag, she noted with surprise. Which meant either he was seriously God's gift to women or she had gone without sex too long.

He crooked his finger. "Now, babe."

The gruff ambiguity of his demand set off a lustful ripple that shimmered through her body without so much as a nod to good judgment. And rather than tamp down the wholly inappropriate response, with equal injudiciousness, she offered him a teasing smile. "What if I said no?"

His dark lashes lowered faintly and he didn't smile. "Don't fuck with me."

The man was definitely all business. Or had that been a fleeting flash of amusement in his gaze? Whatever it might have been, his look was deliberately no-nonsense and hurry-the-fuck-up right now. "You really are serious about this," she said, handing over her backpack.

"Gotta be," he said, taking out her laptop. He looked it over carefully—front and back—weighed it for a second in his hands, then slid off the battery cover. Lifting out the batteries, he put each of them up to his nose and took a good whiff.

"All the batteries are strictly from Best Buy," Zoe offered. "What are you looking for?"

Handing her the laptop, he kept his eyes on her face and said, "Turn it on."

"It won't blow up."

"Lucky for us. Run through your directory for me."

"This must be what the Inquisition felt like," she sardonically murmured, booting up her laptop.

"I don't have a dungeon."

She glanced up. "I hope that was a joke."

This time he actually smiled. "More or less."

If Janie hadn't vetted Nick Mirovic, she might have been seriously thinking of bolting for the door. He was definitely not the standard hunk next door. "These people after you," she queried. "Are they more dangerous than Willerby's hired help?"

"Hard to say. I don't know how badly Willerby wants you out of the way."

"Please—if you don't mind . . . no out-of-the-way insinuations. I want to sleep tonight." She still couldn't quite get her head completely around the fact that someone would actually harm her. Although, she wouldn't be here now if she had discounted it entirely. "Okay, here's what I have," she said, having pulled up her directory. "Take a look. Everything's pretty much related to my book."

A lengthy interval later, after having opened all her files and looked them over, Nick said, "Okay, we're good."

As she shut down her laptop, she gave him an appraising glance.

"You don't believe me, do you?"

He glanced up and offered her a bland smile. "Let's just say I'm not a hundred percent there yet." Returning to the task at hand, he pulled her toiletries out of her backpack—shampoo, conditioner, deodorant, perfume—held them up to the light, uncapped them, sniffed, capped them again, and put them away. He hesitated for a moment when he lifted out her pink razor, and then her purple vibrator, but a second later, he returned them, zipped up the pocket, and sitting back on his heels, said, "You *are* traveling light."

There was something in his tone, or maybe it was in his dark gaze. "Are you implying *for a woman* or is it something else?"

He was seriously thinking about frisking her.

She stared back at him. "What?"

"I was thinking I'd better do a quick body search. I'm not hittin' on you. I just don't like to take chances."

"Janie said you were in some military hospital. Did you learn this stuff in the military?"

She'd come to her feet, so she wasn't going to take offense. Good, he thought, rising and moving toward her. "I wasn't in the military, but I was mixed up with them for a while. And

I'm still dealing with the blowback." He slid his palms down her arms.

"Like how?" She should be more nervous about this strange man checking her out for weapons.

"Depends."

She was about to question him further. That was a nonanswer if she'd ever heard one. But he bent over just then, slid his hands down the outside of her legs, then quickly up the inside, brushing lightly over her crotch with businesslike efficiency and she instantly reacted in a decidedly unbusinesslike way. Her breath caught in her throat, a warm rush of pleasure zipped through her body from that brief point of contact and settled with lightning speed in her highly receptive pussy.

She almost said *Wow*, but stopped herself just in time.

And a good thing she did, because Nick straightened up and said, temperate and cool, like he was some eunuch, "Thanks for your patience. I'll show you your room."

Picking up her duffle bags, he walked into a living room dominated by a lake view and a large fieldstone fireplace. He moved down a hallway illuminated by a window at the far end and, stopping before a door, shoved it open with his foot. "This bedroom has a nice view of the lake."

Indeed it did. Floor to ceiling windows faced the lake, the casements open to a light breeze coming in off the water. The windows were obviously a recent addition to the original log cabin, as was the small bathroom.

"It's lovely," Zoe said, surveying the room. It was cozy and cabiny: a handmade bed covered in Hudson Bay blankets; a desk and chairs constructed from sturdy pine logs; a hooked rug with a pale background and pinecone motif covered the varnished floor—the floor's age evident in its deep golden patina. "Janie said this was your grandfather's home. Did he build it?"

"Uh-uh. My great-grandfather did. It was built in the 1930s. It's still solid." Not to be discounted when considering possible firepower directed at it. "I'm in the room next door," he added, dropping her bags on the floor. "Would you like a drink or iced tea or coffee while I find us something for lunch?"

"I'll take you out for lunch."

He shook his head. "I'd rather not leave the house. And I'm an okay cook," he added with a quick smile. "Don't worry."

As his footsteps receded down the hallway, Zoe moved her duffle bags from the middle of the floor. She thought about unpacking, but decided against it since Nick had said they'd make plans in the morning. Instead, she pulled a chair up to the window and, calculating the time in Trieste, decided Joe would still be up.

The phone rang and rang and rang. She was just about to hang up, when Joe breathlessly answered. "Sorry, I was in the shower. Are you staying in Ely or not?"

She heard a woman's voice in the background. He obviously had company. She'd make her conversation brief. "I'm staying—at least tonight. I'll let you know if my plans change tomorrow. That's it. End of report."

"I met someone from the museum here and some interesting facts have come to light," Joe said, apparently willing to chat. "She knows two or three of the site diggers and some intriguing details."

"Great—score for our side," Zoe replied. "Does that mean we have pertinent facts to cover our asses in case of legal problems?" A decided possibility since the visit of Willerby's two ambassadors of ill will.

"We have shipping receipts. Detailed ones—times, dates, descriptions, destination names, and addresses. And site photos. How's that?"

She could hear the buoyant cheer in Joe's voice. "I'd say we've got them in a corner."

"You'd better believe it. All you have to do now is stay safe and finish that manuscript."

"I'm doing what I can, but nothing's certain yet up here."

"Stay in touch, babe. Wait a minute . . . wait—hey—don't do that," he whispered. "Gotta go," he crisply said.

And the phone went dead.

Having heard the sound of Zoe's voice as he'd walked away, Nick had quietly retraced his steps and, stopping just short of her doorway, eavesdropped. Already suspicious of her sudden appearance in his life, what he heard of her conversation made him even more dubious. Her words, *end of report*, had an ominous ring, as did talk of *covering their asses*, and having someone *in a corner*. Her last comment about nothing being *certain yet up here* really got his attention.

Moving away toward the kitchen once she'd finished talking, he reminded himself that it wasn't as though he'd trusted her before. Her story about being threatened by Willerby was impossible to substantiate short of checking with Willerby himself. Which she no doubt knew.

He could interrogate her he supposed. He certainly had seen his share of the tactics used to gather information.

So—what would it be? Full steam ahead or punt?

He glanced at his grandmother's red teapot clock above the sink as he walked into the kitchen. It was going to be a long day and a longer night if he didn't toss out his new neighbor right now.

No sense in taking chances, the reasonable part of his brain pointed out.

You're overreacting, his libido quibbled. *Think of those beautiful long legs wrapped around your ass. Why send away centerfold material without valid evidence she's Harry's executioner?*

He exhaled softly, wavering between risk and due diligence.

Shit.

When in doubt have a drink, his psyche prompted—a decided habit since Kosovo. Moving to the fridge, he opened the freezer door, grabbed the Stoli Cristal, unscrewed the cap, lifted it to his mouth, and took a good slug. Okay—so booze wasn't the answer to every problem. But it served to smooth out the worst of the speed bumps on the road of life.

"I'll have one, too."

He turned around and saw her standing in the doorway, her smile killer, her heavy-lidded gaze oozing sex, her boobs awesome like the rest of her. Any inclination he might have had to kick her out bit the dust.

"It's been a not-so-good day," she said.

He'd lost count of his not-so-good days years ago. "Things'll get better," he politely said, even though the truth was uncertain and most likely unpalatable. "Wanna a glass— mix—ice cubes?" he asked, waving her to a seat at the Formica- topped kitchen table from the 1950s.

"A glass would be nice and a few ice cubes."

He carried over two glasses with ice cubes along with a small mason jar of raspberry juice he had in the fridge and, setting them down on the table, mixed a couple of drinks. Pushing one toward her, he took a seat opposite her, lifted his glass, and said with a smile, "To things picking up—benevolent-wise."

"Hear, hear." Smiling back, she raised her glass to her mouth and finished her drink in one fell swoop.

His brows rose. "Thirsty?"

"Frustrated. Willerby has really screwed with my schedule. By the way," she added, putting out her hand across the table, "we haven't been formally introduced. I'm Zoe Chandler."

"Nick Mirovic, as Janie already told you," he replied, shak- ing her hand. "And this is where I say, too bad we didn't meet under more pleasant circumstances."

"No kidding." She held out her empty glass. "Who would have thunk—right?"

He was too polite to say *you* should have, but maybe she was playing Little Miss Naive for a reason. "You could be right about Willerby's guys taking off," he said instead, taking her glass and pouring her another shot of vodka. "Who knows, come morning, your life might be back on schedule."

"I seriously hope so. What is that?" She pointed at the mason jar he was pouring from.

"My aunt picks wild raspberries every summer and puts up a few jars of this juice. She treats it like gold."

"I can see why. It's fabulous."

He gently shook the glass to mix the liquor and juice and handed it to her. "Just a warning. She believes in charms and hexes, too."

Zoe grinned. "As if things could get any worse."

He wasn't too sure about that, but he grinned back and lied. "You got that right."

They each had another drink and talked. Or rather Zoe talked and Nick mostly listened. She spoke of her initial trip to Trieste, and he wondered again if he was being set up. How many people traveled to that part of the world? Did she know he'd done extensive linguistic research only a short distance away in Croatia? Could be, he thought, and on that unsettling note, he poured himself another drink.

"There's a slew of court cases pertaining to stolen art on the dockets around the world right now—particularly in Italy," she explained. "Source countries are becoming more proactive in protecting their cultural heritage from tomb raiders and thieves in general. They're also demanding the return of antiquities that were spirited away in the past."

"I've seen the stories in the news. It seems at least once a month you read about some long-lost artwork being restored to the original owner's heirs."

"Like the Klimt paintings." Zoe's brows flickered. "Austria fought their restitution for forty years."

"Nice."

"Depends on your point of view, I suppose. The Nazis appropriated every major collection that came within their purview and carted most of it away to Berlin."

"And other less accessible points."

She smiled. "Yup. Some of it has never surfaced."

"Or it's in some private collection."

"That, too, but then it can never be publically sold or those holding the artwork will be slapped with a lawsuit."

"So why do the Willerbys think they can get away with their illicit purchases?" She'd mentioned the questionable sources for many of their antiquities when she'd first asked for his help.

"They bought a good deal of it before the mid-1990s, when museums and dealers were put on notice that they needed bona fide provenance credentials for any art sold. Also, most of their pieces came from newly excavated sites where no oversight was in place. But Joe found a museum employee who has incriminating testimony from some of the site diggers, as well as shipping manifests, dealers' sales records, actual sequential photos of pieces from the moment they came out of the ground. All of that should put added pressure on the Willerbys to relinquish the objects."

"Will the law require them to give up the art?"

"The Italian TPC—the carabinieri charged with protecting Italy's cultural heritage—will pursue the case. I've spoken to one of the investigators, but they prefer that stolen art be returned without litigation. It's less time-consuming for them. Court cases often last for decades. So the TPC offers deals to collectors and museums: If you give us this, we'll do that for you. The policy has been pretty successful."

"How did you decide to focus on the Willerby collection?"

As she spoke of the first bits of information that had come her way at a cocktail party in Milan of all places, and of the subsequent clues she and Joe had uncovered, he watched her from under his lashes. He preferred that she hold center stage and to that purpose, he continued asking her questions and re-filling her glass.

One thing he'd learned both from working on intercepts and watching Harry's stupidity was that people who talked a lot generally gave something away.

Once he had a moment to himself, he'd see what he could find on her with a Google search. If she was an investigative reporter, there should be byline stories on file.

"So how do you think this case is going to come down?" he prompted. "Do these TPC guys stand a chance against someone like Willerby, who's richer than God?" Willerby was always named to one of the top spots on those richest-men-in-the-world lists. Which meant if this Zoe Chandler was for real she knew the odds.

She smiled faintly. "My source in the TPC has leaned on any number of prominent collectors—all of them richer than God. So I have a good feeling Roberto will do what he has to do to win this one."

"What do you win?"

She shrugged. "It's not about winning for me. I like un-earthing all the clues until everything falls into place. Most reporters are playing the same game. It sounds as though you might be in some kind of win/lose situation though," she added.

He looked at her over the rim of his glass. "That remains to be seen."

"Apparently, you don't intend to lose."

"Nope."

Blunt as a hammer.

She smiled and changed the subject.

Eleven

George Harmon had been trying to get in touch with Bill Willerby for several hours. It was afternoon now and he was sweating even in the air-conditioned hotel room with the air turned up to the max.

He wasn't looking forward to their conversation.

Bill Willerby was a ruthless tyrant, although you wouldn't know it looking at him. All mild calm and smiles, he could turn on a dime and rip you apart with a verbal riposte you didn't see coming. Or if his temper was at flash point, he might order some of the muscle he kept on retainer to scare the shit out of you.

Or worse. George had heard the stories.

Not that Gwyneth ever saw that cutthroat side.

She was special to Bill Willerby—forty years younger, of course—which was a major factor in her specialness. And as

Bill—perhaps mellowed by three previous marriages—put it, "She was his last and best wife." It helped that she rarely argued with him . . . at least in public. Although, if George was a betting man, he'd say in private, too. Bill Willerby didn't like people who argued with him. He went through subordinates at a record pace even in a corporate culture that rewarded those who best understood the nuances and subtleties of sycophancy.

Toadying, no matter the degree, wasn't going to be enough to satisfy Willerby when he heard of Zoe Chandler's rebuff, however. So, while waiting to speak to Willerby, George and his colleague Trevor Sanders had been brainstorming possible ways to convince an uncooperative woman that accepting Bill Willerby's offer would be to her advantage. And ultimately, much healthier.

Although, since Willerby was the ultimate decision maker, they were in limbo until they talked to him. Or more aptly—anticipating Willerby's displeasure—in purgatory.

Not that George hadn't foreseen the Chandler woman's response.

Anyone who scrutinized and probed the underbelly of the art world for a living was, by definition, a crusader of some stripe. Personal gain couldn't be discounted, of course, but he rather doubted it was the prime motive for Zoe Chandler. She lived a comfortable but unassuming life in Connecticut. She didn't cavort in jet-set circles when many in the art world chose to. Nor did she have any vices that required large sums of money. He'd checked her out rather thoroughly before coming here.

Which meant he hadn't been surprised at her answer, he

reflected, punching Redial on his cell phone for the umpteenth time that day.

When Hannah, Willerby's receptionist, finally put him through, his pulse rate went postal.

Christ, I'm getting too old for this. Even his accountant told him he had more than enough to retire and God knows accountants never thought you could have too much money.

"Why do I have the feeling this isn't going to be good news?" Bill Willerby sarcastically said without waiting for George to speak.

"Could be because Zoe Chandler isn't for sale," George retorted, frustrated and sweaty enough to take issue with Willerby's sarcasm and bullying. *Unlike the women in your life, who have always been for sale.* "She threatened to call the sheriff. This is a small town and if the sheriff had become involved, I couldn't guarantee your name wouldn't come up. So Trevor and I withdrew. What do you want us to do now?" he finished grumpily, thinking of his wife out sailing while he was in some outland doing Willerby's dirty work.

"Everyone's interested in money," Willerby said sharply, impervious to the exasperation in George's voice. He gave orders, others took them. Their inconvenience or unhappiness didn't register on his radar. "Offer her more for Christ's sake."

"I don't think she's susceptible to bribery, regardless of the sum."

"What the fuck—is she brain-dead?"

"No, Bill, she isn't." Suddenly Willerby's stolen artwork was no longer high on George Harmon's list of priorities. If the man was stupid enough to buy plundered antiquities why was it his problem? Especially on a beautiful summer weekend.

"Then see that she comes around and takes the money." Ice-cold words.

The *or else* vibrated over the airwaves.

Maybe it was too late to become principled at fifty, George decided, flinching before the all-persuasive authority of fear. And what the hell—as a partner in the firm, at least he'd get his share of Willerby's fees. "Perhaps some other avenues might prove more fruitful."

"Such as?" An acid query. Bill Willerby didn't take kindly to being overruled. He liked to win, but at his game, his way.

"Chandler's publisher might be more amenable to pressure if they were told they were going to be sued for defamation should they publish the book. Like every other business, publishing is about the bottom line. If the profits from her book were impacted by a court case, even with their in-house staff of attorneys, the publisher might reconsider the cost. They could find her book unacceptable and negate her contract. You wouldn't have to pay her a penny for her silence."

"If only Freddy Macintosh wasn't the biggest muckraker in publishing and a sworn enemy."

"Regardless, he has to consider the best interests of the corporation. Litigation is not only expensive, but if rumor suggested that Freddy had taken on this project as a personal vendetta, his reputation at least within the corporation might also be compromised."

"He doesn't care about his reputation. He's so pure in any event, no one would believe such a rumor. His staff worships the ground he walks on; the man gives his entire salary to charity for Christ's sake."

"Then, perhaps a threat to her assistant, Joe Strickland, might stop the Chandler woman. Strickland has a daughter in college he dotes on."

"Finally—you're earning your keep. Tell the Chandler bitch that the girl is in danger."

Not a second of contemplation, or guilt. But then Willerby was a sociopath—without conscience. He was also a man of enormous charm, which accomplished as much as his lack of conscience—both traits common to sociopaths. If George Harmon had a dollar for everyone who had told him that Bill Willerby was one of the most charming men they'd ever met, he'd be a whole lot richer. George glanced at his watch. Three thirty. "Do you want us to tell her today?"

"God damned right," Willerby snapped. "I wanted this taken care of fucking yesterday. And make sure I get the right answer this time, or I might become unhappy with you."

George Harmon was left holding a phone that had gone dead.

"What the hell did you expect?" Trevor Sanders murmured, turning from the golf he was watching on TV. "You didn't mention us shooting the Chandler chick," he added with a grin. "Willerby would have given you a bonus for that suggestion."

"Just because you don't have a stake in this, don't look so smug. I could say you'd screwed up the deal by threatening her. Which you did. Not that it would have made any difference either way," George generously added. He liked Trevor. The man had a sense of humor—a quality sadly lacking in the law firm. "Get your shoes on. We have to go back and threaten Zoe Chandler."

"Do you ever feel like a hit man?" Trevor mused, reaching for his shoes. "Funny how no one ever tells you this in law school—that success and good fortune are achieved by ass-kissing swindlers and thieves in bespoke suits."

"You could always do pro bono work in the ghetto."

Trevor glanced up from tying his shoelaces, his Hugh Grant hair falling over his forehead. "I'll let you know how I feel about that after we scare the daylights out of this gorgeous blonde."

Trevor had a sense of altruism not yet fully extinguished by the allure of money. But then he was young. "Look at it this way. The sooner we put the fear of God in her, the sooner we can go home. Your wife and kids will appreciate that." Talk about someone doting on their family. Trevor was the poster child for family man of the year.

Coming to his feet, Trevor mimed a fast draw. "Hit man ready to ride, boss. Although I hope like hell the lady's not carrying. She looks like she might be faster than me."

A prescient thought, had he known.

Although it wasn't the lady who would be carrying.

And the weapon was far superior to any imaginary six-gun.

Twelve

"Is the team in place?"

"They will be soon. They've landed at the air base in Duluth. It's an hour and a half drive from there to Ely."

Harry Miller leaned back in his leather chair, a view of the Potomac framed in the window behind him, his smile as sunny as the weather outside. "It never pays to leave loose ends. You heard—the votes are there. I've been guaranteed CIA director. The Senate confirmation hearing will be only a formality."

"Yes, I heard. And may I say, Congress couldn't have found a more accomplished and deserving man."

Harry surveyed his aide across his broad desktop with un-abashed good humor. He knew flattery when he heard it, but like so many men with huge egos, he believed it, too. "Winning at all costs, Pete. That's the name of the game. Don't ever forget it—not in this town—or you'll be eaten alive."

Pete Dickenson made a mock bow. "I've watched a master at work. And learned from the best."

"Damned right you have. He's a sick fuck, you know. The world will be better off without him."

You don't have to convince me, Pete thought. He'd seen Harry Miller go after more than one of his enemies. Nick Mirovic was just another person standing in the way. "I agree. Some people are damaged beyond redemption." He knew what Harry wanted to hear. That was his job: to tell Harry he was right—all the time, in every way. And some day, should Harry become a liability—well, it was a dog-eat-dog town, wasn't it?

Pete Dickenson knew where all the bodies were buried, figuratively and literally. And he kept records.

He had his eye on Harry's new job—eventually, of course. But he had to pay his dues first. Everyone did.

So—in the interim—he followed orders, never made mistakes, and fetched and carried like a goddamned serf instead of an Ivy League graduate with a polished resume from all the right think tanks. "I told the team to check in once they reach Ely. You'd be wanting an update, I said. Where the target is, et cetera."

"Excellent. What time is the hearing Thursday?" It had been fast-tracked because of some immigration bill that was going to be debated to death in the coming weeks. His mentor, Senator Ward, didn't want Harry's confirmation hearing to be postponed until after the summer break.

"Ten." As if Harry didn't know. "I sent out press releases to every news outlet in the world."

Harry reached for one of his Cuban cigars brought over by personal courier. "You do a good job, Pete. A super job."

"Thank you, sir."

"Hold my calls for an hour." Harry snipped off the tip of the cigar with a silver cutter.

That meant he was going to watch one of his porno tapes. Talk about sick fucks. Harry was into snuff films. Gruesome stuff. "Yes, sir. One hour it is."

"Get yourself some lunch or something. Emily can hold my calls. It's not as though she's good for much else." Because she was the daughter of a congressman, Harry had been forced to employ the stupid bitch—as he referred to her—as a favor to her father.

"I'll tell Emily, and I'll be back in an hour."

Harry grimaced. "I suppose you're going to that sushi place."

"It's healthy, sir."

"Whatever." Harry struck his lighter and held it to his cigar.

As the door closed on Pete, Harry picked up his remote and jabbed it in the direction of a bank of TV screens.

Thirteen

Unaware of the actions arrayed against them, Nick and Zoe ate lunch. Nick made a simple salad of tomatoes, olives, and peppers in a vinaigrette, cooked some walleye fillets that he'd caught yesterday when he and Chris had gone fishing, sliced a loaf of bread—from his aunt, he said—and offered chocolate cake for dessert.

He didn't mention who had made the cake, Zoe noticed, although there was no doubt it was homemade.

He ate twice as much as she did, maybe more, but then again a body like his required considerable fuel to keep it fine-tuned, she suspected.

He made them both an espresso afterward, using a small Italian pot that had obviously seen much use.

"Everything was delicious," Zoe said. "My compliments to

the chef," she added with a smile. "Even the espresso is fabulous and I'm an expert on the subject."

"I get my coffee beans from Sicily. They're Ethiopian." Since he was anticipating a sleepless night, espresso was on the menu today.

"So do we just sit and wait now?"

"Not for long, I'm guessing. Willerby will send his errand boys back with another offer—sooner rather than later. Tycoon types don't like to wait."

"What about your—as you put it—issues? Is it wait and see on them, too?"

"Can't say," he replied with a shrug. *Although you might be able to.*

"It's up to you, of course," Zoe offered with a polite smile. "But if I have a vote, I'd like to go out in the bush. It's safer."

"I'll think about it tonight and let you know." What he should do was make sure he cut her loose in the morning. His libido was putting up one helluva fight, though, especially when she leaned on the table like that, her boobs resting on the red Formica tabletop like lush ripe fruit, sending rational decision making pretty much on vacation. Intent on dodging temptation, he pushed away from the table. "Let's go sit outside. I'll clean this up later." He stood. "Or would you rather work?" The sensible part of his brain was hoping she'd choose the latter.

"I can't concentrate on work," she said, rising. "All I think about is Willerby's men coming back—what they might say or do." She grimaced. "This trouble from Willerby definitely wasn't in my plans."

"Maybe there's a way around him. Let's see what they're up to next." *Or what you're up to next.* He motioned to a door opening onto a deck. "After you."

The small deck had no railing, offering an uncompromised view of a wildflower garden spreading out to the edge of the woods. "You live in a little paradise here. The lake, the birch and pines, those lovely flowers out there."

"Can't complain. Those were my grandma's flowers," he added, dropping down on a chaise. "I mostly try to keep the weeds out."

She sat down on the other chaise, a 1950s souvenir like so much in the cabin. "My Lord, these are soft. I feel like nap time," she added with a smile. "Are these down cushions?" She patted the faded Hawaiian flower-print fabric.

"I have no idea. They're about a thousand years old." Leaning back, he stretched out his legs and squinted against the sun, not feeling like nap time at all—unless it was an X-rated one, and that was unlikely unless he lost it completely. "So tell me about this Joe who works for you. How did you two get together?" He needed a diversion for his running-on-overdrive libido.

While Zoe explained Joe's research role, how they'd first collaborated and found they were on the same wavelength when it came to understanding the need for painstaking authentication, she, too, was struggling against intemperate desire. Her libido was humming along full speed ahead as well. In fact, she was hard pressed not to openly gape at the gorgeous hunk of man lying beside her. Seriously, who wouldn't be tempted?

It was a heavenly warm afternoon; she had just been served a delicious and *healthy* lunch, chocolate cake included. Was not chocolate *vital* to good health, after all? Not to mention the delectable espresso, clearly of a superior quality. Superior in every way—like the man beside her.

How would he respond if she were to jump him, she wondered as she rambled on about Joe's daughter, Amanda, who was interning at an advertising agency in San Francisco for the summer.

With any other man she wouldn't have hesitated. Men did not, as a rule, ignore her. Nick Mirovic was different though. Off-putting even. And far from offering the usual engaging vibes, he was almost restive.

"Is your family anywhere Willerby can find them?"

The question was so unexpected, she stared at him wide-eyed.

"He might use them as pawns," Nick said, assessing her look of astonishment for authenticity. "Or Joe's daughter."

She sat up, lascivious thoughts dismissed. "You can't be serious."

"I couldn't be more serious." He knew what *he* was up against, knew Harry's depravities and favorite MO. With Willerby he wasn't so sure. Or with her.

"My parents are in Peru."

Conveniently distant. "Sisters, brothers?"

"Uh-uh. I'm an only child."

And maybe a good actress, too. "Willerby probably can't get to your family then," he said, his expression closed. "There's Joe and his daughter though." If she wasn't a spook, he had to mention it at least.

"Joe can take care of himself. He used to do surveillance work at one time."

"The way you talked about his daughter I'm guessing he's divorced?"

"For years now. His ex lives on a ranch in Montana and has a second family."

"What about his daughter? Do you have an address for her—the company she works for?"

"I have her cell phone number."

"Good enough. I'll check with a friend of mine tonight. He could put some security on her if need be." Alan had useful contacts up and down the West Coast. As for his own uncertainties, he'd run this babe past Alan before morning.

"This is getting *way* out of line," Zoe murmured, feeling her shoulders beginning to tense. She could understand Willerby trying to buy her off; she could even understand him threatening her. Good God, congressmen were threatened every day for their votes. She wasn't completely naive about how powerful interests protected their turf. But if Willerby went after Mandy that was too cold-blooded for real life. For *her* life.

"The daughter may not be in danger. It never hurts to be cautious though. And with your man Joe in Trieste, he isn't much help stateside." Everything was all still in limbo, including tonight; come morning, he'd probably have Tony take over. *Who are you kidding*, the little voice inside his head chided. *Why not get Tony to come over now if you're for real?* "Look," Nick said, pointing upward. "An eagle." Avoidance was a cop-out, but what the hell. He didn't have to think about tomorrow until tomorrow.

"How beautiful!" Zoe exclaimed, not entirely averse to changing the subject either. "Look at that huge wingspan."

"The eagles nest on that island in the middle of the lake. The same pair comes back every year; lately, they've spent most of the winter here. Global warming, I guess. The lake doesn't freeze as early as it used to. Their brood started flying a couple weeks ago." Nick smiled. "Watching their trial-and-error learning was something else. Oh, shit." The smile vanished from his face. "You've got company," he murmured, coming to his feet without making a sound. *Or we've got company.* "Go inside." *If she's just another innocent babe, she'll go inside willingly.*

Whether frozen in place or curious, Zoe stayed where she was. Then she saw them, too. Willerby's men were on her dock.

"I'll handle them," Nick said. "You'd be better off inside."

This time his voice was well-mannered and tactful. She shouldn't have spurned such a polite suggestion. "I'd like to hear what they have to say. I don't like secondhand information—if that's okay with you," she replied, speaking in an undertone. "Or do you think they might just go away?"

She didn't really mean if it was okay with him. She had no intention of moving. So now what? Even if she was who she said she was, even if Willerby's men did go away, Nick knew they'd be back. If she was Harry's girl, he'd be better off keeping her close where he could see her. "At least come inside while I grab some hardware." Without waiting for a response, he grabbed her hand and pulled her into the house. Regardless of who she might be, he needed some defense pronto.

He kept her in sight while he opened his pantry door and grabbed a MAC-10 and two extra clips.

"Wow. That's some arsenal." Zoe's doubts about Nick Mirovic came rushing back like a tidal wave. How many normal people had twenty guns in their pantry? She wasn't just talking hunting rifles or twenty-twos. There was some serious arms-dealer stuff in there.

"Part of my paranoia," he said. "Pick something out if you like."

"God no." She took a step backward and shook her head.

Christ, he wished he could dab her with something that would turn red if she was lying. This uncertainty was a drag—and dangerous to boot. Shoving the extra clips in his pocket, he said, "This way," and gestured toward his driveway with the barrel of the MAC-10. "We'll come up behind them."

I don't know much about firepower, she thought as she followed him, *but that is definitely an assault weapon.* The way he held it loosely in his grip gave her pause. On the other hand, maybe she should consider his obvious expertise as a plus.

"I don't suppose I can talk you into staying here," he said, glancing at her over his shoulder before opening his front door. *One last trial balloon.*

"Sorry, I'm too nosy."

Fucking A, she was either really, really naive or an Academy Award–caliber actress. "Curiosity killed the cat, babe." He held the door open for her.

"But then the cat might not have had the advantage of

that." She pointed at the ominous-looking weapon. "Would you actually use it?" Snappy answers aside, she found it hard to contemplate anyone shooting . . . another *person*.

"Depends on those guys," he replied, following her through the door and shutting it behind him. *And you.*

Oh God. He was serious. "What about the neighbors?" She was frantically searching for logical reasons *not* to shoot someone.

"The silencer works pretty well."

A silencer? Did normal human beings even *own* silencers? *Not in my world*, came the quick answer. She blinked twice just in case this was the old TV *Twilight Zone* and everything was in black-and-white. Nope. Glorious Technicolor. Seriously, her book wasn't worth actually shooting a real person. "Tell me you're only going to scare them. This is turning out to be way the hell out of my league."

Nick came to a stop. "Now's the time to say yes or no. It's up to you. This ain't my dog fight." His gaze was laser sharp.

She hesitated when she shouldn't. Then she blew out an indecisive breath when any normal person probably would have called the cops. *As if Willerby's two errand boys would admit the truth to the cops.* "Would you let Willerby roll over you?" she muttered, half to herself. "Silly question," she added, looking at his face.

"It's your life, not mine. It's your decision." *And I'm armed and ready whichever way things go.*

"Do I sound like some self-righteous prig when I say I really resent being strong-armed when I'm in the right? Willerby's the one in the wrong!"

"He's not gonna play nice, though. He might not even know the difference between right and wrong. I've known a few of those in my day. Maybe you should think about taking his offer. You said you wouldn't be losing income-wise."

"It's still not right," she mulishly said. "Other collectors have seen fit to respond appropriately when asked to relinquish their illicit artworks."

He smiled. He didn't know any spooks who spoke like that. "You think you can change Willerby from a predator to a pussycat?"

"Okay, okay." She drew in a breath, still feeling a little like an actor in a crackpot movie. "Either I stand up to him or not. Right?"

"That's about it," he said, beginning to feel good about her. "Not that I'm suggesting you do anything you don't want to do. Nor that taking on Willerby will be a walk in the park." As he spoke, he realized he was going with his gut. He was betting she was with the good guys, and that meant he was willing to take on her battle even though it had nothing to do with him. He was actually feeling some bona fide emotion again—and that wasn't all that bad.

Could be it was just moral indignation directed at Harry Miller as much as this bozo hounding her. Or maybe it was just pure lust. Perhaps he'd finally been forced to crawl out of his cave, and he'd seen there were parts of the world that needed shaping up. "Look," he said, simply. "I can deal with these people. Guaranteed. If that helps."

In for a penny, in for a pound, the die is cast, et cetera, et cetera.

Mostly, he liked that he felt alive again.

"Come on, babe." He grinned. "Let's see if they're packing."

"You're taking this much too lightly," she muttered, holding his gaze.

"Sorry." He tried to suppress a grin and failed. "Seriously, I doubt either of them has ever held anything more lethal than a golf club in his hand." And if he hadn't been so paranoid that morning, he would have noticed their haircuts were a half inch or so too long for spooks or the military. As for her, if his gut was wrong, he could probably take her down—much too lightly like she said.

She looked at him dubiously. "Am I supposed to be reassured?"

Another smile. "I'm trying my damndest."

"I suppose if we can take any pressure off Mandy, that would be good."

"There you go."

"I've never done anything like this before. I've only seen a weapon like that"—she jabbed a finger—"in the movies."

"With luck, maybe Willerby's men will feel the same way."

"You think?"

"Let's go find out."

Fourteen

George Harmon said afterward that he'd thought he'd been hallucinating when he'd seen that huge man standing on the hill above him, his broad-shouldered form silhouetted against the sun, the glint of the assault weapon cradled in his arm shockingly out of place on an idyllic summer day.

"Looking for someone?" Nick inquired with exaggerated courtesy.

The hallucination spoke. Equally terrifying. "We've come to see Miss Chandler." George managed to keep his voice from trembling only with extreme effort. This would cost Willerby combat pay. He hoped he lived to collect.

"Let's get the fuck out of here," Trevor whispered.

Since the only way out of there was through the hulk with the Uzi or whatever it was, George screwed up his courage, hissed, "Not yet," and then, raising his voice so he would be clearly heard, said, "Our employer has reconsidered his offer. He would be willing to double the amount to six million, Miss Chandler." Fuck Willerby. It was all fine and dandy to threaten Joe Strickland's daughter from the safety of the Hamptons. Right now, he'd do the negotiating and leaning on the young girl was off the table.

Nick glanced at Zoe. "What do you think? That's a lot of money."

"Why can't Willerby just give back his looted antiquities?"

He shrugged. "Ask the dude."

"I don't want money," Zoe called out. "I want Willerby to comply with the Italian government and give back the pieces that were stolen."

Maybe when pigs fly. "I believe he's talking to the Italian government about doing just that," George lied, slowly walking toward them up the slight incline, hoping to close the deal. Hoping even more that the man with the gun wasn't deranged. "Nevertheless, in the interim, Mr. Willerby is still willing to pay you not to publish your book."

"Why?"

"This may sound ridiculous, but he's trying to please his wife." Another lie, accompanied by a slick smile. "She's young and concerned about the scandal."

"If they give back the stolen art, there won't be a scandal."

"And you won't have a book."

"I don't see why that matters to you or him."

Nick raised the MAC-10 barrel slightly so George's head

was in his sights. "That's close enough," he said. Turning to Zoe, he gave her a lifted brows look. "Do you want to do this deal?"

"No. I never did."

"Look, guys," Nick said with a silky smile, "much as we'd like to visit with you and get the lowdown on your employer and his young wife, Miss Chandler is of the opinion that she can write a book and have it published without your boss's interference." His smile widened. "Land of the free, right? So why don't you two get in your car, drive out of town, and catch the next plane back to wherever you came from."

"And tell Willerby everyone isn't for sale," Zoe added.

"The girl," Trevor whispered, having conquered his fear when it appeared as though Miss Chandler and her backwoods boyfriend weren't going to shoot first and talk later. "Tell her about the girl," he prompted. Willerby would fire them if they failed; this wasn't the time to hold back.

"Shut up," George shot back, sotto voce.

Nick frowned. "What girl?"

Christ, how had he heard? "He doesn't know what he's talking about. It's nothing."

"Maybe if I shoot up one of your knees that might kick-start your memory," Nick said. "What girl are you talking about?" He was getting a bad vibe about that word, *girl.*

"It's a misunderstanding," George said in his most professional, soothing attorney–client voice. "Trevor didn't talk to Willerby, I did, and no one said anything about a girl."

Nick squeezed off a round that hit the ground an inch from George's polished wing tip and sent grass flying. "I heard what your partner said so don't fuck with me. The next one's for your knee and the nearest emergency room that could competently handle a mess like that is an hour away."

"Willerby wanted us to tell you Joe Strickland's daughter is at risk if Miss Chandler doesn't comply," Trevor quickly interposed, recognizing he'd been wrong about the talking/shooting time frame, mainly concerned now with keeping his head and knees intact.

"You were right!" Zoe exclaimed.

"Sit down you two. Right there on the ground." A cold, brusque command only a lunatic would disregard.

They sat. Even George, who normally wouldn't have considered getting his creme linen slacks smudged.

Pulling a cell phone from his pocket, Nick spoke two syllables into the mouthpiece. A second later when his call was answered, he said, "Hey, Tony. I've got a couple of trespassers here on the Skubic property. If you could come out and pick them up, I'll press charges. Some big-city boys looking for trouble. Maybe you could lock them up for the night. Sure, take your time. They're not goin' anywhere." Flipping the phone shut, he smiled at Zoe. "My cousin Tony is sheriff here. He's on his way."

When Tony and his partner arrived, George Harmon vehemently protested that they were being wrongfully imprisoned. He knew his rights! This was a preposterous injustice! He should be allowed to make a phone call to his lawyer! He *insisted* on it!

"Not a problem," Tony said, cool as a cucumber, holding

George's head as he shoved him—still shouting—into the backseat of the patrol car. Trevor, pale and silent, was being *helped* into the other side of the backseat by Tony's partner, Keith. "First thing tomorrow morning, dude, you can call anyone you want." Tony winked at Nick over George's head.

"Tomorrow morning! That's a gross infringement of my rights! I'll have you sued! I'll have your badge! I'll have you thrown in jail!"

Tony slammed the back door shut. "The guy has some lungs. I'll have to put him down in the basement. So—is tomorrow good enough for you, Nick?"

"Yeah. Thanks. They were harassing the lady. Zoe Chandler, my cousin Tony Mirovic."

Zoe smiled. "Thank you so much. They were really unwelcome and threatening."

"Looks like they're used to having their own way."

Nick's brows flickered. "New York lawyers."

"No shit. Well, we'll have to see that they get a feel for a North Country jail tonight. Do you want them to have Betty's meals or did they piss you off?"

"Nah—they might as well eat a good meal. I owe you, now."

"Like hell." Nick had pulled Tony out of a burning car years ago and saved his life at no small risk to his own. He had literally bent the steering wheel back from the column to free Tony from the car crash. "Have yourself a nice day, you two." And with a thumbs-up sign, Tony pulled open the driver's door and slid behind the wheel.

As the police car disappeared down the drive, Zoe gave Nick a searching look. "Your cousin could get into trouble over this. Willerby's men *will* sue."

"Not a problem. Our uncle is the local judge, another cousin is the district judge. I'm guessing they'll get tired of pursuing their case by the time they lose in those two courts."

She smiled. "You know they'll lose?"

"Let's just say as a betting man I wouldn't put a dime on them winning."

"If they weren't such asses, I might think that they were being denied their rights."

Nick grinned. "Yeah, if only. Come on now. I have to make a few calls. Joe's daughter better have some security, just in case."

"You're being really sweet," Zoe said, walking beside him as he strode down the road to his place. "I appreciate all you've done for me." She grinned. "You and your entire family."

"Forget it. Willerby overstepped. Things like that piss me off." Although, they hadn't for a long time. Not that he was knocking the fact that he was back in the real world—fucked up as it was.

It was better than being half-dead like he'd been.

And you couldn't fault the company, he thought, shooting a sideways glance at Zoe. Even if he wasn't a hundred percent sure about her. Still, he didn't have to say sayonara to her until morning.

Possibilities existed.

He *might* even take advantage of them.

It wouldn't hurt to have some pleasant memories for his coming hermitage in the bush. It would give him something to think about besides the approach of Harry's liquidation squad.

Fifteen

 Chris's car was outside the workshop when they returned.

"A local kid works with me sometimes," Nick said, setting down his assault weapon outside the door. "Come on in. I'll introduce you and tell Chris I'll be out later."

"I saw you on the road a couple days ago," Chris said, after Nick had introduced them. "Nice car."

"Thanks."

"I'll bet it has a pretty cool top end."

Zoe smiled. "It's not bad. You're helping out, Nick says. The canoes are beautiful," she added, surveying the large interior. It was half museum, half full-scale production center. Several old canoes were hanging on the walls, along with other wilderness paraphernalia—trapping gear, fishing poles, snowshoes, skis, several boat motors. Some objects were obviously vintage, while others were state-of-the-art.

"Someday I'll know what I'm doing."

"He's learning fast," Nick interposed.

"I could use a little help boiling these cedar ribs if you've got a minute," Chris said.

"How many do you have in the vat?" Nick asked, moving to a large rectangular cauldron on legs with bubbling liquid inside.

Fifteen minutes later, he looked up and offered Zoe a rueful smile. "Sorry. This must be like watching grass grow for you. Let me take you inside. We're gonna be here awhile."

"I can let myself in. Keep working." She'd lived in the art world a long time and wrestling with a canoe's structural framework was a lot like working on a large sculptural piece. Time often became irrelevant.

"Obviously, you didn't tell her about the alarm," Chris drawled.

"Chris politely refers to me as the human security screen. And she saw some of it already, Chris, so lay off." Nick nodded toward the door and smiled. "He's right though. I'd better lead you back to the house. And you can get me Mandy's number, too. Alan can find her with that and a name."

Zoe followed him on a path to the house that looked perfectly normal. No obvious boobytraps, although she hadn't seen the one earlier in the day either, so what did she expect? Whatever Nick's *issues* were, apparently they required these measures. And why she wasn't more freaked out would no doubt require some time with a therapist.

"There you go," Nick said, opening the front door and stepping aside so Zoe could enter. "I need Joe's daughter's phone number."

He waited while Zoe went to get her purse and when she returned, he punched the number into his cell phone. "I'll take care of this. She'll be fine with Alan on the case. Don't look at me like that. Better safe than sorry." He smiled. "You're shocked to find the world isn't all sunshine and roses?"

She made a face. He was way the hell too cheerful when the world she thought she knew was crumbling around her feet.

"Sorry," he said. *And if you're for real, I really am. No one likes to be terrorized.* "Look, I won't be gone long. Why don't you give Joe a heads-up and if you need me, pick up the phone in the kitchen and hit the intercom button. There's a line to the workshop. Otherwise, I should be back in less than an hour."

After the door shut on Nick, Zoe called Joe and explained about Willerby's threat, that Mandy had excellent security thanks to Nick—some CIA types, she understood. "Mandy should be fine," she finished.

"Easy for you to say," Joe grumbled. "I'm halfway around the world from my daughter and not so damned sure everything's fine. I should probably come home."

"It wouldn't hurt."

"Christ, I was going to go to the site tomorrow with my informant."

Zoe knew that Joe's parenting had been pretty much long-distance since the divorce. It wasn't that he and Mandy didn't spend vacations together and the occasional holiday, but Joe's ex was the primary caregiver. "Would you like Nick to call you and explain the security in place?" Zoe asked, politely giving Joe a way out.

"Why don't I talk to Mandy. See how she's doing. Fucking Willerby, threatening my daughter," he muttered. "We're gonna take the son of a bitch *down*."

"I'm really sorry, Joe. If I hadn't started this . . ." Zoe's voice trailed off.

"It's not your fault Willerby's a douche bag."

"Still, I'm sorry."

"Nah, don't be. I'll call you later."

The phone went dead. Joe wasn't Mr. Diplomacy.

Zoe found herself standing in a front hall lined with deer antlers, feeling as though she should be doing something other than hanging out.

And waiting.

For what, she wasn't sure.

She wondered if she would be better off returning home, hiring bodyguards there, and having Joe come back to the States to help protect his daughter.

She blew out a breath. Damn—everything was so unsettled. If only Willerby wasn't such an unknown. Or rather, if her experience with men like Willerby wasn't so limited. Actually, nonexistent.

Where was that good fairy with the magic wand when you needed her?

Uncooperative fairies aside though, she really *should* work on her book. The sooner she finished it, the sooner Willerby would be checkmated. But after all the commotion today with those visits from Willerby's men and the increasing uncertainty of should she stay or should she go—and where exactly she should go if she did—her stress level was pretty high. Which seriously curtailed any motivation to write.

Chris looked up and grinned as Nick reentered the workshop. "Nice houseguest. You must have changed your mind."

"About what?"

"You gave me the impression you were going to pass on the lady next door."

"Stuff came up."

"Good for you."

"It's not that." Nick smiled. "Sorry to disappoint you." Chris's concern for his love life was well-intentioned but unnecessary. "Zoe's writing some book that a tycoon in New York doesn't want her to write. He sent out his goon squad to lean on her, she asked me for help." Nick shrugged. "I'm thinking about it."

"What kind of help?"

"To push back for her, I guess."

"How hard?"

"Dunno yet. I might head up to one of my outpost camps instead."

"With her?"

"Good question."

Chris flashed another grin. "Why are you even debating it?

A babe like that? If I didn't have a thing for Dee Dee, believe me, I wouldn't hesitate a second."

"But then you're eighteen and I'm not. And—"

"There's some problem," Chris presciently finished.

"*Maybe* there's a problem. She could have been sent here by a guy who doesn't exactly like me."

"Do you want me and my cousins to go with you out in the bush?"

Now there was a good kid. And not to be discounted was the wilderness expertise of the Smith family. Like him, they could survive in the boundary waters with a knife and a fishhook. "I think I can disappear more easily if I'm alone. Which is part of my dilemma concerning the lady."

Chris had been hanging out with Nick since he'd come back to care for his granddad, and with the exception of Lucy Chenko's brief visits, no houseguests had ever been invited in. The fact that Nick was even considering taking his neighbor lady north was a monumental shift in policy. "You don't seriously think a good-looking babe like that could be dangerous, do you?"

Ah, tender youth. "Hard to tell," Nick murmured. "I've run into some bad asses who don't live life like the rest of us. They look like you or me. They just don't act like us. But— whatever," he added with a shrug. "I can take care of myself."

Chris had seen the pantry. He figured Nick could probably take care of a whole lot of things. But friends helped friends. "If you change your mind the offer's open."

"Thanks. I appreciate it. Now let's finish boiling these ribs and get them in the clamps."

No way was he letting Chris and his cousins get in Harry's line of fire.

Rather than stand in the entry hall, Zoe drifted into the living room. Looking around for a place to sit, she surveyed another room from the 1950s. White walls, beige couch, two beige chairs—all three with cushions only slightly worn considering their age. But the living room probably hadn't had much use—a common enough case. The chartreuse rug didn't show wear either, while the needlepoint cushions scattered on the furniture were all pristine variations on a theme. Each exhibited a profusion of flowers and a verse from a nature poem. Nick's grandmother was the embroiderer, she guessed.

Over in one corner a small spinet piano holding an array of framed photos caught her eye. Crossing the room, Zoe sat down on the piano bench and studied the interesting profusion of Mirovics.

She picked out Nick's pictures first. There he was as a youngster—perhaps six or seven—a fishing pole in one hand, holding up a large fish with the other, his gap-toothed smile radiant with pride. He wore jeans, sneakers, a Spider-Man T-shirt, and the same workshop where he was at the moment served as backdrop to the picture. He must have been an only grandchild. There were photos of him as a child—with a trike, a bike, then a motorcycle—always smiling into the camera.

The latest was a college graduation picture showing a handsome young man with his arm around a petite, pretty, dark-haired woman also in cap and gown. The ex-wife or just a friend? Picking up the photo, Zoe studied the woman's face as if the image might give up its secrets. But no, just a smiling face, rosy-cheeked and young.

Replacing the framed picture, she scanned the rest. There were photographs of Nick's grandmother and grandfather, their wedding portrait, them with a baby, their son, Nick's father, she decided from the date of the clothing. In the very back, leaning against the wall, was a large picture of Nick with his parents, his mother holding his hand, his father standing behind them, his features almost identical to Nick's. The family was posed on a lakeshore, framed by pine trees, a canoe pulled up beside them, the sky still a vivid blue in the old photo.

She found herself slightly envious of the small photo gallery. Her family had traveled extensively, rarely staying in one place for any length of time. She didn't have a family home with photos on display, or even a grandparents' home where memories were stored like this. Both sets of grandparents had retired early, sold their homes, and moved to condos in Florida. And if not for satellite phones, she wouldn't have much contact with her parents. Even then, there were times they were in areas where phone service was uncertain.

Jeez—enough with the melancholy. Willerby was to blame for that, too. As of this morning, she'd been happy as a clam in her rented cabin with her manuscript going along swimmingly.

She had been fine. Joe had been fine. Mandy had been fine.

Crap.

She blew out a breath, swung around on the piano bench, and gazed at a large paint-by-the-numbers lake scene hanging over the couch. Now that had been *some* project for whomever had painted it. Coming to her feet, she walked over to it and read the name painted on the bottom right: Peg M. '58.

Nick's grandmother probably.

Then out of nowhere—prompted no doubt by her retro walk down memory lane—her mouth began watering for chocolate chip cookies, or maybe brownies. The kind with lots of frosting.

Or perhaps it was just her usual reaction to stress—reach for carbs and chocolate.

Would Nick mind, she wondered, if she made some brownies? Did he even have the ingredients? On a sudden mission from God, she swiftly walked to the kitchen and began opening and shutting cupboard doors. She was kind of hoping she could find the ingredients without having to look in the pantry. It wasn't that she was a coward, but the idea of that much firepower in an ordinary house was just slightly disturbing.

Yeeessss! There it was, everything—flour, sugar, spices, vanilla, Hershey's cocoa. She rummaged through the shelves but didn't find chocolate chips. Not that she was surprised, with a guy who could bench press a Mack truck. He might drink cocoa maybe, but chocolate chips for cookies—not so much.

She was just putting the finishing swirls on the frosting atop the brownies when Nick walked into the kitchen.

"Remind me to invite you over anytime," he said with a grin. "I'll pour the milk."

"Good. I was afraid you might not like me going through your cupboards."

"If this is the result," he said, glancing over his shoulder as he opened the fridge, "feel free."

"I was stressed. Chocolate seemed the logical solution."

"That or booze. We could do both. I have a sweet French red a friend of mine sends me from Paris that's good with chocolate."

Zoe shook her head. "I drank enough before lunch. Maybe milk will help me sleep tonight."

Sex always helped him sleep, but since he was trying to stay on the straight and narrow, he decided to settle for milk, too. "Try not to be stressed. You're safe here." A relatively truthful statement unless Harry sent in the heavy artillery. "And I'll make us some supper later. Maybe pudding for dessert. That should help you sleep." He set the milk carton on the table.

Zoe's eyes lit up. "What kind of pudding?"

"What kind do you like?"

"Coconut cream."

"No shit. Same here." He didn't exactly believe in Karma— correction, he didn't believe in it at all—but there was some kind of voodoo rapport going on with this babe next door. Next thing she'd be saying she spoke Croatian. *Wait, wait, wait. If she's Harry's spook, maybe she knows I like coconut cream pudding.*

Christ, the ambiguity and suspicion were beginning to hurt his brain.

"I'll get some glasses." Right now, he didn't want to think about Harry.

While Nick was jettisoning thoughts of assassins, Zoe was thinking there was something about sitting at an old Formica table with a dishy guy like Nick, eating brownies and drinking milk, that triggered some hitherto unfelt sentimental sense of contentment. Maybe it had been too long since she'd indulged in such simple pleasures. Or maybe the contrast between her previous apprehension and the dependable ecstasy of chocolate in any form accounted for her unusual feelings. Perhaps it was nothing more than coming within the sexual force field of a super-gorgeous man like Nick Mirovic.

She was beginning to feel like a fifteen-year-old with a crush.

Obviously, the retro-brownies and milk were to blame.

She should have taken him up on his offer of wine—a more mature beverage.

"I probably shouldn't say this." Nick's voice was ultrasoft.

Better you than me. She was very near to propositioning him. "Say whatever," she casually replied, not feeling casual at all. She was, in fact, very close to abandoning discretion altogether. *Really, he could be in an ad for one of those home exercise machines—you know the ones . . . a halfnaked guy that's all hard, glistening muscle telling you for only twenty dollars a month you can look like him.* Not that Nick's muscles were glistening, but maybe later after some hot sex, she luridly thought.

"I was thinking, maybe you could come along with me—at least for a week or so." He was probably being stupid, but she had a thin smear of chocolate frosting on her bottom lip that was just crying to be licked off and his hard-to-control libido was pressing him to do just that. For starters.

"Really?"

She smiled, and her face lit up like some artless, unspoiled, Renaissance Madonna. Not a good analogy in his present lecherous mood—maybe more like a real grateful chick. "Sure. We'll give it a try." Ambiguous words, although his dick interpreted them differently, his erection surging upward in anticipation.

"I probably shouldn't say this," Zoe murmured, lifting her brows slightly in indication of the identical phrase, "but you turn me on." She grinned. "Or maybe it's the chocolate. It's supposed to be an aphrodisiac, right? Although I apologize," she quickly added, his expression so completely neutral she figured she'd blundered, "if I seem too pushy. I'm perfectly fine with platonic, too."

He leaned back in his chair and studied her from under his lashes.

As the silence lengthened, her cheeks turned pink, then cherry red. "Say something," she finally muttered, unconsciously licking away the smidgen of chocolate on her bottom lip. "'No thanks' is fine."

"I'm trying to figure out if Harry sent you. If you're supposed to proposition me. If I'm supposed to fall for it."

"This is where I say, 'Harry who?' Not that you're likely to believe me, but I haven't a clue who you're talking about." She smiled. "But thanks, I thought you were blowing me off for other reasons."

The corners of his mouth lifted faintly, his smile slightly

cynical; his dark gaze, on the other hand, beaucoup sexy. "It's strictly self-preservation, babe. A man would have to be dead to blow you off."

"How sweet."

"That's me. Sweet as hell."

"So what do you think?"

He softly swore.

"If I was naked, you could see I wasn't carrying any weapon." *Good God where did that come from?*

At this point his libido was practically frothing at the mouth, reason was crumbling fast, and a man of less restraint would have succumbed. *She is making this way too easy.* "I'll think about it," he said.

"Is thirty seconds long enough?" The pulsing had accelerated to a hard throbbing rhythm; she was seriously horny and it was all his fault.

The smallest hesitation and then he said, "Yeah. Show me what you got."

Her eyes flared wide for a second. "Here?"

"Here's good."

It was a take it or leave it tone.

Under any other circumstances, i.e., one where she hadn't gone without sex for almost a month, and the man eyeing her wasn't God's gift to women, she would have selected the leave-it option.

Unfortunately, her body was seriously revved up for reasons that mostly had to do with the magnificent specimen of male virility seated across from her. Okay, so that was an unbelievably shallow reason—pure physicality should never be such a driving motive. Even thinking of the word *driving* catapulted a delicious, lustful ripple straight up her vagina.

Or maybe the chocolate was to blame.

"Are you still with me, babe?"

His low, raspy tone effectively sealed the deal.

She smiled. "Yeah—I'm here."

Sixteen

"Are you finished eating then?" she asked, as if anything mattered but consummation in her current ripe-for-sex mood.

"For now."

His smile was pure machismo. She felt the heated insinuation of future possibilities in every quivering sexual nerve ending, particularly those that were busily flooding her vagina for easy access.

"If this show's actually getting on the road"—he lifted his chin just a bit—"stand over there by the fridge where I can see you. And undress slowly." His brows rose faintly. "I want to survive this roll in the hay."

"You should talk." She shot a glance at his pantry as she rose from her chair, astonished to find that a hint of menace was curiously beneficial to sexual arousal. "I should be the one who wants to keep you in my sights."

Not a phrase he cared to hear under the circumstances. "What if I said I wanted to handcuff you?" A deterrent to assassination—*not without its prurient element*, his libido pleasantly reflected.

"If you didn't have an arsenal in your kitchen," she replied, moving the two steps to the fridge, "I might be open to the idea. But since you do—no thanks." Pragmatism was still nominally in charge.

"I'm not playing then." No way—screaming libido or not—was he about to take a chance of dying for a fuck.

"You can't say that." Peevishness in every word.

"I just did."

Christ—that take it or leave it tone again. There were times a smart-ass, take-charge kind of guy was a real pain. "I could use my vibrator." She gave him a pointed look, her version of an ultimatum.

He smiled. "Okay if I watch?"

"You're pissing me off," she muttered, glowering at him.

"I wish I could help you out. You have no *idea* how I wish I could help you out," he murmured.

"Yet handcuffs are a requirement?" Followed by a petulant little sniff.

He ignored the petulance. He even understood; he was under ruttish duress as well. "There are people from my past who won't allow me to make mistakes—sexual or otherwise. It's just a fact. Believe me, if not for them, I'd be fucking you right now."

"You're talking about this Harry person."

"I'm not sure he's a person."

"And I could be working for him?" She was beginning to understand.

"Yup."

"And he would want me to do something not so nice to you," she said in an almost normal tone.

He laughed, a harsh, guttural sound. "Yeah—something lethal."

"You don't mean *kill* you?" she breathed in disbelief.

"That's the general idea."

Her face went pale and she sank onto a chair. The thought of people killing people could really take the wind out of one's sexual sails, not to mention rattle one's sense of personal mortality. "You don't think Willerby might be planning that for me, too, do you?"

He was staring at the face of fear or that of a very good actress. "I don't know him," he answered honestly, not in a position to offer blanket assurances even if he wanted to. "So I don't know what he'll do."

"Joe told me Willerby was dangerous, but I never imagined he meant *seriously* dangerous."

"I'm sorry. I didn't mean to frighten you." Her fear looked genuine. Or at least he thought it did. He wished there was a way to know for sure.

She went silent, hands folded in her lap, her fingers clenching and unclenching.

He didn't move or speak, determined not to get anymore involved than he already was. The practical part of his brain was hoping she might decide to hire some real security and let him off the hook. The impractical part was focused on the pink flush beginning to color her cheeks and the gentle rise and fall of her bodacious breasts. Predictably, his hotheaded libido was yelling at him to pick her up, carry her to his bedroom, and take her mind off her troubles with some mutually gratifying sex.

"I have no idea what to do," she finally said.

"That makes two of us."

She offered him a rueful smile. "That's not comforting."

"Sorry."

She grimaced faintly. "With a closet full of firepower, you're supposed to know what to do when bad guys threaten people."

"Even if I did, I doubt you'd want to hear about it."

Sliding down, she looked at him from under her lashes. "How is it possible that my life has fallen apart in only a few short hours?"

"Don't look at me. I have nothing to do with any of it." And if he was smart he'd steer clear.

"I know." She softly sighed. "It's my own fault, as Joe pointed out to me. He warned me against taking on this investigation," she muttered, making a small moue. "And of course I didn't listen."

"And now your ass is in a sling." Nick suddenly grinned. "Nice ass though."

She smiled back. "Thanks. A couple minutes ago, I was going to eat you alive and now—well . . ." She blew out a breath, wrinkled her perfect nose. "Okay, so maybe I still feel like a little nibble."

"I wouldn't want to be accused of taking advantage of a lady," he drawled, clearly amused, "but the simple facts are, if anyone's gonna come after me, it's not gonna be in broad daylight, and Willerby's stooges can't get through my security. So if you'd care for a nibble or maybe more, I could take your mind off say"—his brows lifted ever so faintly—"this current unpleasantness."

She sat up, leaned her elbows on the table, and looked at him with an appraising and decidedly droll expression. "That was one smooth and, may I say, lucid invitation."

He leaned forward, so their faces were close. "If you're interested in additional lucidity—pleasure-wise, sex-wise, orgasmic-wise—I'd be happy to oblige."

"Such confidence," she purred, warmed by the smoldering heat in his eyes, aware that he was effectively finessing her fear and misgivings.

He grinned. "Some people just have the knack."

"Lucky me." It was nice to feel the piquant shimmer of arousal again instead of quailing panic. How kind of him to take her mind off the disagreeable Willerby dilemma, not that his motives were completely altruistic. Still. "You're ever so polite," she murmured.

He laughed softly. "I have my moments."

"I want to kiss you."

His brows flickered upward in surprise. Even as he was thinking it had been a long time since he'd heard so innocent a request, his less ruminative self said, "Go for it."

"Are handcuffs required?"

He couldn't tell if she was teasing or not, but he said,

"Maybe later," because he didn't as a rule let down his guard completely.

"Not now though."

"Uh-uh."

He watched her push her chair back, rise to her feet, walk around the table, and as she leaned over to kiss him, he abruptly shoved his chair back and pulled her down on his lap. "Let's do this my way," he said, running his palms down her back. "So I can feel you."

"And me you," she whispered, shifting her bottom against his erection in a tantalizing little wiggle. "Ummm . . . lovely," she murmured, as he sucked in a breath. With an enchanting little smile, she moved again in a slow, leisurely seesaw vacillation that, in contrast, spiked through their senses at lightning speed.

Fingers splayed, he grasped her hips and exerted pressure downward, holding her against his engorged cock for a silent, protracted moment, his dark eyes close and flame-hot.

Then she kissed him or he did her, the exact convergence mutually inspired and willful. Neither of them was a person of restraint, or perhaps a certain urgency was at play after so many hours of holding out against temptation. A distinct impatience suffused their kiss—a ransacking, ravenous devouring of each other, not a taste but a gluttonous prelude of what was to come.

Impatient for more, he tried to pull away.

"No, no," she cried, gripping his face. "Not yet."

He could have easily broken free, could have done whatever

he wished to do considering their relative strengths. But glancing at the red teapot clock, he saw that it was only four. At least five hours until dark. If Harry's people came, it would be at night. Maybe not tonight, but some night. So what the hell— he had time for kisses.

He gave her his full attention then. Gently curling one hand around the back of her neck, holding her lightly captive in turn, he tempered his fervor. His kisses were less forceful now, his tongue exploring in a lambent, grazing rhythm, his free hand drifting softly down her back, sliding upward again, his fingertips coming to rest on the plump outer curve of one breast.

The feel of his fingertips sinking ever so slightly into her flesh shouldn't have ignited such flame-hot desire. He was exerting the merest pressure, restrained, delicate—without intrinsic demand. And yet a quintessential authority somehow sprang from that gentle touch, causing her breathing to change.

Gratified, he inhaled her fluttering, erratic breathiness, drew her closer. A moment later when he tenderly cupped her breast and slid his index finger back and forth over her taut nipple, she arched her back, pressing into his hand, asking for more.

Flexing his hips, he thrust upward, ramming his cock against her cunt.

A skittish cry broke from her lips.

His hands clamped down hard on her hips this time, exerted a rough downward pressure, needing more than teasing foreplay.

They both groaned at the wild rush of pleasure inundating their senses.

No longer in the mood to wait, Nick debated where he'd left his handcuffs. Lucy was into S&M, so handcuffs were a regular adjunct to their sex—not that he was averse when in one of his black moods. But rather than moodiness, he was driven by necessity this time, and he needed them.

"I'm done," Zoe murmured, abruptly pushing him away.

His heart skipped a beat until he saw that she was reaching for the zipper on her slacks.

"Done kissing?" he inquired, just to be sure. Not that he couldn't have persuaded her to his way of thinking regardless, but it never hurt to know the terrain.

"Yup." The zipper was down and she was standing up.

The smokin' hot blonde next door was full of revelations. First she was on, then off, then on again, and this time in an impatient, purposeful way that was both gratifying and rare. Women sometimes preferred a less imperious facade—not that there weren't always exceptions. But, Christ, Miss Chandler was treating this fuck like a trip to the grocery store.

Not that he gave a damn one way or the other as long as the payoff was beneficial.

And it sure looked as though it would be. Her shoes were already off and she was sliding her slacks down her hips.

He was about to come to his feet and start stripping off his clothes when some inner voice of reason stopped him. Instead, he checked out the table—no knives or other lethal weapons—noted that the counter was too far away to reach, made a point of shoving away the closest chair that could be used as a weapon, and decided this particular sex act was gonna play without handcuffs, due to extenuating circumstances . . . like a fast-approaching orgasm. He sat back to enjoy the view.

She didn't appear to be performing some prescribed role. She was clearly frenzied, aroused, her nipples jewel hard under her T-shirt, the expeditious removal of her slacks and panties not the actions of a working woman for hire. Her cheeks were flushed a rosy pink, her lush mouth partially open as if the feverish heat within required egress. And when she jerked her T-shirt over her head and dropped it on the floor, the room went silent, save for her rough breathing and Nick's suppressed gasp.

She heard and smiled. "You like—this?" she noted, reaching behind her back to unhook her bra.

An ambiguous phrase, but he knew what she meant. "Where did you get that bra?"

"In Paris—where else?" Slipping the straps down her arms, she tossed the Spider-Man bra to him. "Boys aren't the only ones who like Spider-Man," she murmured.

He turned the silk fabric in his hands so the cartoon figures under the half cups were fully visible. "Nice job for Spidey," he murmured. "Holding up those big boobs."

"Thanks, but I don't feel like talking—if you don't mind."

She was moving toward him, nude, voluptuous, eager for sex, and no man this side of the grave would have argued with her. Unzipping his shorts, he jerked out his cock; she wasn't the only one in a rush.

"Wow—every woman's wet dream," she breathed, stopping before him momentarily to take in the splendid sight of his huge, upthrust penis.

"Back at you, male version." She was tall and slender with all the right curves and lovely, pillow-soft breasts.

"I'm really, really glad we met—even under the circumstances. That gorgeous dick goes a long way . . . toward mitigating . . . my not-so-good day. You must have women lined up at your door for a piece of that."

He smiled. "Flattery will get you everywhere with me."

"I'm serious." She was. She could hardly wait to feel that magnificent erection inside her. At which point her body reminded her to stay focused by sending a little hysterical gimme-gimme paroxysm spiking through her fevered, pulsing vagina.

He crooked his finger "No line here, babe. Just you."

As if she needed an invitation with the pearly fluid of arousal oozing down her thighs in little rivulets and her frenzied heartbeat pounding in her ears.

As she came within reach, he leaned over slightly, slid his fingertip up the trickle of white fluid running down one thigh. "You're making this real easy, babe," he whispered, touching his fingertip to his mouth, pulling open a small drawer under the table with his other hand and taking out a condom.

"What's with that?" Surprise—perhaps the veriest shade of pique.

"This?" He held up the foil pack.

"No, the always-prepared-for-every-eventuality Boy Scout. In the kitchen even."

"Does it matter?" He wasn't sure he liked her tone. For sure he didn't want to explain Lucy's anything-but-the-missionary-position mentality.

Why was she even questioning him? On the other hand, she had this picture of Lucy Whoever spread out on the table and . . . *and nothing* she reminded herself. She and Nick were very recent acquaintances, and if she wanted to get to know him better and profit gratification-wise from the experience, she would do well to ignore mental images of Lucy Whoever. "You're right. Doesn't matter," Zoe said, smooth as silk.

He grinned. "Don't wanna rock the boat?"

She shot a glance at his erection, then met his amused gaze with one of her own. "Let's just say I have a real incentive to mind my manners."

He laughed. "So we're gonna do this politely?"

"Right now, style doesn't matter so much as speed." Her brows rose. "If you don't mind, of course."

The only thing he minded was if she was Harry's girl, but even that wasn't going to stop the show at this point. "It sounds like I'd better get a move on," he said with a smile. Ripping open the foil packet, he slipped out the condom, dropped the foil on the floor, and rolled the sheath down his cock with the speed of considerable practice. Then, looking up, he opened his arms wide. "Come talk to me, babe."

Steadying her as she straddled his thighs, he adjusted her position slightly in order to bring the crest of his erection in line with her wet, throbbing pussy. As interested as she was in speed, he gripped her waist and, fingers splayed, began deftly easing her down his sizeable erection.

A taut, hushed silence accompanied her slow, gradual descent, both of them intent on absorbing the full sensual impact—slick electrifying friction, sleek tissue ever so slowly yielding to the compelling invasion, overwrought, prodigious sensation bombarding their brains. When she came to rest at last, blonde hair juxtaposed against his black, her bottom warm on his thighs, her ripe cunt chock-full of cock, they were both scarcely breathing. Unprepared for the raw intensity assaulting their senses, they were momentarily held hostage by a disorienting delirium.

More wary, Nick's survival instinct kicked in first. Conscious of his surroundings once again, he briefly took note of the woman currently in custody of his cock before scanning the kitchen—carefully, with an eye for detail acquired long ago in Kosovo.

Everything in place.

Including his cock.

Which brought him back to the business at hand.

An orgasm was on the agenda—preferably sooner rather than later.

Although, gentleman that he was, he'd see that she came first. Intent on expeditiously reaching the promised land of sexual bliss, he focused his attention on the lady's impressionable sensibilities, because the quicker she came, the quicker he'd get off.

Slipping his hands under her bottom, he took care to slide her honeyed cunt back up his cock in a deliberate, leisurely ascent, so she was sure to feel every soul-stirring, quivering degree of sublime friction. In her hot-to-trot pussy, in her lush, trembling body, in her fingertips clutching at his shoulders, and most of all in that primary female pleasure center—her clitoris.

Not that he didn't experience equivalent voluptuary stimulation.

He found himself holding his breath at the apex of the ascent.

The lady was panting, clearly impatient for more.

He obliged her. She was fantastically hot inside and out, always whimpering on the upstroke, panting on the downstroke. Frenzied in the most disarmingly sexy way.

Although, he had to admit, there was always that moment at the very depth of her descent when he lost it, too. When they both caught their breaths and waited for their nerve endings to stop flipping out.

"You sure know how to push all my buttons," she murmured once, when they'd both started breathing again.

"My pleasure, babe." He didn't say he was restraining his rampaging libido by sheer brute will. Instead, he lifted her up again so they could both feel the edgy rapture.

It wasn't long before he realized the lady impaled on his cock was seriously approaching the brink. He wasn't counting, but say on the following fourth or fifth up-and-down transit, she suddenly brushed his hands away and gasped, "I can't wait."

At which point, she proceeded to go directly to orgasmic heaven, bypassing GO and any expectations he might have had.

Her scream bounced off the kitchen walls, and sinking downward, she bottomed out on his cock, and feverishly rolled, twisted, undulated her hips in a trembling, overwrought search for Nirvana.

Wasting no time—getting off was high on his priority list as well—he jumped on her speeding freight train. Ignoring her indignant cries, he lifted her upward again, rammed her down hard on his cock, and suddenly recognizing the peaking franticness in her voice, held her there and gave her what she wanted: his stiff cock motionless inside her, stretching her to the limit, pushing her headlong toward the orgasmic finish line.

Or his nominally motionless cock, discounting the steady, rhythmic gush of seminal fluid into latex.

This was, after all, about mutual self-interest.

In time, her screams tapered off.

He could tell because his ears stopped ringing.

Not that he had actually been conscious of the clamor, too intent—once his orgasm began—on his own pleasure.

Her body's warm, he thought afterward as he held her lightly in his arms. And soft and welcoming, along with any number of other fondly earnest, maybe even sappy, designations.

He must have been amusing himself with Lucy too long, he thought, to find himself so inclined to sentiment. Then again, S&M wasn't likely to bring out the tender emotions. Not that he was into coercion with his sex, but he knew how to be obliging. And let's face it, he hadn't exactly been in a hearts and flowers mood lately.

Whatever the reasons, he preferred feeling what he was feeling now.

Contentment, perhaps even something more.

Astonishing.

"You know, I'm thinking there might be a real upside to my troubles," Zoe murmured, lifting her head from his shoulder and licking a warm path up his cheek. "That was pretty fabulous."

She was smiling sweetly at him. "Definitely gratifying, I agree," he said, smiling back. "And if you're in the mood for more, we could forget our troubles in the comfort of my bedroom. Whaddya say?"

"I say, yes. I haven't had nearly enough of you."

He grinned. "Same here." Lifting her up and away, he set her on her feet. Stripping off his condom, holding his shorts up with one hand, he rose from the chair, disposed of the condom, and wiped himself off with the kitchen towel.

"How much time do we have?"

He didn't ask her what she meant. It didn't matter. "At least until dark," he replied, zipping up his shorts. *After that, there are no guarantees.*

She exhaled softly and held out her hand. "I'm glad there's time."

They must have been on the same weird wavelength because he understood the carpe diem implication in her words. "No problem," he murmured, taking her hand and drawing her close. "Just for the record, I'm in a greedy mood."

"Just for the record, I haven't had the advantage of a Lucy type in my life lately. I may be more greedy than you."

He grinned. "I must have died and gone to heaven."

She wrapped her arms around his waist, rested her chin on his chest, and gazed up at him. "Is this sexy or what? You clothed, me not. I must be here to serve as your afternoon nymphet."

"Christ," he said in a husky rasp, "as if I need more provocation."

"You must like having a nymphet around," she purred, rubbing against his rising erection. "He seems to be ready again."

"If you're gonna be naked and within reach, I guarantee he's gonna always be ready."

She playfully fluttered her lashes. "How *very* lovely to hear."

Seventeen

His bedroom was like so much of the house, pure retro, including the green chenille spread on the bed and the 1950s furniture. It surprised her that he lived here and nothing of himself was evident. No personal items lay about or adorned the walls. Not even in the bedroom where he slept.

Or maybe he didn't sleep here. Maybe he just fucked Lucy here.

Which thought was perversely carnal.

It shouldn't be of course. Then again, everything about him was a turn-on, from the top of his handsome head to his Teva-sandaled feet. In particular his enormous cock that she'd just had the pleasure of ramming up her.

A little thrilling quiver fluttered up her vagina in memory and anticipation of more to come. She came to a sudden stop, clenching her thighs to staunch the going-off-the-deep-end tremors.

He looked at her.

Drawing in a small breath, she exhaled carefully as though she dared not move. "I seem to be on a short fuse with you."

The *with you* part struck some weird, machismo nerve, or perhaps anything she said would have been equally arousing in his current horniness. He was in the mood to fuck *no matter what*. "I'll carry you," he said, as though understanding her reason for stopping. Gently placing her on the bed a moment later, he unzipped his shorts and let them slide to the floor.

"You don't wear underwear." She unconsciously licked her lips as she gazed at his full-blown erection.

He half smiled. "Is it a problem?" He jerked off his T-shirt.

"God no."

She wasn't looking at him, she was laser focused on his cock. "It's hot in the summer," he said in explanation, thinking her half-open mouth was damned tempting. If he wasn't worried about Harry's girl biting off his cock, he might have followed through.

But figuring he liked his dick intact, he pulled open the drawer on the bedside table instead and lifted out his handcuffs. Not the normal kind—something Lucy brought over. Single cuffs, gold, with long velvet ties for fastening purposes.

Zoe's eyes flared wide briefly, then narrowed. "Lined in pink velvet. Your favorite color?"

"Not really. I hope it's yours," he returned, grasping one of her hands and snapping a cuff around her wrist.

"And if I were to say I don't like pink?"

"Too bad." He smiled faintly and held her gaze. "But you're not gonna say it, are you?"

"I should."

He snapped a cuff on her other wrist. "And I should send you packing." His brows rose. "But neither of us is going to do what we should."

"If you didn't have such a big dick," she muttered.

"If you didn't have the perfect cunt for it," he softly drawled, raising her hand slightly higher than shoulder level so he could secure the velvet ties to a bedpost.

As he lifted her other arm and fastened the cuff to the bed, Zoe felt as though she might come without any help from him at all. After her recent introduction to his physical splendors in the kitchen, she knew exactly what pleasures were in store for her; her body apparently knew as well and it was jazzed up and ginned up and seriously oversexed.

Also, his quiet authority and purposeful movements, his willfulness and calm intent were profoundly erotic. He didn't ask for directions; he didn't ask her permission. He was self-ishly intent on his afternoon entertainment.

And she understood why he was tying her up.

He didn't trust her.

Some impetuous, primal force within her was apparently in tune with his unceremonious divine-right theory of sexual gratification. She was already audibly panting, an ache of long-ing pulsed hard and deep between her legs, and her engorged labia were slippery wet in welcome.

Having secured her and protected himself, Nick became aware of Zoe's increasing agitation. *Join the club*, he thought, gazing at her. Her skin was flushed, her eyes half shut, the minute, suppressed undulations of her lower body, the clenching and unclenching of her thighs, quintessential hot and bothered impatience.

He sucked in a breath in an effort to curb his more headstrong impulses. It wasn't as though this was the first time he'd tied a woman to his bed—but there was something about this switched on, give-it-to-me woman that triggered his brutish instincts. It was an unprecedented sensation, as if seeing her shackled and ready for him prompted some latent depravity.

He counted to ten, tamping down the wildness.

Then he counted to ten again.

"You're not doing me much good standing there," Zoe muttered, high-strung and overwrought. Perhaps still petulant as well over pink handcuffs when she shouldn't give a damn. When she'd known Nick Mirovic for less than a day and it was none of her business.

"You want this?" He gestured toward his erection stretched hard against his stomach, his voice like hers taut, heated.

"Or my vibrator. I don't really care," she said, unreasonably. Neither of them was in a rational mood.

Turning, he walked from the room.

"Don't you dare!" she screamed.

This was the time to turn her loose, he thought, striding down the hall. Cut his losses, do himself a gigantic favor, and not knowingly look for trouble. *If only*, his libido smugly mused as Nick walked into Zoe's bedroom.

He returned with her vibrator. "Lady's Little Helper and I'll take turns," he said, holding her purple vibrator aloft as he approached the bed. "I'm guessing you won't mind coming a few times."

"You could be nicer, dammit," she said, pouty and peevish.

"So could you."

"I thought you were leaving."

"I live here." He sat down on the bed as if to underline the point.

"I suppose I *could* apologize"—she glanced at his glorious, upthrust penis—"considering."

He spread her thighs with a sweep of his hand. "Considering I can make you come?"

"Among other things."

He looked up, his hand holding the vibrator arrested inches from her crotch. "Meaning?" *Harry's threat returns with a vengeance.*

"Don't look at me like that. It's scary."

He shot a quick look at the bedposts, checking to see she was still securely tethered. He offered her an imitation smile. "How's that? Better?" Then he smoothly slid the vibrator up her vagina and effectively curtailed further conversation. He wasn't in the mood to exchange possible falsehoods with her. At the moment he didn't give a damn if she was Harry's girl or not as long as she couldn't escape her bonds. He was gonna fuck her until he didn't want to fuck her anymore and in the morning, he'd hand her over to Tony.

This was strictly playtime.

No conversation necessary.

Holding the vibrator in place, ramming it slightly upward with the palm of his hand, he bent low to draw one of her nipples into his mouth. He sucked gently at first as she whimpered and writhed beside him, as her body took a real fancy to him, glowing with the heat of arousal, turning liquid around the vibrator, the scent of sexual fervor pungent in the air. As her breathing shifted, became increasingly frantic and her hips rocked wildly against the pressure of his hand, he sharpened the pressure of his mouth. Sucking and nibbling, devouring her tenderness, taste, and texture, he tested the tensile elasticity of her nipples, perhaps tested his own self-control as well as she gasped and cried out in seething frenzy.

As he tugged and stretched her nipple, a fierce, thrilling ecstasy swept downward through her body, met the torrid, seething pulse of nerves stretched taut around her vibrator, and rolled over her in great, glorious pleasure waves. Her orgasm approached like a tidal wave, quickly—too quickly, but inexorably.

She screamed at the shocking rapture, her orgasmic cries exploding in the quiet room, and Nick sucked harder. But his mind was multitasking, every nerve on full alert, monitoring her progress. And the moment she finished coming he was going to replace her vibrator with his cock.

He was already reaching for a condom as her orgasm diminished and when he slid between her legs seconds later and plunged deep inside her, she sucked in a shocked breath.

He didn't move for a second, not necessarily out of courtesy. He was trying to decide if he was light-headed because all the blood in his body was in his cock or whether being buried in Miss Chandler's delectable cunt was somehow affecting his senses.

But suddenly, Zoe curled her legs around his ass exactly like his libidinous fantasies had divined and, shifting her pelvis upward, she whispered with heartfelt fervor, "Finally the real thing."

"Speaking of real things," he whispered, nominally back in the real world, although the pleasure was so stupefying he wasn't altogether certain he wasn't experiencing some crackpot out-of-body event. Not that it was going to impinge on him climaxing. That presumption would survive a nuclear attack. "I'd suggest you hang on."

As she quickly complied, he considered himself a very lucky man for the first time in a very long time. No games, no pretense with Zoe Chandler. She wanted it as much as he did.

He slid his hands up her arms, grabbed her wrists and exploited her availability, eagerness, and the highly salacious fact that on occasion—like now—she was definitely subject to his whims.

Her skin was hot to the touch, her cunt perfection as in a perfect fit, the scent of her in his nostrils outrageously aphrodisiacal.

Or was it his response to her, rather than her particular flesh and blood humanity? Not that it mattered. Not that he was about to debate cause and effect when currently *effect* was scorching and vaporizing everything but pure, megalomaniac sensation. This was about *raw feeling. Intense, profound feeling.* The kind of feeling previously absent from his life.

At the moment, Zoe was quite willing to forgive him for any and all past, perhaps future transgressions as well, because the explicitly carnal, glorious pleasure heating her body to fever pitch was unprecedented. Seriously, she reflected, she didn't know she could feel this good. This hot. This shameless level of ravenous desire. And apropos of nothing but her own gratifying ravishment, she noted he had the most gorgeous butt, currently oscillating like a pile driver on steroids.

Halfway through what turned out to be a wild, rampaging, plunging, pounding—reciprocal—quest for orgasm, Nick took note of his highly unusual conduct. He didn't normally approach sex with untamed fury. Correction—he never did. And if he wasn't fast approaching climax, he might have given more than a fleeting consideration to the possibility that Harry's girl had drugged him.

He couldn't help but grin at the transient thought as his climax exploded with such violence he thought his head would blow off. If she'd slipped him something, he decided, it must have been a doozy.

He didn't even notice that she'd climaxed along with him until his brain shifted from automatic pilot back to normal function and he felt the small, diminishing ripples of her vaginal muscles fluttering over his cock.

"Jesus H. Christ," he murmured, blowing out a breath as he lay braced above her. "That was one helluva ride."

"I hope you're up for more."

He chuckled. "Don't be shy."

She met his gaze and raised her brows infinitesimally. "I never am."

"No kidding. Not that I'm complaining."

"I can tell." She shifted her hips as his penis swelled inside her.

"I hope like hell Harry didn't send you," he said, softly. "You're really fun to play with."

She heard the unspoken menace in his words, however soft his tone. "I prefer playing with you to whatever your alternative might be. And seriously, I don't know any Harry."

"Whatever. I just can't take chances."

"At least these cuffs are velvet lined."

That was carte blanche if he ever heard it. "Let me get a fresh condom," he said, withdrawing in a smooth, supple movement that brought him to his feet beside the bed. "Do you want a drink or anything?"

She laughed. "A polite wild man."

"I apologize for that head-banging shit. I'm not usually like that. You're way too sexy—what can I say?"

He disposed of the condom in a convenient wastebasket, Zoe noticed, not sure why his former love life annoyed her. It did, however—perversely making him even more attractive. As if he wasn't alluring enough already.

"I'll be right back," he said, breaking into her sexual reverie. "I need a drink."

He returned with a frosted, half-empty bottle of vodka, offered it to her, and when she shook her head, he sat, cross-legged, at the foot of the bed, facing her. "Break time," he said, and lifted the bottle to his mouth.

"It doesn't look as though *he* needs a break," Zoe murmured, pointing her toe at his engorged dick.

"One of us does. Don't worry, I won't keep you waiting long. Tell me how you don't know Harry."

"Let me count the ways," she teased, thinking that he looked exactly like those workout machine ads she'd considered earlier. His body was slick with sweat, every muscle vividly accentuated as if he were oiled down for some bodybuilder contest—his rigid cock the picture of vigorous, bracing good health. "I don't know Harry, not yours, not anyone's. Sorry. Tell me how you came by that scar." It didn't stop at his waist. Now that he was naked, she saw that the ragged scar ran down the entire length of his body and halfway down the outside of his left leg.

"Someone shot at the Humvee I was riding in."

"It must have been more than a rifle shot."

"Shoulder-fired missile."

"Jeez. You're lucky to be alive."

"My driver wasn't so lucky."

"I'm sorry." His eyes had gone blank.

He didn't answer. He took another slug of vodka, waved the bottle in her direction, and said brusquely, "Spread your legs."

"Maybe you should ask nicely."

"Please spread your legs," he said, not nicely at all.

"When you growl like that, I'm not inclined to oblige you."

"Then again," he said, leaning over and placing the bottle on the floor, "whether you choose to oblige me or not doesn't really matter." Drawing himself back into a seated position by his abs alone, he leaned back against the footboard of the bed and held her gaze.

"I suppose it's easy to be a prick when I'm trussed up and can't hit you."

"I suppose it is." No way was he taking the bait. He had plans for the night, and they didn't involve him getting killed.

"But I'm thinking you won't care if I'm a prick when you're coming so hard your screams raise the fucking roof."

"So you're good. I never said you weren't. You're still a prick."

"Sorry. I've got lots of shit going on right now."

He actually sounded contrite. "I understand," she said more civilly than she'd planned.

"I'd uncuff you if I could," he quietly said.

She abruptly smiled. "And if I didn't want your big cock, I'd get the hell out of here."

"And go where?"

"I have places I can go. Friends Willerby doesn't know about."

"Good," he said, enormously relieved. He was off the hook. Come morning, he'd help her pack her car. "So, are we done?"

"With you being a prick you mean?"

"Whatever you say." He smiled. "Feel better now?"

"I do. Thanks for apologizing."

Little bitch. But he only smiled. He could see her cunt from here and it looked ready for action—slick and receptive. "You're more than welcome," he said, smooth as silk. "How about we take it a little slower this time?" He grinned. "You know—get to know each other better."

His idea of getting to know each other better turned out to be a world-class talent wedded to a professional expertise that any accomplished yogi would envy. He knew exactly how to move, how slowly or quickly, how deep and when, with the kind of delicacy and virtuoso technique that could only have been acquired through diligent practice.

He seemed willing to let her take the lead, as if he'd squandered his sum total of wildness and was content to relinquish the reins. And when she was ready to come, he gave her what she wanted—once, twice, three times in relatively swift succession. He came with her the third time, as though he understood before she did that she was momentarily sated.

He untied her hands afterward, although he didn't uncuff them. And he sat across the room with his vodka bottle while her breathing returned to normal.

Pushing herself up on the pillows after a time, she smiled and said, "Thank you. You're very good, although I expect you know that."

"Thank you, too. You feel like heaven."

She held up her cuffed hands. "Maybe later I could feel you."

He smiled faintly. "Maybe in the next lifetime."

"You're not given to rash impulses, I gather."

"Au contraire. You're my rashest impulse to date."

"Are you getting tired?"

She spoke softly, politely, unlike her earlier imperiousness. "No, I'm good," he said, setting the bottle on the floor, understanding what she meant. "You ready again?"

He was so incredibly courteous, she wanted to shower him with kisses and hugs and endless gratitude for the pleasure he'd given her. "You really are nice," she said, as he neared the bed.

"Thank you." He was watching her closely. "Now be a sweetheart and lie down."

She obeyed because it was decidedly to her advantage. She didn't even care anymore who was right or wrong, in control or not. She was only looking forward to the intense pleasure he offered—with expertise and largesse.

He retied her hands to the bedposts and stood looking at her for a moment afterward.

"What?"

"I was just wondering what your pussy tasted like," he said.

Oh God, oh God, oh God. She was going to die of pleasure before the night was over. But she was still rational enough to say in a relatively neutral way, "Be my guest."

He moved the pillows so he could push her up to the head of the bed and give himself more room. While she was already beginning to pant in anticipation, he gently shoved her legs apart, then taking her feet, eased them upward until her knees were bent. "It's close quarters," he murmured. "Bear with me."

As if she wouldn't. As if she was about to complain when he was going to entertain her so gloriously.

And when he'd finally gotten into position, lying half on his side so he'd have room for his legs, draping her left leg over him so he could get in close, he looked up and grinned. "Now, make sure you let me know if I'm doing something you don't like."

"Arrogant bastard," she muttered, but she was smiling.

"Insatiable bitch," he grumbled, but he was smiling, too.

He didn't actually touch her clitoris for the longest time. He licked and sucked every other portion of her genitalia, every fold and crevice, every sleek surface and aperture. His tongue was gentle, thorough, sometimes fast and other times slow. He nibbled at her pulsing flesh with a tantalizing delicacy that managed nonetheless to bring a cold sweat to her skin and a jolt to her senses.

She had long since grabbed the velvet ties and was holding on for dear life, overcome with a near hysteria. Wanting more.

And when she couldn't wait another second, she sobbed, "Oh God, please, please, please!"

He finally obliged her, playing a tune on her clitoris until she found a song she liked and climaxed with an uncharacteristic little soft sigh.

Then he played several of the other songs he knew until she finally gasped, "No more . . . no more . . ."

He gently lifted her leg off him after that, rose up to kiss her tenderly on the cheek, then coming to his feet, uncuffed her wrists and returned to his chair and his bottle.

"I am speechless. I am without words," she whispered, her eyes still shut, her body immobile, her blonde hair frizzy from her sybaritic exertions. "You are . . . incredible."

"Then we have a mutual admiration society going here," he murmured, lifting the bottle to his mouth, begrudging his feelings. Struggling with an inclination to keep the lady for a few more days and fuck his brains out.

He could wait until morning at least. He'd probably be more rational with the light of day. Or maybe Tony could talk some sense into him.

"Would you like something to eat or drink?" he asked, thinking she'd been using a fair amount of energy in the last few hours.

Her eyes opened and she smiled. "You'd be on my list."

"Maybe later," he politely replied. "I need a little downtime."

"How much downtime?" she playfully queried.

He laughed. "Not too long—okay?"

And so it went throughout the afternoon and evening, both apparently in the mood for a sexual marathon. Zoe finally fell asleep after ten and Nick rolled up in a blanket on the floor. He hadn't said he wasn't planning on sleeping with her. He just figured he'd wait for her to doze off.

There was no point in going over old ground.

She was who she was or who she said she was.

And he wasn't taking any chances.

Eighteen

That afternoon, while Nick and Zoe were on mile five of their marathon, Harry Miller was talking to his crew chief, Bob Hanover, who was in a car traveling north on Highway 53.

"You understand now? Don't go in earlier than three. I want everyone in the neighborhood down for the night."

"Gotcha." Bob and his driver were close facsimiles: square-jawed, military haircuts, tanned, both dressed like tourists in jeans and sweatshirts.

"Mirovic will have traps out."

"Not a problem."

"He's no amateur."

"He's not CIA." Translation: Everyone else *was* an amateur.

Harry frowned, debating whether to offer additional

warnings. But a moment later, he decided Hanover was one of his best men. He should be able to deal with Nick Mirovic—competent bastard or not. After all, he was sending in an entire team to kill one man. How hard could it be? "Call me when it's over."

"Roger that."

A teenager mowing the weeds in the parking lot of the long defunct Sweet Sue's Café in Cotton paused his John Deere tractor and watched the caravan of unmarked black sedans speed by. *Just like in the movies*, he thought, but the idea of government agents in his backwater neck of the woods was way too weird to be real. Maybe some car dealer was moving his drab lease cars to Enterprise rental in Virginia.

He let out the clutch and went back to his mowing.

Nineteen

At 3:05 Nick's motion sensors activated the flood-lights, set off the alarms, and brought Harry's assault team to a momentary standstill in the woods.

Zoe shot upright in bed, stifling a scream. Why . . . she had no idea since she refused to buy into the whole freaky situation where people were out to get her or Nick or both. Her stalwart defiance began to vaporize, however, when she suddenly realized she was alone in bed.

Oh God. She'd been left in the lurch to deal with possible killers all by herself!

Most women would scream at a time like this, Nick thought, watching her from the window. "Looks like some of your friends are outside."

Thank God she wasn't alone! She didn't even care that Nick's voice was grim. "They're definitely not *my* friends. In fact, I've never been more scared." She squinted into the darkness . . . there! Nick's shadowy form materialized from the shadows across the room.

"And I'm supposed to believe you?" he muttered, his gaze trained on the floodlit yard outside the windows. He'd seen scared before and she didn't quite fit the bill.

"Look, I don't have a clue who the hell is out there," she snapped. "And I'm guessing you do."

"Maybe," he said, figuring anyone Willerby hired would have been amateurs. This assault had paused to make adjustments. Professionals. "Okay—let's say I believe you," he heard himself saying, knowing full well what was driving him. Sex, sex—and sex. He hoped his libido wouldn't make him a dead sucker. "Get dressed. We have to get out of here."

He'd shifted his stance slightly, giving her a glimpse of a deadly looking sidearm holstered at his hip, and all of a sudden, she really, really, *really* wanted to go back to her old safe, pre-death-threats life. Unfortunately, that possibility wasn't likely with whomever was outside. "My clothes are next door," she said, trying to keep her voice from shaking.

"Bring in your duffle bags and dress here," he directed, turning back to the window as a floodlight suddenly went out. More correctly, was shot out. "I suggest you hurry."

Tossing the covers aside, she leaped from the bed and moved toward the door. "Could this be Willerby's operation?"

"I doubt it. It looks like professionals." Another floodlight went dark.

"Oh, God, don't say *professionals*. *Professionals* for what?" she squeaked.

"Just get your gear," he gruffly replied, ignoring her question, as the ping of another round hitting a light echoed inside and the lakeside went black. "We don't have much time. I'm gonna check the other side of the house and I'll meet you back here in five. Go."

He hadn't raised his voice, but she understood authority when she heard it.

By the time she'd fetched her luggage from the bedroom next door, he was back, carrying a slim leather bag in one hand. "I'll carry your bags. It doesn't matter what you wear. We're just going down to the boathouse."

"Why the boathouse?" Unzipping a bag, she pulled out jeans, a T-shirt, and a pair of tennis shoes.

"I'd like to get out of here before they get too trigger-happy." Harry's assassins were into overkill. Finesse wasn't a factor in their testosterone-driven world. He'd counted ten goons out there at least—all armed. He'd once seen this crowd pour ten thousand rounds into a farmhouse—that turned out to be empty.

Grabbing Zoe's backpack, Nick slung it over his shoulder along with his laptop bag, zipped up the duffle bag, and picking up both the bags, waited grim-faced for her to dress.

She could have won a prize for fastest dresser in the world.

But then she had incentive.

She didn't want to be anyone's target—particularly if real bullets were involved.

Nick was halfway through the bedroom door the second she tied her last shoelace. Racing down the hall to catch up with him, Zoe breathlessly said, "Tell me everything is going to turn out all right so I don't die of a heart attack. Lie if necessary."

He shot her a look over his shoulder. "We should get out of here safely enough. But we have to hustle."

While it wasn't exactly the assurance she was looking for—like *this is all a dream and you'll wake up soon*—at least he sounded bluntly determined.

Since she didn't actually have a choice—it was go with Nick or wait to be shot by men with guns—she followed close on his heels without further self-examination or questions.

They took the basement stairs at a run, entered an underground tunnel, its entrance hidden in an abandoned coal storage room, and raced down a timber-lined passageway that sloped downward. Toward the lake presumably.

When they reached a small doorway, Nick put out his hand to halt her. "Stay here. I'll see what's going on outside first." Setting down the baggage, he slowly opened the door, the hinges silent and obviously well-oiled. He disappeared from sight only to reappear a moment later. "We're clear. Stay close."

As if, she thought, but she didn't say it, given the circumstances—such as the fact that her life was in mortal danger.

She just stuck to Nick like glue as he dashed across a small stretch of grass between an old root cellar and the boathouse. He carried all the bags as if they were weightless, leaping onto the dock with a light-footed tread.

Shoving open the boathouse door, he waited until Zoe was inside, then locked it behind them and moved toward a large seaplane. Jumping onto a pontoon, he opened a side door and tossed in the luggage, while Zoe was trying to come to grips with the notion of *flying away*. It seemed a hundred times more dangerous than *driving away*—like to the police, for instance. Like to Nick's cousin, the sheriff, for a real good instance.

"Untie that mooring strap," Nick said, pointing to the opposite side of the plane as he moved to unlock the large door facing the lake.

She obeyed because her brain was short-circuiting and alternative escape plans didn't seem to be rushing to her rescue. "Couldn't we just call the sheriff?" She had to at least make the effort.

"He wouldn't get here in time." Nick tossed the padlock on the deck and shoved open a large accordion-pleated slat door, the panels sliding smoothly over a metal track.

Oh God! He won't get here in time meaning before we'd be killed!

"We'll call him later—once we're out of here. How would that be?" She was frozen in place. This was the time for lies. "Everything's okay. Don't worry."

A second later, Nick was unfastening the strap she was supposed to untie. And a second after that, he picked her up, swung her onto the pontoon, opened the plane door, and said, "Get in . . . please, right now," he softly added.

More or less in shock, she wasn't capable of speech; she did as she was told. It wasn't as though a better choice was available or even *any* choice.

Once Zoe was inside and seated, Nick climbed in, slammed the door shut, and sat down in the front of the cockpit. The R-985 Pratt & Whitney nine-cylinder engines of the Twin

Beech 18 roared to life a second later, and the seaplane slowly taxied from its berth. Nick flashed her a quick smile over his shoulder. "You're doin' good, babe."

She tried to smile, not very successfully.

But Nick had already turned back and was checking the gauges and easing the throttle forward.

As the propellers cleared the open portal, he advanced the throttle another small measure. The nose of the plane slid past the door, the cockpit next, and suddenly the lake opened up before them—shimmering under a moonless sky and dark, scudding clouds.

"Buckle up," he ordered, shifting his grip on the joystick as the tail cleared the doorway. He glanced back—left and right, once, twice, then he said as quietly as the noise of the engines allowed, "Hang on. Here's where it gets interesting."

He slammed the throttle into the dash.

The scream of the engines blasted through the stillness of night, the reverberation echoing over the lake like a sonic boom as the plane rapidly picked up speed.

Zoe watched the speedometer needle steadily climb. She could feel the hard *slap, slap* tattoo of the waves as the pontoons sliced through the water, the roar of the engines vibrating through the plane, and she hoped like hell Nick knew how to fly—*really well*—because she'd always been warned about the dangers of flying in small planes. Especially at night. When it was really dark and moonless.

Oh shit.

A flash of light or flame streaked by, inches from the left wing.

"What was that!" she shrieked.

"Shoulder-fired missile!"

"A missile!" she screeched, even as another vivid flash exploded way too close for comfort directly in front of them.

"We're lifting off," Nick shouted over the roar of the engines, wanting to give her some warning because he was going up as sharply as the plane design would allow. He jammed down the flaps and the plane began rising from the water in a precipitous canting slope. If they made it to the security of the cloud bank above, they'd be out of sight and home free. Fortunately the sky was overcast and the moon obscured, making them a more difficult target.

But they'd need more than darkness to outfly a missile. They needed Lady Luck as well. Running full flaps for both speed and lift, Nick flew the heavy twin engine bush plane like a featherweight crop duster. Banking hard left and right, side to side, always climbing steeply, he managed to evade two more missiles before they finally reached cloud cover at ten thousand feet. Exhaling, feeling as though a fifty-pound weight had been lifted from his shoulders, he leveled out the plane and set it to cruising speed—a fast two hundred miles per hour.

"How you doin'? Okay?" he shouted, like they'd just finished a rousing tennis match.

Zoe gave him a thumbs-up because she wasn't capable of politesse when she was so *far* from okay the concept wasn't even remotely in her frame of reference. Nor did she contemplate that okay feeling surfacing anytime soon after having been fired at by *freaking* missiles. Her heart was pounding in her chest, her limbs were shaking, and the only reason she hadn't jumped out of her skin was because she was strapped in her seat.

"You can relax now," Nick shouted, flashing her a smile. "We have about two hours of flying time ahead."

Relax? If she could relax after what she'd just been through, she would have been fully capable of becoming the next astronaut to the moon. No further training required.

"We should be out of range now, and my outpost camp is hard to find even if you know where it is."

He was trying to be nice. He really was. She wished she could join him in happy land, but jeez, this scary shit was way too unnerving for her to quickly switch gears.

Missiles had never figured prominently or otherwise in her sheltered world.

She offered him a smile that was more like a grimace, but she couldn't help herself. Right now, she was feeling as though things were only going to get worse and no way, no how, could she dredge up even a modicum of Pollyanna emotion.

In contrast, her pilot was whistling and apparently unconcerned with her frame of mind. He'd switched on a radio and a second later he was talking/shouting in what could only be code to God knew who.

Twenty

Alan Levaro was sitting on the edge of his bed, leaning over his shortwave radio, deciphering Nick's message as he spoke. Harry had sent his attack team, Nick and some woman had escaped and were on their way to his outpost camp in Canada. Nick needed some serious artillery. ASAP.

Since Alan happened to deal in said arms, *and* since he'd been to Nick's camp, and even better since he also flew, he promised Nick prompt action. "Late tomorrow," he said in code. "I'll bring the full package."

Nick reminded him Mandy needed close supervision.

Alan said it was in place—everything was copacetic.

The men signed off, and Alan turned to his wife, who had come awake when his message center had started buzzing.

"Someone should eliminate Harry," she said, having heard the conversation. "He's out of control and has been for way too long."

"He still has friends in high places, sweetheart, but his lease on life is getting shorter. And I won't be gone long. Nick needs some ordnance at his outpost camp."

Alan's wife had been an analyst at the CIA before she resigned five years ago. She knew Harry and despised him, as did most people who had the misfortune to cross his path. She was also Alan's source for information within the agency. Many of her former colleagues were disgruntled and willing to cooperate with those with more reasonable convictions. The upheaval within the CIA was unprecedented; morale was at an all-time low. Almost everyone was opposed to Harry Miller's appointment to director.

In personal terms, with the mass resignations and defections from the agency to private security firms in the last few years, Alan's field of contacts had expanded. As had his business.

"I'll pack you a lunch. Which camp are you going to?" Ginny Levaro had met Nick years ago when the three of them had been in Kosovo, and they all vacationed together from time to time.

"The one on Jackfish. He has a woman with him."

"Nick brought along recreation at a time like this?"

"I couldn't tell. Probably not."

His wife smiled. "Make sure you ask. I adore gossip."

Twenty-one

"I don't *fucking* believe it! You *lost* him? *Ten* of you lost *one* fucking man!"

"He had a bush plane in his boathouse. It was a boathouse. Who knew?" Bob Hanover had been listening to Harry scream for years. It never rattled him, because he knew Harry was a wuss and if anyone dangerous needed to be wacked, Harry sure as hell wasn't going to do it himself. "We'll find him, Harry. Don't get your pants in a bundle."

"The congressional hearing is in five days! He has to be gone in *five* days! Do you fucking understand?"

"Yeah, yeah, save your breath. I'm not looking for a promotion so I don't have to kiss your ass. Remember, Harry, you need me more than I need you. In fact, you need me real bad right about now."

"Point taken," Harry muttered. "Accept my apology. But you do understand the very limited time frame."

"Apology accepted," Bob Hanover said just to piss Harry off. "And we'll get him. It's not a problem."

"Allow me to be skeptical after the recent malfunction."

"Things don't always go like clockwork and the bastard had his house covered from every angle. I never saw such a security layout other than, say, your house, Harry," Hanover drawled.

"Very funny. I hope you realize now, he's not going to be an easy target."

"I never thought he was. You forget, I met him once in Pristina—right after he broke your jaw. So listen up, Harry. Here's what I'll be needing. And don't give me any shit about having to go through channels. You and I both know there isn't time. Gotta pencil?"

Twenty-two

They glided in for a landing just as the first rays of the sun broke over the horizon. The air was still, the lake deep blue and mirror-smooth, dark pines and green poplar stretched far as the eye could see—the scene that of tranquil nature with a capital *T*. On the distant shore, a small assortment of buildings were the only sign of human existence—not just here, but in the wilderness they'd flown over ever since crossing the border. Not that the line between the United States and Canada had been distinguishable in the vastness of forest and lakes below them.

But Zoe was willing to take Nick's word for it.

Nick brought the aircraft down lightly on the placid surface of the lake, the silver plane glistening in the morning sun. Slowly taxiing to a long dock, he cut the engines shortly before reaching it and was out the door and onto a pontoon in a flash. Jumping onto the dock, he secured the bush plane to mooring rings with a few efficient twists of the wrist.

Returning to help Zoe alight, he said, "I'll run the plane into the boathouse later. I'll bet you're hungry."

Disoriented maybe, frightened surely, hungry, not so much. "Not really," she replied, stepping onto the dock, wondering how he could think of food when their lives were in crisis. "Maybe later."

"How about a latte?"

He was so damned chipper, she found herself mildly resentful. Not that she wasn't grateful to be alive—thanks to him. But she also was in the middle of a bloody wilderness that she couldn't find her way out of in a million years, people with lethal motives might still be after them, and she wasn't altogether sure her pilot and savior was entirely stable. So sue her if she wasn't a happy camper.

"Sorry, I really like this place," he said, recognizing her restive, frazzled air. "But this isn't business as usual for you, is it?"

"Not exactly," she retorted, a tad snappishly.

"Let me show you around and you might feel better," he graciously offered, taking her hand, forgetting in his pleasure at reaching his favorite spot in the world that she was still a partial unknown. Although the percentages that he believed her were definitely on the rise. "Once you're settled in, you'll be able to relax." He smiled and started walking down the dock. "And this is a helluva lot safer than Ely."

"They still could follow us," Zoe muttered, not ready to smile yet.

"We're hard to find."

"Because we're at the ends of the freaking earth."

"The good end though," he pleasantly replied, ignoring her sulkiness. "Wait and see."

He pointed out two boathouses as they moved down the dock, one for the plane and one for boats and once they started up a small incline of granite outcropping and wild grasses, he indicated a woodshed with a wave of his hand, then a gazebo perched on a rocky point, and the sauna on the shore, painted brick red with white trim. On reaching the crest of the hill, they approached a sizeable log cabin with a porch running across half the front. "Welcome to my Batcave."

"No joke. It's just as hidden."

"That's the idea—for me at least," he replied, leading her up a wide staircase. "Although my Grandad bought this lake for the fishing."

"You have a whole lake?" In her surprise she forgot her pique. It was a big lake.

"It didn't cost much at the time. Grandad got the Twin Beech as war surplus after World War II so he could fly in. By canoe, it's at least a two-day trip depending on whether you take time to sleep or not."

"It looks as though you've done work here, too." Portions of the buildings were obviously more recent than sixty-some years.

"Yeah, I've built a fair amount here—construction therapy,"

he added with a grin. "Come on in." He opened a green door hung on huge black wrought iron hinges.

Once inside, Zoe's gaze widened. "Nice therapy," she murmured, awed by the size and beauty of the cathedral-ceilinged room. A dramatic fieldstone fireplace stood dead center, a wall of windows sparkled in the morning sun, the log walls glowed an aged honey gold, the furniture was over-sized to complement the spacious area. Large mission-style chairs and sofas, made for men she suspected, were scattered about while the pine floor was covered with colorful hooked rugs like those at the lake place in Ely. "Your Grandma's rugs, I'll bet."

"Yeah. She never sat still. She was always busy making things. Nice things," he softly added. "I'll show you the kitchen," he offered in a different tone of voice, conversational and bland. "I have an old woodstove that makes the best pan-cakes. They end up kinda smoky, but really good. I'll make you some later."

He was proud of his cabin, as well he should be, Zoe decided after being given the grand tour. It had all the amenities: solar heat and light; a propane generator for backup on cloudy days; indoor plumbing; two cozy bedrooms and a little gem of a library that overlooked a sea of pink and white sweet william outside the window.

"This is an absolute paradise." Experiencing a sense of snug comfort in contrast to her former misgivings, she did indeed feel better as Nick had predicted. "A person could live here comfortably for a *very* long time. I see why you like it. And I didn't need batteries for my laptop after all," she added with a grin.

"I was trying to discourage you." Nick lifted his brows faintly. "You can't blame me. I had no idea who you were."

"And now you have a little better idea?" Zoe playfully noted.

"Yeah, you might say that," he said, soft and low. But thoughts of sex instantly triggered all the pesky unknowns—including the possible risk in fucking the seductive Miss Chandler. *And no handcuffs here.*

"I feel sooo far away from all the nastiness of the Willerbys of the world," Zoe breathed. "You were right. One feels safe here." Overcome by a genuine well-being—their recent perils left behind—she opened her arms wide and offered him a dazzling smile. "I'm *very much* in your debt, Mr. Mirovic." Closing the distance between them, she leaned into his body, wrapped her arms around his neck, rose on tiptoe, and kissed him lightly. Leaning back slightly, she whispered, "That's a thank-you."

"You're definitely welcome," he whispered, holding her gently and kissing her for a long, lingering moment. Then unwinding her arms from around his neck, he stepped away. "I have to take a rain check," he said to the surprise in her eyes. "My security needs a look-see first."

"You're not *serious*! We're the only human beings for hundreds of miles."

"Maybe, maybe not."

"Couldn't it wait?" Lush, sultry invitation in her tone.

"Not really."

She held his gaze. "You still don't trust me, do you?"

"I don't trust anyone."

She blew out a small breath. "Tell me what I have to do to make you understand I am who I say I am."

His lashes drifted downward and he gave her an assessing look. "Probably not much of anything. Don't take it personally. Harry's the kind who doesn't give up until he gets what he wants. Although, you might already know that."

"Jeez Louise, I *don't know* Harry! I have *never* known a Harry in my life! I don't even know who the hell would name their kid Harry. And consider, my suspicious fellow traveler, why would I be stupid enough to even think about doing you harm when, at the risk of possibly adding to your conceit," she said with a beguiling smile, "you've given me sexual pleasure a thousand times better than anyone I've ever run across."

Even as he reminded himself she was probably lying, his libido was already stoking up, his erection was readying itself for action, and his brain was racing through possible options for on-the-spot sex that didn't include him dying. "Look, I'd like to believe you," he said, his voice taut with constraint, "but since I can't for a bunch of reasons you couldn't begin to understand, let's just keep things the way they are."

"You mean sex with handcuffs."

"Not exactly. I don't have any here."

She glanced at his crotch, his arousal obvious. "I'm sure you can improvise," she murmured with more than a touch of sarcasm.

"Don't be a bitch. I'm not in the mood."

She sucked in her breath. His dark eyes had gone cold, his mouth was set in a harsh, unyielding line, and suddenly conscious that she was alone in the remoteness of the Canadian wilderness with a possibly dangerous man, she quickly said, "Forgive me. I didn't mean to offend you. You know best. You call the plays."

His smile was instant. "Don't freak. I won't hurt you." Another quick smile, boyish and sweet. "You're white as a ghost."

"It's a long way to civilization."

He exhaled softly. "Maybe I was a little curt," he said, his tone ultraconciliatory. "I'm on a short fuse." *Harry has a lot to answer for, including, perhaps, this sexy babe. Then again, maybe she is clean; wouldn't that be fucking nice.*

"We're both tense," she acknowledged with a smile.

"Look, why don't you call Joe or some friend of yours on my shortwave and give them an update. You can't talk long, because I don't want to give anyone time to get a fix and lock onto the signal. But you can tell them you'll call back tomorrow. That way you know you have someone on your side— you're not completely alone in the wilderness."

"But I am," she retorted, thinking she shouldn't be so mouthy, but then that would require a personality change. "You know as well as I do that no one could *ever* find me out here."

He shrugged. It was impossible to argue the reality. "Regardless, you're safe. I'm harmless. Should I put that in writing?"

"Since I saw your idea of 'harmless' stacked up in your kitchen pantry, do me a favor and cut the bullshit."

He softly sighed. "Let's put it this way. You, personally, are safe from me," he said, very, very softly. "Guaranteed. Cross my heart and hope to die," he added, his gaze amused.

Call her a pushover for atonement in a man. Although honestly, Nick's glorious erection may have been more of a mitigating factor. "Does that mean I'm safe from sexual advances, too?" she purred.

He grinned. "Now you're jerkin' my chain."

"You're not going to give me an opening line I could drive a Mack truck through, are you—like maybe there was something else I could jerk off?"

"Cute."

She lifted her chin slightly, directed her heated gaze at him, and said, hushed and low, "Perhaps if you made me feel really, really good I'd forget about being afraid of you."

He laughed. "Does anyone ever say no to you when you look at him like that?"

She smiled. "Not usually."

Pulling her close, he slid his hands down her bottom and hauled her against him so she could feel the full extent of his erection. "You win. But seriously," he added, brushing her mouth with a kiss, "I have to check my security first, so you'll have to wait awhile."

"How long?" she whispered.

He dragged in a breath, exhaled, and said, "Fifteen minutes. I'll hurry." His smile would make any woman weak in the knees. "But if we have incoming because you need sex ASAP, it's gonna be all your fault."

"I'll get undressed and wait in your bed," she whispered,

every sexual nerve in her body racheting up. "You just take all the time you need," she purred.

"Bitch." But his voice was husky and without umbrage this time.

And his security system was reviewed in record time.

Twenty-three

Nick went through the flight bag in the plane and came up with a few condoms. He normally didn't bring women to his outpost camp. However—like everything else with Zoe Chandler—*normal* had taken a hike.

So when he entered the bedroom, condoms in his pockets and a small bouquet of pinks in hand, he was pretty much in carpe diem mode. And when the condoms ran out, he'd just have to punt. "Here, babe, I come bearing gifts."

"How sweet. They smell wonderful. You look even *more* wonderful," Zoe murmured, lying tantalizingly nude and expectant on his bed.

He held up the flowers. "Water," he said. A moment later, he'd put them in a glass from the washstand and brought them back to the bedside table.

"You constantly amaze me," Zoe said, coming up on one

elbow to sniff the fragrant little bouquet. "You're not all Mr. Tough Guy."

"I never said I was." He kicked off his sandals. "You were the one who came looking for a bodyguard. Perception, babe," he said with a grin. "It's in the eye of the beholder."

"Speaking of perception," she murmured, as he stripped off his T-shirt, "you are really, really *fine* Mr. Mirovic."

Taking in the view, he lifted his brows and said, "While you babe, are looking—"

"Eager and impatient?"

He laughed. "I was gonna say, you're looking real fine on my bed. No shit, I must live right." Zoe was lying on top of his patchwork quilt, looking like some bucolic Daisy Mae centerfold, although her blonde pubic hair was glistening in a ray of sunshine as in a consummate porno shot. Staged or real? Right now, he didn't give a damn.

"Just hurry," she whispered. "I am sooo hot—here, feel." She put her hands to her cheeks. "And it's all your fault."

"So you're not this hot all the time. Yeah, right." *I haven't just fallen off the last turnip truck. This chick could come on a dime.*

"*No*. I'm not!"

She actually looked affronted. "Fine," he said noncommittal and circumspect. "I'm glad." *This is no time to insist on the truth.*

"It's some Karma thing or some weird sexual affinity. I haven't a clue which or why, but I want you—constantly." She smiled. "Except when people are shooting at us."

Speak for yourself, he thought. When his adrenalin was spiking, so was his libido. "We have plenty of time right now," he said, unzipping his shorts. "So why don't we test out that *constantly* thing." Pulling out the condoms before he dropped his shorts to the floor, he tossed them on the bedside table.

"Is that all?" Zoe said with alarm, silently counting the condoms.

"No, I have more," Nick lied. *No way am I getting in an argument now.* "Move over." *I should have tied her hands.* He should have done any number of reasonable, prudent things, starting with leaving her behind. But at this precise moment, it didn't look like he'd have to fight off an assassin. She was beginning to pant.

The instant he lay down on the bed, she rolled on top of him, threw her arms around his neck, and showered him with kisses.

Death by kisses, he thought, smiling against her mouth. *Not a bad way to go.*

She was soft and warm blanketing him, her skin silky smooth under his hands, and he genially returned her kisses because they had nothing but time until Alan arrived. He gently traced the curve of her spine, skimmed the ripe curves of her bottom with his palms, held her for a tremulous moment against the hard, rigid length of his erection and figured Karma or whatever—he liked the kick-ass rush.

"You have to give me *that* . . ." Zoe whispered against his mouth, moving her hips gently back and forth over his erection.

"In a minute, babe." He smiled faintly. "I'm having a Zen moment here."

"You're always so take-it-or-leave-it calm and I'm ravenous, insatiable." Her pale brows drew together in a frown. "How do you do it?" Then her mouth lifted in a sudden smile. "Who cares. I'm just sooo glad you brought me along."

"Me, too," he said, in lieu of the truth. They both knew he almost hadn't.

"For your information, I might take advantage of you while I'm here," she playfully teased.

He laughed. "I hope like hell you do."

"Oh, good," she said, brushing a kiss over his mouth before pushing herself up and straddling his hips. "Although, you're much too handsome, you know," she grumbled, wrinkling her nose. "You must have women throwing themselves at you all the time."

"Nah," he lied, quickly grabbing a condom and ripping open the foil, because he could see where this was going. "But believe me, I'm more than happy if *you* want to."

"What a darling," Zoe purred. "And him, too," she softly added, running the pads of her fingers up his taut erection lying flat against his stomach, the engorged veins pulsing under her fingertips. "I'm ridiculously jealous about where this gorgeous cock goes," she said, coming up on her knees while Nick rolled the condom down at record speed. "And there's no reason in the world why I should when I didn't even know who you were a day"—and before she had time to reach for Nick's rampant penis or finish her sentence, he'd helped himself to her hot, wet cunt, impaling her on his flagpole of an erection and curtailing her speech.

Save for what was becoming a familiar little satisfied moan.

Holding her hips motionless, his fingers stretched wide, he whispered, "Try coming without moving this time . . ."

Her lashes lifted marginally so he could see the stormy green of her eyes. "Don't want to," she muttered, sulkily.

"Try it. You'll like it."

"No I won't." Pouty, begrudging his assurance.

"Maybe you don't have a choice. I'm stronger than you . . . bigger . . . feel how big I am. Your hot little cunt is crammed full." Maybe he was more intolerant of her ripe and ready passions than he'd admit. Perhaps he was feeling a perverse need to chastize her. "Think of it this way," he said, raspy and low, "if you do as you're told, I'll let you have my cock for as long as you want."

"Nick, no. I can't—really I can't," Zoe heatedly protested, struggling to break free, squirming against his hold, chock-full of his enormous cock and so feverishly aroused, she was quivering.

"When your boobs bounce and jiggle like that it makes me really horny," Nick whispered, softly. "Are you teasing me with your big boobs?"

She shook her head, feverishly tried to pry his fingers loose.

"You're turning me on anyway, babe," he murmured, ignoring her clawing fingers. "Can you feel that? My cock's getting bigger and harder."

She softly groaned, her eyes half shut, her cheeks flushing pink.

"There—see—you're almost there." She was clearly trembling on the brink. "See if this helps," he whispered, and flexing his hips, he thrust upward with brute force.

She gasped, then whimpered, frenzied, shockingly in heat. "Please, Nick . . . oh God, please."

"Please what?" His voice was rough, harsh, an outlandish *jealousy* suddenly manifest in his thoughts. *She's ready to fuck anywhere, anytime, damn it.* "You want to come, right?"

"Yes, yes, yes!"

"Then you're willing to do whatever I want?"

"Yes," she panted. "Anything."

It was amazing how a single word could be such a powerful aphrodisiac. It felt like his dick swelled a foot. "You sure?"

She quickly nodded, eyes shut, breathing hard, her entire body flushed with passion.

"You can't say no to me."

She shook her head. "I won't, I won't."

"If I want you to beg me to fuck you, you will."

"Yes, yes."

"If I want to fuck you all night, you have to let me."

"Yes."

"Yes, what?"

Her eyes snapped open, bewilderment in her gaze.

"Say, 'Yes, master.'" He was so outside the pale, the voice couldn't have been his. Nor the thought. Denial in extremis.

She hesitated.

He tightened his grip on her hips, his fingers pressing into her soft flesh.

"Yes, master," she whispered, shuddering, her gaze focused inward once again on the wild, sensual prodigality overwhelming her senses.

He smiled, an austere, cryptic smile. "That's a good girl." Then he raised her up his erection and controlled her downward descent, prolonging the exquisite, agonizing pressure, determining the degree of honeyed friction as pulsing nerve met overwrought tissue, further inflaming the seething, turbulent sensations.

But as he well knew, once she was resting on his thighs again, once she was so gorged full of cock she was uncontrollably shaking, she climaxed.

Violently.

Wildly.

Headlong, unaided by judgment.

Like I knew you would.

Brief moments later, he tumbled her onto her back and fucked her again the old-fashioned way—perhaps in apology for his small tyranny, perhaps to convince himself that he hadn't done what he'd just done. Telling himself his perverse need for her submission probably had to do with the coming assault whipping up his libido.

He was particularly gentle, tender, kissing her like an adoring lover might, making sure she was utterly sated and replete before allowing himself to climax. Holding her face between his hands at the end, he held her gaze and whispered with a disarming smile, "Wanna go steady?"

"No, you're too mean."

He knew what she meant. "You could have said no," he blandly replied, rolling off her onto his back, stripping off his condom, and tossing it.

She punched him. Hard.

She punches like a girl, not like someone trained to kill. And she definitely wasn't faking her orgasms. Two points for my side. He wiped himself off on the sheet.

"And here's for being such an ass!" she said, slamming her fist in his arm again.

He shot her a look, thinking he probably should apologize. But she jerked his chain in ways he didn't particularly like. So maybe they were even when it came to frustration. Seriously, he didn't like this have-to-have-it crap with sex. He didn't want to *crave* a woman.

"You should apologize," she muttered, coming up on one elbow and glaring at him.

He turned his head on the pillow. "What for? Your five orgasms?"

"It's not just about orgasms."

"Excuse me. Weren't you the babe begging to come?"

"Take me home."

He gave her a slit-eyed look. "You're joking, right?"

She came up into a seated position so fast, he braced himself for another blow, but she only crossed her legs and smiled down at him. "I suppose I am."

"Fuck. You're crazier than I am."

She made a face. "Au contraire. I'm addicted to that." She nodded in the direction of his—wouldn't you know it—fully tumescent erection. "Jeez," she murmured, half in awe, half bewildered, "you must be popping Viagra."

"Au contraire," he mimicked. "My Viagra is in bed with me."

"Really," she said with a wide smile and a playful flutter of her lashes.

"So don't talk to me about addiction," he growled. "I should have left you in Ely."

"But you can't live without me."

"I can't live without this," he said, coming up off his back at warp speed, pushing her down, shoving two fingers up her vagina, and delicately stroking her G-spot like he hadn't just growled, like he was the sweetest lover on the face of the earth.

Lying in a blatantly sensual sprawl, her senses on fire, she whispered, "Maybe we shouldn't think too hard about any of this."

"You got my vote," he grunted, reaching for a condom.

They made love leisurely this time, as if they were abstemious personalities, as if they had momentarily jettisoned their mainline addition to sex. He kissed her everywhere—up and down her body, in every crevice and fold and heated orifice. And when she attempted to return the favor, he held her gently at bay and said, "Later, babe." He still wasn't sure of her and keeping his cock intact was high on his list of priorities. Especially with hours to go until Alan arrived. But when she screamed his name at the last as she climaxed, he experienced a rare, singular pleasure. Analogous to the inexplicable pleasure he felt when he came a few moments later.

At a loss to understand his extraordinary fondness for Zoe Chandler, Nick resorted to his habitual remedy to uncertainty and doubt. "I'll be right back," he murmured, rising from the bed. When he returned he was carrying a bottle of Stoli Cristal.

She recognized his familiar palliative. "Therapy time?" she said with a grin, resting against the pillows.

"Old habits," he said, sitting at the end of the bed. "Want some?"

"No thanks," she said, moving her legs over to give him room. "I'm good. Temporarily, of course," she added with a teasing smile. "I hope you don't mind."

"As if," he said, leaning back against the footboard. "Cheers." He lifted the bottle to his mouth and drank a generous portion.

"You can tell me it's none of my business, but I have this strange compulsion to want to know everything about you; it's a girl thing. Do you have a trust fund, a secret job, a benevolent mentor? You don't seem to work."

"I build canoes."

"I see," she politely said, not believing him for a minute. "Do you have family—mom, dad, brothers or sisters, aunts, uncles—do you like pizza or pasta, dogs or cats, Dostoyevsky or Dickens, Britney or Annie Lennox—tell me everything." In the aftermath of extra-lovely orgasms with an extra-lovely man, like every female she wanted to know all there was to know, including his favorite toothpaste. So sue her.

"It's none of your business." Like most men he didn't feel like telling her.

"Never mind then." She'd settle for sex instead of conversation.

He smiled. "It looks like you can be polite if you're not hungry for sex."

"And you can't, sexually or otherwise," she said in more of a teasing voice than a serious one. "Mr. I'm-the-Fucking-Boss."

"Sorry. That was an aberration for which I apologize."

"Well, it all turned out excellently in the end," she noted with a smile.

"I noticed," he drawled.

"If I didn't appreciate the incredible benefits, I might be pissed at your virtuoso skills."

"Why? They make you feel good."

"I don't know why—okay?"

"Fine with me. And to answer your questions," he said, as if he hadn't recently blown her off, "I don't have any immediate family left. My mom and dad died in an accident when I was twelve, my grandparents are gone, too, and the reason I don't work," he added, "is because I sold the north end of Burntside Lake after my grandpa died. They're not making anymore lakeshore in case you haven't noticed. The developers went crazy."

"So you're independently wealthy."

"Comfortable." He lifted the bottle in her direction. "Feel like sitting outside for a while?" *I'm done giving out information.*

"Sure." She could tell he was done giving out information.

He came to his feet, and offered her his hand.

When she rose from the bed, she said, "Aren't you getting dressed?"

"There's no one for miles. If you're worried though, we can sit in the gazebo."

It turned out to be a heavenly venue for making love. The gazebo had two big chaises and a view to die for. With the cultivated grace Nick exercised more often than not, three orgasms later, he brought her out a lemonade and vodka, along with chocolate-chip cookies from his freezer—suitably zapped in the microwave.

"You sure know how to charm a woman," Zoe said, lounging back on her chaise, the sun warming her skin, a cookie in one hand, a drink in the other, and the man responsible for both her creature comforts and her sexual gratification lying on an adjoining chaise—close enough to touch.

He turned to her with a really sweet smile. "Life's good—no doubt about it."

A sudden hush fell.

Ripe with tenderness.

"Shit," he muttered, a heartbeat later and lifted the Stoli bottle to his mouth.

Zoe emptied her glass as if she needed a quick antidote to untoward feeling.

A moment later, she calmly said, "Look at that lovely red-tailed hawk in that Norway pine over there."

He smoothly replied, "There's another one over there by the dock."

They were careful after that to avoid comments that might be construed as overly emotional. They both understood that sexual craving was by its nature a physical manifestation.

Despite carnal desire and lustful passions, however, neither was inclined to relinquish their avid pursuit of *that* pleasure.

It turned out to be a memorable night in terms of physical gratification.

As for their previous, impulsive tenderness, they both dutifully repressed any further embarrassment in that regard.

Twenty-four

That same evening, in Virginia hunt country, in the bedroom of a small Tudor-style cottage—slate roof and all—the sound of gently falling rain outside the window was drowned out by Harry Miller's harsh, breathless gasps. He was sprawled on his back on sweat-soaked Frette sheets, panting like a hound dog in a heat wave. His face was bright red, his paunch was shaking, and he was seeing blue spots before his eyes.

Damn the bitch, she'd done it again. But he was smiling.

The bitch in question was smiling, too, although a Miss Alabama would never be so gauche as to openly pant after sex. But the half capsule of Viagra she'd put into Harry's scotch had done its magic. She'd finally had a chance to come.

Much as she enjoyed Harry's largesse and her life of leisure, Harry's thirty-second fucks did on occasion require some personal adjustments. She deserved a mind-blowing orgasm every once and awhile, too.

"I should cut your allowance," he muttered, "for doping my drink."

"Harry, darlin'," Abigail—don't call her Abby—Cathcart sweetly murmured. "I only put in half a capsule. I'm always looking out for your health, sweetums. You know that. And admit it, you really got off."

He shot her a sideways look. "Fucking A."

She slid up on the pillows so her boobs looked better. "Then, see," she brightly declared, "mission accomplished."

Harry half smiled at her obvious pose, although he liked that she didn't have silicone boobs. "Bring your pussy over here, Alabama," he gruffly murmured, running his fingers up his cock. "I still have a boner from the Viagra. We might as well make use of it."

Harry's vulgar and crude, Abigail reflected with an inward sigh, *but he is generous with his money*. CIA money, she suspected. She'd found two suitcases full of hundred-dollar bills in neat packets in the back of the closet downstairs, a few of which she removed from time to time. Her Cayman Islands account under her cousin's name was increasing nicely. "Do you want me to be the French maid or the lady steeplechase rider?" she whispered in a sultry contralto as she came up on her knees and moved toward him. "You jus' tell little ol' me what your little heart desires . . ."

"Don't worry about my heart, Alabama, just ram your cunt down my cock before I lose this hard-on. Or come to think of it, you can play my secretary, Emily. Say something stupid—

something prissy like a tight cunt from Vassar would say if I asked her to suck my cock."

"Oh, Mr. Miller, sir," Abigail replied in a little girl voice as she settled on Harry's thighs, "what would my *daddy* say if I told him how disrespectful you were to me?"

"He'd say let *me* suck your cock," Harry said with a chuckle. "Lance Baskville and I have an understanding. I don't out him and as chairman of the Intelligence Committee, he never questions my requisitions."

"You're so very, very smart, Mr. Miller," Abigail purred, raising herself over Harry's hard-on and guiding it to her pussy. "Would you like me to stay after work and help you with any special projects?"

"I've got a special project for you all right." Harry grunted with satisfaction as Abigail slid down his cock. "You can ride my dick till I come and then lick it dry."

Eeewww . . . Harry is sooo gross.

Most of the time she had to shut her eyes and think of Tiffany's when she was having sex with him.

If I had the nerve, I'd sleep with that hunk trainer from Merry-weather Stables who's always ogling me at the polo matches. Those jodhpurs of his are a real turn-on. Every inch of his cock is out there for the world to see. And that cock I wouldn't mind licking.

But she valued her life.

She'd overheard enough of Harry's conversations to know that he gave his enemies short shrift. She didn't want to be targeted by one of his hit squads. And really . . . her vibrator was excellent.

Twenty-five

The next morning, Tony personally unlocked the holding cell door in the basement of the courthouse. "You're free to go," he said, surveying his two prisoners, who were in need of a shave and a change of clothes. "A word of advice, though. Go back to wherever you came from and leave us alone."

"Screw you! I'm suing your ass!" George Harmon snapped, bolting to his feet. Stalking through the cell door a moment later, Trevor on his heels, he said with a sneer as he brushed past Tony, "You're fucked. You have *no* idea who you're dealing with."

"Actually I do," Tony replied. "I did a little background checking. Nice families—both of you. You wouldn't want anything to happen to them."

Both men spun around on a dime.

A moment of shocked silence vibrated in the air.

"Are you threatening us?" George softly hissed. *Who the hell does this hick think he is?*

"I'm not threatening anyone." Tony certainly didn't look threatening. He wore jeans and a T-shirt with a Burntside Lodge logo on it, and if not for the badge clipped to his belt, he could have been anyone. "I'm just pointing out," he calmly noted, "that you may want to think about what your employer is asking of you. This—Willerby—that's his name, right?—he's asking you to put your and your families' lives on the line. According to my sources, it looks as though he doesn't get a lot of good press and that's an understatement," Tony said with a small smile. "Willerby also makes sure he never actually dirties his hands himself, although he expects others to. All I'm sayin' is you gotta ask yourselves if the price Willerby's paying you is worth the risk. Not that I'm suggesting there's any risk," he murmured, amiably. "But stuff happens all the time. Accidents, things like that."

George Harmon was about to respond with his usual intimidation and threats, point out to this nobody from nowhere that he and Willerby, in particular, had more power than God, but the words died in his throat at the look in the sheriff's eyes. Fuck, that was one eerie look. Cold as ice, ruthless. Even Willerby at his worst didn't strike such terror in him. Then again, Willerby wasn't capable of snapping your neck like this man obviously was.

Grabbing Trevor's arm, George turned and hastily withdrew, hightailing it down the basement hallway full tilt. He didn't even dare turn around to see if they were being followed, fearful of what he might see.

Did we stumble into some North Woods version of Deliverance?

George didn't stop running until he and Trevor were standing in the sunshine on the sidewalk outside the Iron Range granite-sheathed version of a Palladian villa courthouse. Feeling more in command—in the full light of day, within sight of passersby, his pulse rate subsiding—he spoke in a close to normal tone of voice. "We'll discuss what to do next with Willerby in New York, not here. I think we've outstayed our welcome in this burg."

Trevor gave him a jaundiced look. "You think? I'd say that was one helluva blunt warning."

"Sometimes these small town sheriffs have a Napoleonic complex," George countered, more courageous now that he was removed from immediate danger. "There are ways to deal with a man like that."

"You have my blessing to deal with him any fucking way you want, but I'm opting out. You heard what he said about our families. Fuck Willerby's art collection. His money can't buy my personal security. And Sims and Sims has been wooing me lately. I'm taking their offer."

"You're probably being sensible."

"No shit," Trevor vehemently replied. "As if Willerby would go to the mat for me—or you, for that matter."

George Harmon knew better than to actually express his feelings. The world of New York attorneys was an incestuous sphere and gossip spread faster than it did in Hollywood. "I understand your position," he said, neutrally. "Far be it from me to counsel you otherwise."

"Christ, George, do you ever say what you think?"

"It's been awhile." He wasn't sure he remembered how. "Let's get the car."

Twenty-six

Alan flew in early, arriving at midday.

"I'll help him unload and then bring him up to meet you," Nick said, getting up from the table where they were having lunch as the plane was taxiing to the dock.

Zoe looked up. "Is that a tactful way of telling me to stay here?"

"If you don't mind."

She smiled. "What if I do?"

"Then I'll have to be tactless. I have to talk business with Alan. Sorry."

"Yes, sir." She gave him a mock salute.

He rolled his eyes. "I won't be gone long."

He left by the kitchen door.

She watched Nick run down the hill and surprisingly greet

Alan with a hug. She wouldn't have thought him so unrestrained; he was the prototype for machismo in so many ways.

The men laughed over something, then spoke only a moment more before turning to the airplane and beginning to unload official-looking military green crates.

"Must be nice," Alan said, as each carried a box of rocket launchers to the boathouse, "having someone warming your bed up here in the bush."

"It wasn't as though I had a choice. Not that I'm complaining. You'll see when you meet her. She's easy on the eyes."

"I have orders from Ginny to get the scoop on this babe. Serious, not serious, true love or just sex."

"She was more or less dumped into my lap," Nick replied, not answering the question. "I still haven't decided if Harry had something to do with her or whether I can believe her story."

"Which is?"

Nick went on to explain about Willerby, the stolen art, the unfinished book, and the men who had threatened Zoe. "So," he finished, "you know as much as I do about what's true and what isn't. She could just as well be Harry's setup—like that deal in Kosovo when he sent in a female agent to zap the mayor of that town who was threatening to notify the UN about Harry's strong-arm methods of interrogation."

"How do you find out what's true?"

"Wait and see I guess."

Alan's brows rose. "That's a little dicey."

Nick smiled. "But not without side benefits in the meantime. But look, it's a waste of breath talking about this. I'll find out about her soon enough when Harry makes his next move. Either she helps him out or she doesn't."

"His hearing is next week."

"Then his hit squad should show up soon to see that he doesn't get any bad press from me."

"Ginny's keeping her ear to the ground. If she hears anything definitive, she'll let us know. But you know how Harry's off-the-record operations work. Most never see the light of day for obvious reasons."

"Understood. Which is why I needed extra firepower. Thanks for bringing me some high-class ordnance." Alan had brought rocket/grenade launchers, some heavy-duty shoulder-fired missiles, two antiaircraft field pieces, and perhaps most useful, a small radar station.

"Not a problem. I figure I need help some day, I'll call on you."

Nick nodded. "Anytime." The two men had worked together in Kosovo originally, although Alan had twice since called on Nick for some backup on arms deliveries to areas of the world where life was particularly cheap. Alan had been an Army Ranger when they'd first met, Nick had been chaffing at the bit under Harry's reign of terror in the Balkans, and the two had drunk away the night on more than one occasion, trying to anesthesize themselves from the brutality of that particular peacekeeping mission.

"I'll give you a hand with Harry's goon squad, too. You can't do it alone."

Nick turned from setting down a box of ammo. "Don't. Ginny wouldn't appreciate it. I'll be fine with the radar and this firepower. I can see them coming and take them out before they get close enough to touch me with the range on these weapons."

"Don't give me any shit. Two's better than one and you know it."

That's a tough one to argue. "You sure?" Nick grimaced. "I don't think it's such a good idea, and for sure your wife won't think so."

"Look, you're leaving yourself open to have this woman wack you while you're playing defense against Harry's crew. You can't watch your back when the shit starts flying. And I already told Ginny I was stayin'," he lied, "so don't give me any crap."

Nick didn't answer right away. "I'll owe you then," he finally said.

"Hell no, I'm still one behind after that Chechen deal. If not for you, we wouldn't have gotten out of that war zone alive."

"Knowing local dialects comes in handy at times," Nick said with a grin. He'd been able to hire a phalanx of unemployed ex-KGB to guide them in and out of Grosny for that particular transaction. The men were locals who had come back home: some were retired with government pensions that didn't cover much, a few of the young guys had decided freelancing paid better, and a couple turned out to be Chechen nationalists interested in liberating their country. They were more than happy to see that Alan's high-tech missile launchers got into the right hands.

"Knowing a dozen languages is fucking invaluable, too, my

friend. I still have nightmares about the time only your fast talking got us away from that Serbian mob in Derventa."

"You saved my ass more than once. Including now. My hunting rifles wouldn't have done the job these babies will," Nick said, carefully setting down a box of rocket grenades.

"Wait till you see my new radar. It's French, still experimental, and megasweet. We'll set it up in the house," Alan said. "We're about done here," he added, picking up two black metal cases the size of small suitcases. "Now, show me your lady. I admit a certain curiosity if Harry sent her."

"If he did, we'll find out pretty quick. Come on, I'll introduce you to the lovely Miss Chandler and you can give me your take on her."

Twenty-seven

 Seeing the men walking around to the back of the cabin, Zoe went out on the kitchen porch to greet them.

Wow—Harry knows how to pick 'em, Alan thought, *if indeed she's been sent. Not that a beautiful blonde with a killer body isn't from spy-world central casting.* But his expression gave nothing away when Nick made introductions.

"And before you ask," Nick added, "Al says Mandy's safe. Her security is in place and so far not a sign she's even being watched."

"Might Willerby have been bluffing?"

"Could be. Or maybe Tony put the fear of God into his advance men and they talked Willerby out of doing something stupid." *Tony can always be counted on to do his duty for the family.*

Zoe shot Nick a puzzled look. "Fear of God?"

"It's an expression." Turning to Alan, he deliberately changed the subject. "How about some lunch?"

"Sounds good. Ginny packed me a lunch, but I ate it about an hour out of Vancouver."

"Need a drink, a beer, something more interesting?" Nick offered, holding the door open for Zoe and Alan.

"A beer, thanks."

After following his two companions into the kitchen, Nick waved Alan toward a table set under the window. "Make yourself at home."

"Everything looks the same," Alan murmured, setting down the suitcases and glancing around the kitchen. "Peaceful as usual."

"That's the point of being isolated." Nick shot a glance over his shoulder as he took two beers from the fridge. "Or maybe *semi*-isolated."

"We'll find out," Alan said, taking a seat. "Not that you don't have a great defensive position here."

"Yeah—it's prime." Nick set two Labatt Blues on the table, took a seat, and casually said, "With that high ground behind the cabin, if anyone approaches from any direction, we have a clear shot."

Zoe looked up, the plate she was placing before Alan arrested midway to the table. "Talk of clear shots is making me nervous."

Alan and Nick exchanged a glance.

"Sorry, babe. It's only a remote possibility anyway," Nick added. "With luck, no one will find us." *And with that kind of luck, I'm sure to win the next Powerball lottery and live happily ever after in a land of milk and honey.*

"That's better." Zoe set the plate down. "I prefer denial if you don't mind. I'd like to enjoy the rest of my lunch."

"Nick's right," Alan observed, lying through his teeth. "This place is pretty far off the beaten path. I doubt anyone can find you." He smiled. "Nick tells me you're writing a book."

"I was until I was interrupted by some big-city lawyers who had been sent out to threaten me." Zoe sat down and picked up her napkin. "Apparently the subject of my book took issue with my exposé."

Alan half smiled. "You can't blame him, I suppose."

"I guess. Call me naive though—I was surprised at the style of his reprisal. Please, help yourself." Zoe indicated a bowl of pasta with red sauce. "Nick made it; I heated it up a minute ago."

"Zoe made the biscuits," Nick offered. "And we both worked on the salad," he added with a smile for Zoe.

The intimacy of Nick's smile as well as Zoe's was intriguing, Alan decided. He'd never seen an affectionate side to Nick, and when he'd first met him, Nick had been married, although the marriage had been in need of resuscitation by that point. While Nick was in Kosovo, his wife decided she wanted to live in L.A. and took a job teaching Slavic history at UCLA. He'd been pissed at her unilateral decision, but stuck halfway across the world wasn't in a position to alter the circumstances. Then he'd gotten Trish's Dear John, we've grown apart letter. She'd added the classic, it's not you, it's me, *and him and him and him* Nick had found out later. Anyway, it would be nice if Zoe Chandler hadn't been sent by Harry considering the obvious warmth of their relationship.

But if she had been, Nick would deal with it.

You didn't share life-threatening adventures without knowing the capacity for violence in the man who watched your back. Nick could be merciless if the occasion demanded.

Such grim thoughts were out of place in the current atmosphere of cloudless well-being, however. Alan refocused his attention on the conversation.

Nick spoke of their recent canoe trip to the rapids emptying into Loon Haunt and the repairs his old canoe required after their bumpy white-water ride. Zoe brought up their berry-picking excursion behind the cabin and they both cheerfully argued about who had picked the most blueberries. The loser apparently was obligated to make a pie.

Later, when Zoe asked, Alan explained how he and Nick had met and smoothly lied about the circumstances.

"Alan and I would rather forget we'd ever been in Kosovo," Nick remarked. "Not that it wasn't a good cause, but the day-to-day execution of the mission left a lot to be desired."

"Amen to that and changing the subject," Alan interjected with a grin. "Tell me when the sauna is going to be heated up for me."

Nick glanced at his watch. "I'll fire it up as soon as we're finished eating, so say, four hours from now it should be hot enough for you. Alan likes skin-scalding heat," Nick added, smiling at Zoe.

"Then I'll take second shift since I prefer comfort."

"Why don't you show me your security while the sauna's heating," Alan suggested. "Then we'll find a spot for my new toy," he added with a nod toward the black cases.

"You two go do your thing," Zoe offered. "I'll clean up here and work on my book."

"Thanks, babe. Come on Al. I'll show you the right way to start a sauna fire."

Zoe watched the men walk down the hill toward the sauna. Both were tall and toned, dark-haired, swarthy. *Modern-day pirates*, she fancifully reflected. Neither looked like they'd back down in a fight. But Alan had a sparkle in his eyes.

While no one had mentioned that Alan dealt in arms, she was pretty certain he did. The wooden boxes unloaded from Alan's plane looked like those in the movies—drab military green with white stenciled labels. The two official-looking black metal suitcases by the door also appeared to have been appropriated from some government warehouse.

Not that she cared to speculate about Nick's need for serious armaments. She was sticking with her denial plan. It was less nerve-racking. In fact, she panicked each time she let herself think about them being on the run. Or worse . . . that their pursuers would find them.

Her only consolation was that she had the most gratifying and sexually satisfying personal bodyguard on duty twenty-four seven. Not that world-class sex could completely mitigate the serious hazards facing them, but it went a long way in calming her heebie-jeebies.

"Whaddya think of her—beyond the obvious," Nick asked, squatting down in front of the sauna stove, opening the cast-iron door and tossing in some kindling.

"The obvious is she's A-class centerfold material. Which makes me slightly suspicious. Harry would likely employ a gorgeous babe like her to get your attention."

"Agreed. And? Hand me those two logs on top." Nick pointed through the open door to a wood box in the small changing room.

"And otherwise, you seem to like her and vice versa." Alan came back with the two split logs and handed them to Nick. "You're right though—you're gonna have to watch her." He smiled. "Which isn't bad duty."

"Not for long. If Harry's confirmation hearing is next week, we should expect company real soon." Carefully placing the two pine logs on top of the kindling, Nick struck a match on the concrete stove base and lit the fire. He watched it for a moment until the flame caught, then shut the door, opened the flue wide, and came to his feet. "We'll add more wood in ten minutes or so. Let me quickly show you my perimeter line. I added a few new man traps since you were here. Then we can set up your new toy."

Twenty-eight

Tony left a message on the local radio program that transmitted personal notices into the telephone-free boundary waters from nine to ten every day.

Nick. Your New York visitors went back home. Tony.

Zoe and the men were finishing breakfast the following morning when they heard the announcement. It was sandwiched between *Kathy, Joe will be over tonight to play cards. Do you have enough coffee?* and *The fishing party ill be at the Straw Lake portage at two tomorrow. Meet them. Lou.*

"I'll have to send Tony a thank-you," Nick said.

"Add my thanks to yours," Zoe murmured, exhaling softly. "What a relief."

"They might have an act two somewhere down the line," Nick cautioned.

"I expect they will. But right now, they can't get at me. I can write with a freer mind. My creativity doesn't function well when I'm being threatened."

"Do you have much left on your book?" Alan asked, thinking the threat level was probably going to get worse before it got better.

"A couple of weeks of hard work and I should finish my first draft."

"I should probably leave you alone then," Nick said with a grin.

"Actually, some things *enhance* my creativity," Zoe replied ever so softly.

"Maybe we should take a short break before we start working." Nick's voice was low and heated, his dark gaze covetous. "You know, recharge our batteries."

Her smile was tantalizing. "Is there time?"

"No problem." Whisper-soft and sexually explicit.

"Don't let me interrupt this licentious moment," Alan said drily.

"As if you could," Nick drawled, coming to his feet. "If you'll excuse us."

"While you two are ignoring the world, I'll check on the progress in Washington."

Nick picked up Zoe from her chair and swung her up in his arms. "Give our regards to Ginny."

"Will do." Alan tapped his wristwatch. "I'll be waiting."

Nick grinned. "Lucky I can deal with pressure."

As Nick walked from the kitchen, Zoe murmured, "Maybe we shouldn't."

"Don't worry about it." Nick casually replied. "Alan is risk averse, that's all."

"Considering the circumstances, maybe you should be, too."

"I am, okay? I just don't happen to be *right this second*."

"Because you're focused on sex."

"Oh, yeah." His grin flashed. "Once we're alone, I'll show you how *focused* I can be."

Alan regarded the departing couple with a speculative gaze. If Nick was watching his back with the lovely Miss Chandler, he sure as hell didn't show it. He was careless, headstrong, letting his cock call the shots. If Zoe *was* Harry's agent, Nick might be looking at some deadly sex. But short of becoming a voyeur, he'd have to rely on Nick's instincts and whatever restraint was still operating beneath his hotspur need to fuck.

Nick set Zoe down once they reached his bedroom, then quickly turned and shut and locked the door. "Just in case Alan decides break time is over before we do," he said, swiveling back around.

"He's not going to be angry, is he? Or think us impolite?" Zoe murmured, her mouth faintly pursed.

"Are you saying you don't want to come?"

"Well . . . no—I mean . . . that is—"

He smiled. "Same here. And seriously," he said, beginning to quickly unbutton her shirt, "don't worry about being polite"—his brows flickered—"unless it's to me." Sliding her plaid camp shirt down her arms, he let it drop. "Although, I'm so horny even politeness isn't a requirement." He unhooked her bra with a flick of his fingers, slipped it off, unzipped her jeans with one quick pull, and dropped to one knee to divest her of her jeans and panties.

"I hope you're not planning on wham, bam, thank you ma'am sex," she said, drolly.

He glanced up, his gaze sardonic. "This from the babe who comes so fast, I have to sprint to keep up?"

"That must be why we get along so well," she said with a grin, lifting one foot, then the other so he could pull off her remaining clothes. "Although we're operating under time constraints this morning."

"The only time constraints we're operating under is when you decide to cry uncle." Rising to his feet, he brushed a fingertip down her fine, straight nose. "So you just let me know when you've had enough." He jerked his T-shirt over his head and dropped it on the floor.

"Arrogant man."

"You're hotter than hell—what can I say?" Taking a light weight CZ 100 handgun from his pocket, he tossed it on the bedside table, unsnapped and unzipped his shorts, and let them slide to the floor.

"Speaking of temptation," Zoe whispered, her gaze suddenly avaricious, thinking if ever a man shouldn't wear underwear, he was the perfect candidate.

"Me or this?" he said, with a glance at her favorite toy. *Silly question.* "Hey, babe." He snapped his fingers. "Look at me."

Her gaze lifted, affront in her eyes. "I don't take orders."

"Sometimes you take orders."

"Only if they turn me on."

"So I should reword my statement?"

"It might be wise."

"Or what?"

"Don't be a prick."

"I don't take orders either," he brusquely countered.

For a moment they stood motionless, taut with lust, willful and edgy. Then in a flash, he picked her up, dropped her on the bed, followed her down in a smooth, controlled flow of muscled strength, and shoving her legs apart, settled between her thighs. Resting on his forearms, he pinned her to the bed—although lightly, his weight no more than a hovering presence. "Now, let's make sure I word this properly," he murmured, his dark eyes close as he nudged her slick, cushiony cleft with the swollen crest of his erection. "I wouldn't want to piss you off."

"Too late," she hissed.

"I don't think so," he whispered, knowing any cunt as wet as hers was more than ready for action.

She should have yelled, *I'm not listening to anything you say! Get off me this instant!* and if he wasn't hung like a horse and seconds away from giving her the pleasure her greedy, overwrought senses craved, she might have. So much for principles up against unbridled lust.

"You're really wet, babe," he murmured, like he could read her mind, the sleek head of his cock resting inside the slippery folds of her labia. "I'd say you're ready to let me in."

"Not without a condom." *There. Principle reasserted.* Her independence restored. Insisting on at least a modicum of discipline for her heedless libido that was willing to acquiesce to anything as long as Nick's enormous cock was involved.

"I don't have any condoms left."

"You're *kidding!" Now what, Miss Smarty Pants*, her libido carped.

"Don't worry. I won't come in you."

"Jeez, I don't believe this!" she wailed, every irresponsible, oversexed nerve in her brain busy examining possible options. Principle and independence were in serious jeopardy of being ignominiously jettisoned, overruled by the avaricious ache of desire throbbing through her vagina.

"We left in kind of a hurry. And the condoms I had in the plane are gone. But I'm dependable as hell."

"What if I say no?" she muttered, trying to keep it together even as her body was rolling out the red carpet.

"I'd say you're so wet"—he slid the head of his cock up and down her liquid slit again—"you don't really mean it."

"Maybe . . . I . . . do."

"And maybe I'd believe you if you weren't panting."

"I—am . . . not—panting."

His smile was benevolent. "Whatever you say."

"This . . . can't . . . be . . . happening to me!" she fulminated. But her hips were moving of their own accord, further whetting her already ravenous appetite for sex, her creamy labia were enveloping the engorged head of Nick's erection, and reason and discretion were collapsing under a tidal wave of lust.

"You don't have to worry," he whispered, smoothly easing the head of his penis into her vagina fractionally. Politely pausing for leave to continue. As if her consent was actually in question.

"Oh God, oh God . . ."

Not explicit consent nor precisely his name, but definitely frenzied reception. And figuring that was as good as a yes, he drove in and buried himself to the hilt in her well-lubricated, soft as silk, welcoming pussy. As he came to rest embedded in her lush, tight cunt, he was gratified to hear her exhale a low, sumptuous pleasure sound.

But only a second later, coming to her senses, she frantically pushed at his chest and cried, "Stop! Stop! Get off of me!"

Not likely. But he murmured politely, "In a minute."

"No! No! *Now!*" she exclaimed, more heated still, punching his shoulder.

Even if he'd been considering acceding to her wishes, her hips were still gently swaying beneath him, her hot, slick vaginal tissue was massaging the entire highly sensitive length of his cock—all of which put into question the sincerity of her demands.

On the other hand, he had no intention of stopping.

With masterful finesse, he forced himself deeper.

Touched to the quick, she cried out at the shocking pleasure. Yet, a heartbeat later, struggling to suppress the delirium ravaging her senses, breathless, panicked he might come in her, she pleaded, "Please! Please! Stop!"

"You don't mean that," he whispered. Her arousal was not only obvious but provocative as hell and he could no more stop than she could nullify the flowing succulence of hot desire bathing his cock. "Tell me—do you like this . . ." Driving a fraction more into her soft yielding flesh, the additional, almost minimal penetration was so excruciatingly fine, he shut his eyes against the raw splendor.

And for a hushed moment, mutual rapture held sway, the silence seething with overwrought passion.

Coming up for air a moment later, overcome with a novel tenderness, Nick dipped his head and gently kissed Zoe.

For a nanosecond.

Jerking back, he growled an obscenity and licked away the blood from his lip.

"You *are not* coming in me!" she shrieked, struggling to break free, her self-preservation at stake. "Damn, selfish prick!" Writhing and twisting beneath him, she shoved at his chest with all her strength.

Not that he noticed. He was talking himself out of hitting her and it was taking awhile. *The bitch took a piece out of my bottom lip.*

Equally pissed—*No way am I taking a chance of getting pregnant*—strengthened by fury, Zoe rolled to her right and lunged for something to hit him with.

Her fingertips had just brushed the rim of the bedside table when she was slammed back onto the bed and Nick's fingers were hard around her throat. Stunned, her mind racing, she hoped this was some game he was playing, and then she looked up and saw his cold, merciless eyes.

Oh God! He's gone psycho!

Gasping for air, she fought against his stranglehold.

His grip only tightened as she struggled, the pressure of his fingers curiously delicate as though he knew just how much power was required to extinguish life.

Unable to breathe, her lungs burning, spots dancing before her eyes, she understood death was fast approaching.

Gathering her last remaining strength, she swung her fist wildly upward.

In her enfeebled state, Nick barely noticed the tap on his cheek. But he did for a split second. Staring at her in that brief, stark moment, he took note of her terror-stricken eyes—saw an honest-to-goodness vulnerability.

Both characteristics alien to Harry's hit men.

Slackening his grip slightly, he shook his head like a swimmer did breaking the surface of the water—his survival instinct yielding for a moment to reason. *If she is an assassin why hasn't she tried to break my hold in any of the routine ways known to a professional?*

He further loosened his grip, his fingers light now on her throat.

She frantically drew in great gulps of air, all the while focusing her gaze on his face, fearful he might change his mind.

"What were you reaching for?" His tone was mild, his dark, searching gaze was not.

"Nothing—anything . . . whatever I could reach—to hit you with and stop you from—coming in me. You—asshole," she panted, combative and touchy. Ignoring the reasonable part of her brain that was counseling her to be tactful.

He half smiled at her nerve or temper—he didn't know which. But the fear had suddenly vanished from her eyes; they were on an equal footing once again. "I thought you were reaching for my handgun."

"So I gathered. Not that—your cock—took issue," she sarcastically murmured, any last doubts obliterated by his familiar smile.

"My cock isn't logical. As you see," he murmured, his erection swelling inside her. There was something about danger that accentuated sensation, magnified lust. Surviving death was an aphrodisiac he'd discovered while living in a war zone.

"I'm not so sure—my pussy is logical either," Zoe ruefully noted, as an unmistakable libidinous ripple vibrated through her vagina.

He grinned. "I felt that."

"I can feel *you* clear up to my throat."

His gaze was amused. "So—how do you like it?"

"If you must know," she said, breathing normally again, "I like everything about you. Even though you're occasionally scary as hell *and* a prick and *definitely not* coming in me on pain of death."

"Gotcha. And I'll try to be more congenial," he softly murmured.

"You could start by taking your hands away from my neck."

He immediately complied. "Sorry. I thought you were here—" He hesitated.

"To kill you?"

He shrugged. "Baggage from my past. I apologize." As though to mitigate further crises, he picked up the Czech handgun from the table and dropped it on the floor.

"That was sweet." The rainbow after the storm. As was his apology. Wrapping her arms around his neck, Zoe lifted her hips into his rigid erection and smiled. "So, are you feeling better now?"

He grinned. "Sane, you mean?"

"Sure about me I mean."

"Absolutely," he lied.

"Perfect. Then we can indulge ourselves *properly*."

He grinned. "And how exactly would that be?"

"Nonviolently."

"Like this?" Dipping his head, he kissed her gently.

"Ummm . . . exactly," she purred, the taste of blood perversely erotic. "Although I'm not against a certain brute strength in other areas from time to time."

"How about this?" His ran his hands down her waist, grasped her hips, held her securely, and devoted himself for a lengthy interval to a robust exploration of her vagina—leisurely in and out, side to side, rotating from time to time so as to make contact with every susceptible, quivering nerve and palpitating bit of tissue.

She melted around him, liquid and increasingly frenzied, impatient finally as was her nature, insisting in no uncertain terms that she wanted to come—*now*.

There was something about her wild passions that inflamed him beyond the ordinary. Tantalized and provoked—made sex with her more than a game. In fact, he almost forgot himself and came in her as she climaxed—her piercing screams triggering something primal in his brain and cock and gonads.

He caught himself just in time, jerked out, and came on her stomach.

Fuck that was close.

He apologized. "I didn't quite wait until you finished. Sorry. It won't happen again."

Languidly raising her eyelids, still in the grip of a delicious torpor, she gazed up at him and smiled. "No need to apologize. It was lovely . . . in every way."

Lovely was not ordinarily a word he would use to describe an orgasm, but damned if it didn't apply this time. Along with *awesome*.

Which naturally prompted him, very shortly, to repeat the exercise. And with the sexy Miss Chandler lying in his bed, her hot cunt only inches away, who wouldn't?

So he did and she did and they did.

It was amazing how many times you could come when you were primed, when the lady in your bed was more or less insatiable, when her cunt turned even more velvety soft with each additional fuck.

Or maybe he was just chalking up pleasure points before everything went to shit. A real possibility with Harry's hit men on their trail.

Then again, you couldn't discount Miss Chandler's pure, unadulterated sex appeal, not to mention her equally insatiable horniness. If he actually believed in heaven, he might consider their carnal compatibility as a match made there.

A pleasant conceit until, eventually, inevitably, time constraints *did* put an end to their amorous fun and games.

Although it was Nick who called a halt to the festivities.

"Do we have to?" Zoe pouted.

He was surprised at his virtuousness. Then again, lives were at stake. Perhaps survival trumped sex in the end. "I could find your dildo for you," he politely offered, rolling off the bed. "But Alan's chaffing at the bit by now. I have to go."

"But I want *you*, not a dildo."

"Tonight, babe." He smiled and picked up his shorts. "I promise."

"I suppose we have to be sensible," she grumbled.

"I'll make it up to you. Word of honor." He grinned, zipping up his shorts. "So see that you're rested up."

"Yes, sir," she whispered. "Whatever you want, sir. Your wish is my command."

With a soft groan, he slipped his T-shirt over his head. "You're makin' this really tough, sweetheart." He blew out a breath. "Don't say another word—uh-uh"—he held up a finger—"or you won't get any." If he didn't leave in the next few seconds, he was gonna nail her again. And Alan would really be pissed.

He bolted for the door.

Twenty-nine

 Nick walked into the library, smiling. "Sorry. It took longer than I thought. Did Ginny have any news?"

"She said to say hi. I don't suppose there's any point in giving you a lecture on personal responsibility."

"Go for it," Nick said with a grin. "For your information, I showed up now because I am noble and pure of heart."

"Better late than never, I guess."

"We can't all be prudent *all* the time."

"You'd better start thinking about it."

"I am, I will—seriously," Nick said, suddenly purposeful and solemn. He nodded toward the radio Alan was monitoring. "Have you heard anything?"

"No intercepts from Harry's execution squad, but Ginny had some info," Alan briskly replied, pleased to see that Nick was occupied with their issues once again. "Harry is out of the office today to golf—code for he's away banging his mistress. He keeps a former Miss Alabama in a house he owns in the hunt country. Ostensibly no one knows. In fact, everyone does, including his wife. But such is the way of the world. Don't ask, don't tell."

"It would pay to get the coordinates on that house."

"I already have them. Are you thinking what I'm thinking?"

"Oh, yeah. Provided we survive this assault."

Alan grinned. "With our firepower? Don't sweat it. Pull up a chair. I'll show you how this early warning system works."

Ten minutes later, Nick leaned back in his chair. "What a sweet deal. We should have plenty of time to get into position." He smiled faintly. "Christ, this baby practically tells you how many minutes you've got before the first shots are fired."

"They'll come in on choppers. We have to hit them before they launch their missiles."

"Preemptive strike—sounds good to me, healthy."

"If we're lucky they'll be using some of the local choppers. Old, and slow, no high-tech gunnery."

"I'm not so sure. Harry always goes for overkill."

"You're not thinking Apaches?"

"I doubt there are any around. Everything's in Iraq. On the other hand, if he's been planning this operation for awhile— it's a possibility we have to consider."

"Crap. If that's the case, we *have* to hit them first. They could take out this whole lakeshore with a couple missiles. But, let's think happy thoughts instead." Alan grinned. "Like, will you be needing a copilot on your trip out east—once this is over?"

"Again, if Ginny doesn't mind, sure." *I can look at the bright side, too, and ridding the world of Harry Miller is definitely a happy thought.* "But if Harry sees his mistress with any regularity, he should be an easy hit even for a one-man operation."

"But two's better. Don't think you're gonna have the privilege of taking Harry out all by yourself. Not when I have an account to settle with him, too. He sent our squad into a fucking ambush that first winter in Kosovo. And he knew it, the prick."

"So we'd be doing the universe a favor."

"You'd better believe it," Alan muttered, taking a last look at the radar screen. "What say we get to work and set up our defenses? Can you keep your dick in your pants for a few hours?"

Nick grinned. "I'll try. I can't guarantee it though. She keeps me stoked—what can I say?"

"You *might* want to think about keeping your mind on business for the duration. When Harry gets back to Washington tomorrow, it's countdown time for the confirmation hearing. And for us, my friend."

"I know, I know. Consider me a monk from now on."

"You'd better tell her."

"Well, a monk in the daytime at least. What? Okay, I know, night shift starting today—three hours on, three off." Nick grinned. "So I'll have to settle for a quickie on my hours off."

Alan smiled. "Worst case—you'll die a happy man."

"No joke. I *am* happy."

"I can tell."

"And I never thought I'd say that again."

"I'm glad for you. There's nothing like the love of a good woman."

"Whoa." Nick raised his hands. "I wouldn't go that far. We still don't know for sure if she's for real or not"—he grinned—"the hot sex notwithstanding, which is definitely real. But 'live for the moment' is my mantra. Speaking of which, we'd better get the planes and boats out of target range. They'll want to blast them out of the water."

"Sounds like a plan. I'll follow you."

In the next few hours, Nick and Alan taxied their planes into a cove two miles northwest of the cabin, camouflaged them, and repeated the drill with two of the boats. Nick left his fastest boat in the boathouse in the event they needed it. Then he and Alan set up the antiaircraft guns in commanding positions on the hill behind the cabin and stocked each gun emplacement with enough ammunition to blow anything that came at them out of the sky.

Satisfied at last that they could ride out just about any attack, the men rested on the dock and shared a single malt. "We're as ready as we can be," Nick murmured. Taking a swig out of the bottle he kept in the boathouse, Nick handed it over to Alan.

"Bring 'em on, as those in charge of our body politic say," Alan said with a sardonic grin, lifting the bottle to his mouth.

"We'd better be more successful than those jack-offs," Nick muttered.

"That should be easy enough." Alan handed the bottle back. "We can walk and chew gum at the same time."

"And hit a moving target from seven hundred feet."

"At twelve hundred rounds a minute."

"In a rainstorm with nightscopes."

Alan grinned. "That was some fireworks blowout over Macedonia."

"Impressive, I agree. And good cover for our retreat."

"We lived to drink another day."

"Amen." Nick held out the bottle. "Are you drinking or what?"

But neither overimbibed with Harry's operational threat imminent.

Instead, after a few shots, they made use of the sauna as though purifying themselves before battle. Or at least, that's what Alan did, devotee that he was of a Zen warrior code.

Nick and Zoe took the opportunity instead to engage in some leisured and not so leisured sex. Afterward, Nick was lying on the top bench waiting for his pulse rate to subside to somewhere in the normal range. Zoe had climbed down to open the window and was pouring water over herself to cool off. Each time she bent over to scoop water out of the large washtub Nick's cock recorded the event with a lustful jolt.

"Better not do that, babe," he murmured.

"What?" Bent over, she glanced at him over her shoulder with a studiously innocent look.

"You know what. When you're bending over like that your pussy is damned enticing."

"Like this you mean?" She gave him an even more tantalizing view.

He came down off the top bench so quickly, she squealed and dropped the dipper. Grabbing her from behind, he shoved her head down, lifted her bottom high, and slid his rampant cock deep inside her alluring, bewitching pussy. "Cock teaser," he muttered, thrusting and plunging, engulfed by her silken warmth and ardent eagerness. "What do you have to say now?"

"Thank—you—ever so . . . much," she panted, turning to smile at him. "From the bottom of my heart."

"And from the bottom of your sweet cunt," he whispered, driving deep into her welcoming body, equally gratified, perhaps as avaricious as she. Certainly as willing to see if quenchless sexual appetites could indeed be quenched.

He reached up and shoved the window wide open after a time so they wouldn't die of heatstroke. But it was another kind of heat—voracious and flame-hot—that ultimately brought them prostrate to the floor.

Once he was no longer gasping for air, he turned his head toward Zoe and couldn't help but smile. Her body was shiny with sweat, her hair a mass of curls, her face turned to him and graced with the sweetest of smiles. "Alan's going to be wondering what happened to us," Nick murmured. "You look wonderful," he added apropos of nothing but unreasoning impulse.

"We probably should go, although I sure don't want to," Zoe said, more willing than him to reveal her feelings.

Reaching over, he gently brushed her cheek. "Thank you Miss Chandler, for a mind-blowing experience—several in fact," he added with a grin. Then he pushed himself up on his knees, stood, and helped her to her feet.

He politely rinsed her off first, then himself, opening the door into the changing room afterward and waving her in. They dressed in a companionable, or perhaps lassitude-induced, silence. And with the sun low in the sky, the scent of pine in the air, they walked back to the cabin hand in hand.

Dinner that evening was subdued—initially from sauna- induced lethargy, but as the meal progressed, the gravity of the coming assault could not be ignored. While Nick hadn't openly commented on their operation, Zoe was well aware their defensive arrangements were not without cause.

She wasn't surprised when Nick said after dessert, "Let me show you the escape tunnel in the event it's needed. Al and I will be taking turns with sentry duty tonight. Not that we have any definitive information," he interposed at the apprehension in Zoe's eyes, "but we're erring on the side of caution. Should we come under attack, I want you to take cover away from the cabin." He didn't say the cabin would be the most obvious target because he didn't plan on letting Harry's crew get the drop on them. Zoe should have time to exit the premises.

"I know you're anticipating these people coming soon. You needn't parse the truth. You've been getting ready all afternoon."

Nick scrutinized her face, wanting her to be genuine. "It's highly likely they're on their way. Harry Miller's confirmation hearing is next week. He needs me gone before the hearing starts."

"Couldn't we just fly farther north or west or anywhere but here?"

"They'll come after us wherever we go. We have a better chance of stopping them right here."

"But for how long? This Harry guy must have other men at his disposal."

He'll be dead soon. "Long enough," Nick said.

"Show us the escape tunnel," Alan interposed, curtailing an unwinnable argument. No one was leaving.

"The stairway is hidden behind the pantry shelves." Nick came to his feet. "This way."

A narrow stairway led down to a tunnel that ran behind the cabin into a small sanctuary cut into the hill. The room was fully supplied—food, water, a small bed, a radio, propane light, a chemical toilette.

"Jesus, this is scary," Zoe whispered, thinking this is what they meant by a bomb shelter. "May I go home now? I don't want to play this game anymore."

"Sorry," Nick murmured, not sure even a really good actress could look so distraught. Zoe's eyes were shiny with tears and she was trembling. "You'll be safe here," he whispered, taking her in his arms and holding her close. "Guaranteed. Nothing can touch you."

She softly exhaled, sniffed away her tears, and offered him a tentative smile. "Sorry I'm such a baby," she said, rallying her self-control. "I'm fine again—just a brief meltdown. I don't suppose this danger is much different from worrying about being eaten alive by piranhas. I survived that."

The men exchanged a look over Zoe's head.

Piranhas versus missiles wasn't even close.

"Look, if we're attacked, get yourself out of the cabin and hunker down here while Alan and I head them off at the pass,"

Nick said with a grin. "The good guys always win, you know that."

"Yeah, right, and the Willerbys of the world get their come-uppance instead of becoming billionaires. Oops, I guess not."

"This is different, babe. No one fucks with us and survives."

"Not that we're killing anyone," Alan quickly interposed at the sudden shock on Zoe's face. "We'll just send them packing."

"I know this isn't charitable to say, but if these people are really trying to kill us, maybe you can't afford to be too squeamish."

Nick smiled. "Don't worry, babe. I plan on living a long time."

"Oh, good, then I will, too."

Nick dipped his head and kissed her lightly. "Now there's incentive."

"I hate to break up this lovefest, but I want some eyes and ears on our perimeter."

"I'll take first sentry duty," Nick said, letting his hands drop away and stepping back. "Let's get you into the cabin."

Everyone's sleep was restless that night.

What there was of it for Nick and Alan.

They grabbed a few minutes between rounds, but neither was able to ignore the familiar precombat tension.

Thirty

Nick heard the distant soft *tut*, *tut*, *tut*, *tut*, like beating grouse wings echoing across the lake in the predawn silence.

Helicopters approaching.

And one of them *was* a frickin' Apache.

You never forgot the sound, nor the chilling memories.

"I heard," he said as Alan appeared in the bedroom doorway, and getting up from the chair where he'd been watching Zoe sleep, he walked to the bed and woke her. "It's time to go to the bunker," he said, purposely keeping his voice mild. "I'll get you when it's over. Don't come out until I do."

Then he strode from the room in order to avoid argument.

There wasn't time for debate.

"I've been watching them on the radar for the last forty minutes," Alan said as the men left the cabin and walked swiftly toward the rocky ridge north of it. "They're taking their time."

"We're a soft target. Why should they hurry?"

"They're gonna be in for a surprise."

Nick smiled. "I like your confidence."

"It ain't confidence, dude, it's prime weaponry."

"And for us, it's not just another mission," Nick gruffly said.

Ten minutes later when the Apache attack helicopter swept up over the treeline across the lake, they were ready. Even the second chopper didn't register alarm. But the third brought an exchange of glances between Nick and Alan.

"Fucking A," Nick said. "That *is* overkill."

"And I'm guessing Harry's safe in his office in DC."

"Ya think?" Nick half smiled. "Lucky we have ingenuity."

"And plenty of practice."

"Not to mention a motherfucking grudge for my sixteen months in the hospital."

"It's all about speed now," Alan murmured, his gaze on the approaching aircraft.

"And surprise," Nick said under his breath, his eyes riveted on the Apache chopper in the lead. "They won't know what hit 'em. The range on the weapons you brought is awesome."

"Nothin' but the best—that's my motto."

Nick flashed him a quick grin. "First drink's on me when this is over. Red con one. *Weapons loaded and safeties off*. That Apache is almost in the kill zone."

While the men were trading comments on the hillside above her, Zoe was huddled in the bunker below, freaking out. She'd never been near a firefight before. She'd never had the slightest inkling of what the phrase *die of fright* meant—until now.

The sound of the choppers had been audible as she'd raced for the tunnel and now her greatest fear—besides being killed—was being left alive out here in the wilderness with everyone else gone, maybe even dead.

Although, she wouldn't actually allow herself to contemplate Nick dead.

She couldn't think such awful thoughts.

She prayed instead, harder than she'd ever prayed before.

She prayed for a miracle, because they'd need it with armed choppers transporting killers intent on slaughtering them. She prayed that Nick and Alan were the best shots in the world. She prayed that the bad men coming to hurt them would somehow feel the full fury of God's mighty wrath. She mostly prayed that everything would turn out all right—her usual generic prayer from childhood when she was afraid of the dark and big hairy spiders and snakes that could swallow a whole person.

Jesus, how had her normal, conventional life come to this terrifying impasse? How could this be happening to her? She was a writer—granted, she focused on some of the more unethical people of the world doing unethical things, but wasn't there supposed to be a divide between white-collar crime and all the other ruthless manifestations of thuggery? Seriously, wasn't there a rule about that? She shouldn't be semipanicked in a bunker praying for a miracle; she should be debating chapter titles or zeroing in on all the excellent work the TPC was doing in Italy.

Unfortunately, this was all too real—and scary thought number fifty-two in her increasing list of scary thoughts— what if things *didn't* work out? What if they were overwhelmed by men with guns in helicopters—carrying missiles, too, probably. *Shit.* While Nick hadn't exactly spelled out in detail who was after him and why, they'd already been fired on by shoulder-fired missiles and she knew you didn't buy those at your local Ace Hardware.

Zoe swallowed hard, the thought of actually *dying* suddenly flooding every mushy bit of grey matter in her brain in a tidal wave of fear. And the worst part—if there was a quantitative cringe factor in dying—was the fact that no one would ever know exactly what happened to them. They were hundreds of miles from civilization. They were seriously *into the wild*. And everyone knows what happened to *that* poor guy.

The loud boom of artillery, followed by the clatter of machine-gun fire suddenly erupted above her.

She screamed and started shaking.

By the time Zoe started shaking, Nick and Alan had already taken out the Apache chopper with several well-placed armor-piercing rounds from high-powered Russian sniper rifles. Nick aimed for the pilot's face visible behind the narrow, sloped window and firing full automatic, pumped the entire twenty-round magazine into the pilot's head—blowing it away.

Alan simultaneously unloaded his twenty rounds on the rotors, shredding and slicing them to pieces, sending the chopper into a deadly downward spiral. The copilot riding tandem had had time to fire off two missiles but they ended up blasting holes in the lake bottom instead of Nick's cabin.

Knowing the spitting muzzle flashes had been visible, the men dropped the sniper rifles and raced through the cover of the pine trees to their artillery emplacements dug in laterally a hundred feet out. Quickly aiming two French APILAS 112mm LAW rocket launchers that had been set up on moving tripods, they sighted in on the two lumbering Huey choppers flying in the wake of the faster Apache. The pilots were continuing their approach despite the destruction of the lead chopper.

"Harry must be paying top dollar!" Nick shouted, centering one Huey in his scope. "Motherfuckers are still comin'!"

"They're sitting ducks with no long-range missiles!"

"The one on the left is mine!" Nick was curled over the weapon, his finger hovering over the firing mechanism.

"Roger that!" Hunched over the other rocket launcher, Alan had the second Huey in his crosshairs.

"Light 'em up!"

The men discharged two powerful warheads capable of punching through twenty-eight inches of armor into the squat fuselages of the largely unprotected Hueys and tore them to pieces. As the two choppers exploded in balls of fire and dropped from the sky in a cascade of flaming wreckage, Nick and Alan ripped them with machine-gun fire.

Fragments large and small, materiel, metal, flesh, and blood fell into the lake, throwing up geysers, spouts, spurts until the dark water closed over the shattered pieces of Harry's attack squad. Only the occasional ripple or floating shred gave evidence of the graveyard below.

The sudden silence was eerie.

"We should check on survivors," Alan said, walking over to where Nick was standing looking out over the lake.

"In a minute," Nick said, Alan's voice muffled by the ringing in his ears. "I'm beating back all my fucking nightmares." Drawing in a deep breath, Nick wiped the spattered machine-gun lubricant from his face with the back of his hand and slowly exhaled. "It's been awhile." In the midst of a firefight, time always slowed down for him, detail was starkly heightened, the deafening machine-gun fire only a whisper. He had no feeling while he was loading and firing, muscle power simply taking over. But afterward—it was all too real. "Killing sucks," he murmured.

"It was them or us." Having wiped off his face, Alan folded his greasy handkerchief neatly and put it away in his pocket.

"Ain't it always."

Alan shrugged. "Better them than us, then."

"Yeah. No doubt." Nick half smiled. "Thanks to your hardware."

"And our defenses. Hey, the good guys won. Isn't that the way it's supposed to go?"

"I guess. They were overconfident."

"Typical of Harry's people. They're not exactly rocket scientists. They figure superior numbers are always the answer.

Are you ready for a look-see?" Alan nodded toward the lake. "We can't take any chances."

What he means is we have to kill any survivors. Not that there is a polite alternative. "I'm good," Nick said, issues of morality contained. "All my psycho-devils are back in their cages."

Making their way to the boathouse through the cover of the trees, Nick and Alan took out the boat and ran it out to the area of the lake where the choppers had gone down. Slowly traversing the crash zone, they methodically crisscrossed and scrutinized the water.

Only the lightest debris still floated, some of it human remains.

"It never gets easy," Alan murmured as Nick steered the small speedboat around the floating body parts. "No matter how many times you see it."

"Fuck no. Even if they were trying to off us, you can't help but think of the families these guys left behind. And then there's Harry," Nick added, gruffly. "Safe and sound back in DC. I'm tempted to call him and tell him to get his will in order."

"Not too tempted I hope," Alan cautioned.

"Nah. Do I give a shit if his will is in order?"

"No sense in warning him," Alan said, ever heedful.

"I know. Although it's tempting to let him sweat it for a while."

"Don't worry. Once these guys don't report back, he'll know what happened to them."

"Which means we'd better scatter, too."

Alan nodded. "Does Zoe have someplace safe to go?" *She's passed the loyalty test in not coming to the aid of the attackers.*

"Dunno. She said something about friends who would take her in, so I'll find out. After you check in back home, I'll meet you in the Cities. Zoe should be out of the way by then. That leaves Harry front and center on the radar."

"I have contacts at the Pentagon. We can pick up weapons in DC."

"Harry's sure to be watching his back, so we should avoid commercial airports. I have an off-the-record aircraft available to me in Minneapolis. It was supposedly scrapped a few years ago, so it's safe. Fake registration, fake flight plans, we fly into rural airports—who's to know?"

"How about next Thursday?"

"Thursday's good."

"How will your babe deal with you saying see you around?"

"I'll find out. Not that it matters. We can't stay here. Everyone has to go underground until Harry's out of the way."

Alan lifted his hand slightly, indicating the detritus floating in the lake. "This is gonna wash up on shore. What are you gonna tell her?"

"That we're alive and they aren't."

"Simple enough."

"Yup. A Hollywood happy ending."

Once the men had assured themselves that no survivors remained, they returned to the shore, ran the boat into the boathouse, had a quick shot of single malt, cleaned the gun oil from their hands and faces with a little gasoline, and locked up.

Then Alan went off to send a short, coded message to his wife, while Nick proceeded to the bunker to apprise Zoe of their success.

She hadn't tried to kill them during the firefight. Reassuring. Maybe he could finally write off any further suspicion.

Oh, fuck.

She's gone.

He stood arrested in the doorway, contemplating the silent, empty room. The hairs on the back of his neck rose to attention, his brain was screaming *Alert, alert!*

Swiftly moving from the illuminated entrance into the shadows of the room, he automatically slipped his handgun from his pocket and flicked off the safety. "Zoe?" His voice was soft, expressionless.

"Nick! Thank God, it's you!" she cried, coming out from behind the small storage cupboard. "I heard footsteps and when the door opened, I didn't dare look out in case . . ." Her voice trailed off. "But thank God it's you," she said again with obvious relief.

"We're good," he said in the same mild voice, although he didn't lower his handgun and every muscle in his body was poised to react. "It's over."

"We're safe?"

"For the moment. Stop there."

"Is something wrong?" The softness of his voice was unnerving, as was his command. And the gun in his hand was scarier still.

"I have to check you for a weapon."

"Okay," she said, as mildly as he, not wanting to agitate him in any way. After her near-death experience in his bed, she was wary. As was he, apparently, although she'd never tried to kill him so maybe she was allowed a degree more apprehension.

"Step over there into the light." He waved the Czech handgun toward the doorway. "Hold out your arms and spread your legs." His voice was curt.

"I heard all the gunfire and was really, really scared," she murmured, feeling the sudden need to talk, as if her chatter would soothe the savage beast. "I prayed for the first time in a very long time and seriously . . . more than I've ever prayed before. I asked for everything to turn out okay, and maybe it worked, because here you are. I'm so glad you weren't hurt. Is Alan okay?"

"He's fine."

He'd come up behind her so silently she almost gasped, although she quashed the impulse for fear of spooking him. Forcing her breathing to a normal cadence, she said, "I don't have a weapon."

"That's good." Blunt and cool.

Unlike his hands that were swiftly running down her body from top to bottom. They were warm and gentle. And unexpectedly—arousing. *Damn him or damn my wanton impulses. This is no time to give into prurient desires.*

Somehow he knew, although she'd not so much as moved a muscle.

"You always want it, don't you?" he said husky and low,

turning her around and slipping his hand between her legs. "Your little pussy is fired up even now when you're not sure of me—or what I might do to you."

"I'd like to say *fuck you*," she muttered, returning his amused look with an ill-humored one. "But you frighten me, and not to be discounted, you apparently saved my life. On the other hand, you're way the hell too arrogant and maybe that's why I'd most like to say *fuck you*."

"Even when I can feel your hot cunt pulsing in my palm?" he said with an impudent smile, increasing the pressure of his hand.

"Mostly then," she snapped.

"Personally, I like to have sex after a firefight."

"But then you're—" She stopped herself.

"Crazy?"

"I didn't say that."

"You thought it." He suddenly grinned and pulled away his hand. "Look, relax. I'm not going to jump you. Come on, let's go see Alan and have us a victory drink."

His moods fluctuated so wildly, it took her a moment to get up to speed. But she managed a smile a second later and even though it was barely daybreak said, "A victory drink sounds wonderful."

"And don't worry," Nick said, waving her before him toward the tunnel to the cabin, "I'd never force myself on a woman."

As if he'd have to, her still strumming pussy observed. But she only said, "Glad to hear it." A niggling little voice inside her head pointed out that it would be *really nice* if he wanted her as much as she wanted him.

Apparently, Nick Mirovic could take it or leave it when it came to sex with her.

Shit. Why don't I have as much self-control?

Thirty-one

Over drinks in the living room—on the side away from the lake so the crash site wasn't visible—the men explained their plans and expectations.

"Harry might send in a second team." Nick deliberately spoke in a casual tone. "It's just a possibility," he added with a smile for Zoe, who sat across from him in a large cushioned chair, her feet curled up beneath her.

"He probably won't." Alan was lounging on a couch, his drink resting on his chest. "But we're not taking any chances."

"There's no need to panic though," Nick quickly interposed, noting Zoe's apprehensive expression. "Harry won't be sure the mission failed until late today. And he couldn't get another crew out here in less than two, three days. So we're figuring we'll pack up and leave in the morning."

"We were wondering if you had someplace safe you could

go," Alan inquired, figuring it might be easier for him to ask than Nick.

"If you don't, I'll find you a secure accommodation," Nick quickly offered. While he appreciated Alan's good intentions, he could deal with Zoe himself. "It wouldn't be for long. Al and I have to take care of some business, that's all."

Their taking care of business has nothing to do with economics. Not that I'm about to quiz them on the particulars. "What's the time frame on the someplace *safe*?" she asked, sticking to the essentials, avoiding ethical considerations that would require a complete restructuring of her rules to live by. "I'd really like to go home."

Nick looked at Alan, Alan looked at Nick, and after a brief moment of silence, Nick said, "Probably two weeks."

That exchange of glances pretty much said it all. And after having been way too close to a bona fide, nitty-gritty *battle scene*, she wanted to stay as far away as possible from the next one. "I have a college friend in Chicago who doesn't have any obvious connection to me should someone want to trace my whereabouts." Her brows rose. "I'm supposed to be in an undisclosed location I presume."

Nick grinned. "Yup. Only until everything is resolved."

"Your stuff resolved or mine?"

"Both."

"You can't possibly deal with Willerby. Can you?" she added, part dubious, part not so sure he couldn't.

"I might know someone who can lean on him."

"I don't think I want to ask what that means." *I can't afford years of therapy.*

Nick smiled faintly. "Good idea."

"May I make a suggestion?" Alan interjected. "I say we celebrate our current victory before we start talking about the next one. It's like tempting fate—bad karma for sure. Who's ready for another drink?" He rolled off the couch and walked to a table where a bottle of single malt from a small distillery on the Isle of Skye and a bottle of Kahlua sat on a tray beside a pot of coffee. Zoe wasn't quite up to single malt this early in the morning. She was drinking Kahlua and coffee.

Alan's diplomatic proposal put an end to any further discussion of matters the men preferred not discussing—and Zoe didn't really want to hear.

She wanted to stay *way* clear of further gunfire.

She wanted to forget that they could have been killed.

She really didn't want to think about what had happened to the men coming after them because that meant she would have had to deal with Nick and Alan having eliminated—shit, let's face it—*killed* them. Oh, God, was she going straight to hell? Or did you get points for making the world safe from bad guys?

But even as she struggled to calibrate the dictates of good and evil, she also found herself increasingly aware that Nick was exiting her life. Soon, he and the pleasure he wrought would be gone—the grievous thought looping through her brain in an obsessive rotation, blocking out the men's voices.

Their departure was imminent, only hours . . . at the most, a day remained before she and Nick parted.

And the word *privation* was beginning to flash neon bright in her brain. Despite Nick's occasional psycho moments, he was not only unbelievably gorgeous but absolutely incredible in bed. She'd miss the awesome sex and seriously, she wasn't sure she'd ever find someone as fine as him again. She wasn't exaggerating; she'd dated more than her share of men before and after her marriage. And without a doubt, Nick Mirovic was one of a kind.

"Hey, babe."

Looking up, she realized she'd zoned out, because Nick was smiling that knowing, perceptive smile. Like he knew what women were thinking when they were in a trance. "Sorry, I was thinking about packing," she lied.

"I was just asking if you want steak or fish with your breakfast. Alan and I are hungry."

"Whatever you want is fine with me."

Nick held her gaze for an overlong moment. "Steak then," he finally said, his voice soft and low. "Come sit in the kitchen and keep me company while I cook," he added with a smile, his tone normal once again. *Shape up, dude*, he cautioned himself. "Alan will pour drinks and we'll have ourselves a party."

Breakfast was a convivial occasion, the company excellent, the food superb—pancakes, Canadian maple syrup, steak, strawberries from Nick's freezer with a splash of kirsch and half-thawed cream with little crystals still in it. And of course, Nick's fantastic lattes, which in addition to all his other magnificent achievements were naturally divine.

Alan also kept the drinks coming, in her case Kahlua in her latte.

No one mentioned killing anyone or what had become of their attackers, nor did they speak of anyone's plans for the next two weeks. They ate and conversed like the characters in an Alice in Wonderland unreality—about cabbages and kings or the weather and fishing, books read, favorite TV programs, the state of modern architecture in Europe for some reason. Evil and wickedness didn't exist at the breakfast table that morning. Only cloudless, blue sky pleasantries held sway.

It was close to nine when they finished eating.

"I'm going to start packing my stuff," Alan said, rising from the table. "I might leave today if it works out. Ginny worries when I'm gone."

Nick shoved his chair out from the table. "I'll give you a hand," he offered, coming to his feet. "There's a lot to crate up."

"I can do it myself," Alan said, waving off Nick. "Take it easy."

"Nah, I'll help. Closing up camp is so routine for me, I can do it in a couple hours. Are you okay here alone?" he asked, turning to Zoe.

"Perfectly fine." She was as capable of counterfeit equanimity as her colleagues. "Let me clean up the kitchen since you did all the cooking. Then I'll pack my bags so whenever you're ready, I'll be set. And if I don't see you again, it was a pleasure," she added, smiling at Alan.

"The pleasure was all mine. Good luck with your writing."

Nick nodded at Alan. "Ready?"

As the men's footsteps echoed on the porch, then the stairs, Zoe slid down in her chair, and finally at liberty to dispense with the pretense that everything was dandy, she gave into a significant sense of bereavement.

Not exactly an orthodox emotion after their recent triumph

over evil. But apparently her psyche was capable of ignoring that obvious success and fixating instead on her impending loss.

As if she'd ever had Nick anyway, her unhelpful psyche pointed out.

So get a grip. Another unwelcome bit of advice from the irritating voice inside her head. *Clean up the kitchen dammit*, the bossy voice commanded, *then pack your duffle bags, wait for the plane to leave, and get on with your life*. Affirmation therapy—bulldozer-style—was calling the shots.

She sighed, knowing her subconscious was just being realistic. Once they reached civilization, she'd give Rosie a call and invite herself for a visit.

Not that Rosie would mind.

They had taken turns crying on each other's shoulders through the angst of college romances, jobs that sucked, and their respective divorces. Rosie was happily single now, enjoying her new position as lifestyle editor at the *Sun Times* and living in a darling little house overlooked in the gentrification of the Near North Side.

It even had a patch of fenced-in yard out back where it would be possible to work if she wanted a couple rays of sun.

Completely private.

Perfect really.

Sans Nick and the fantastic sex of course, but that's the way life went sometimes.

It couldn't always be a bowl of cherries.

Thirty-two

 Four hours later, Alan and Nick stacked the last two crates into the hold of Alan's plane.

Nick jumped back onto the dock.

Alan said, "I'm outta here," and moved down a pontoon toward the cockpit.

"Thanks again. You saved my ass."

"Not a problem," Alan said, climbing into the pilot's seat. "See you next Thursday, ten o'clock."

"Roger that. I'll have the plane and flight plan ready."

"Give my regards to Zoe." Holding the cockpit door open, Alan grinned. "And remember, keep your mind on business."

"Will do Mom."

"If only I believed you." With a last smile, Alan slammed the door shut, fired up the engines, and a minute later was taxiing away from the dock.

Nick watched the plane until it disappeared into the high cumulus clouds that were habitual in the summer skies up north. Then he walked back down the dock and closed up the boathouse. He knew what he wanted to do next, but that meant getting involved when he didn't want to get involved, so sex was out. *Fuck*.

Instead, he trudged through two miles of timber and underbrush to the cove where his plane had been stashed and spent the remainder of the afternoon bringing his plane—and two repeat journeys later—both boats back to the boathouses. It had to be done. As did raising the boats in their lifts inside the boathouse and filling his plane with gas, checking the oil, doing all the routine maintenance necessary before they took off in the morning. After that, he locked up the sauna, the woodshed, the gasoline tank and walked back up to the cabin to pack.

Not that he had much to pack. He kept clothes here.

He glanced at his watch as he entered the kitchen. Four thirty.

He inwardly groaned.

It was going to be a long night.

But he wanted to arrive in Ely in the morning. It would not only be more convenient for Tony to meet him, but he needed to store his plane either at Tony's or Shagawa Resort where the usual suspects wouldn't be looking for it. Then he figured he'd drive Zoe to Duluth and personally see that she was safely on a plane to Chicago.

In the course of the day, Zoe had had plenty of time to talk herself into a mature state of mind with regard to Nick. They were both adults. They understood that sex was sex was sex. And the unusual circumstances that had brought them together had moved on to another phase.

In fact, had they not been attacked in the middle of the night, she may have decided to escape Willerby's unwanted attentions in some other fashion. By morning, she may very well have thought of Rosie as a viable option. Or Ann, another friend, who lived in a secure, gated community in San Diego.

Ah, denial.

So after several hours of mental gymnastics that ignored the elephant in the room—in this case, the fantastic sex—Zoe was feeling smugly in control of her emotions. Or perhaps not *entirely* in control, for when she heard Nick come in, she prudently stayed in the library and continued working. Actually, semiworking. Intellectually, she may have been in control, but her brain was less easily persuaded and no matter how seemingly sensible her resolve regarding Nick, she had spent lots of time daydreaming about, let's face it, the awesome sex.

In fact, in the midst of recalling some steamy memories, she almost jumped out of her chair when Nick knocked on the door and said, "Supper in ten minutes."

Fortunately, he didn't open the door since his voice alone had put her in such a dizzy state she felt like a twelve-year-old at her first junior high dance wondering if any of the boys who were huddled in a group across the room from the girls would walk across the gym floor and ask her to dance. *Where the hell did that come from?*

From the indecisive and yet much too willing libido that was go-

ing to be a complete pushover if Nick so much as smiles in my direction at dinner.

He didn't though.

Which should have made her happy but pissed her off instead. That huffiness was *most* helpful though because pissed off she was able to eat and converse and in general get through the meal without making a fool of herself.

As in—asking for it.

Although, wouldn't you know, Nick had cooked some damned cordon bleu version of chicken with Parmesan rice and peas that melted in your mouth, along with biscuits and coconut cream pudding that was almost as good as an orgasm.

Plus, he sat back in his chair, all casual nonchalance, and carried on a polite, easygoing conversation without so much as breaking a sweat.

He was really, entirely annoying.

No man should be so urbane, not to mention drop-dead handsome and expert in absolutely everything—including cooking.

Her pique may have been evident when she came to her feet immediately after finishing her dessert and said, snappishly, "Thank you for dinner. It was excellent as usual. If you'll excuse me."

He didn't move from his lounging pose. "You're welcome. Sleep well."

"Hmpf!" she muttered, and marched out of the room.

Only when she was well out of sight, did he push himself up in his chair, reach for the wine bottle, lift it to his mouth, and drain it in one long chug. Then, coming to his feet, he proceeded to set the kitchen to rights, loading the dishwasher and starting the cycle, wiping off the counters and table, unplugging all the appliances. As if physical activity would take his mind off his relentless cravings.

It didn't, but at least the kitchen wound up clean.

After that he grabbed a bottle of Canadian whiskey from the liquor table in the living room and walked out on the front porch. Slumping down in one of the chairs, he uncorked the bottle, took a slug, and cradling the bottle in his hands, gazed out at the lake. The moon was no more than a faint suggestion in the evening sky. It was summer in the north and light until ten.

Forcing himself to concentrate on knocking off Harry instead of surrendering to lust, Nick mentally reviewed his plans, checking off items one by one, going back over the schedule twice more to make sure he wasn't forgetting anything. He systematically forecast each required step with cool pragmatism. He couldn't afford to let emotion get in the way of scoring a hit.

He couldn't afford mistakes.

Harry was gonna be in full defensive mode.

It was completely dark when Nick finished the last of the whiskey. He still wasn't tired. Nor had the booze numbed his senses or, more particularly, his craving for the woman asleep in the bedroom down the hall. He walked back into the living room, and stood near the door debating his options. Another bottle? A few more hours outside on the porch safety zone where he could ride out the powerful wave of lust rattling his cage?

He remained at a standstill—as though all would be lost if he moved one additional step. Clenching and unclenching his fingers, he drew in deep, calming breaths. Told himself to be sensible. Reminded himself of what was at stake.

Come morning, they'd take off and that would be that.

Don't look for trouble.

Do not look for trouble.

He swore under his breath, the ticking of the clock on the mantel suddenly raucous in his ears.

Out of the blue, the phrase *Where have all the flowers gone?* leaped into his brain. A split second later he thought, *What the hell—life's short.*

Thirty-three

Zoe heard the bedroom door open. She glanced at the clock—a luminous 12:23.

Should she say something, sit up, feign sleep? Would he stay or go if he thought her sleeping?

At the thought of him leaving, her libido quickly took charge. *Sit up, sit up . . . so he knows you're awake! Then the ball's in his court.* What prompted her sudden bashfulness, she hadn't a clue. In the past, she would have simply asked for what she wanted. Maybe it was the effect of having been more or less ignored at dinner.

Apparently, Nick wasn't aware that the ball was in his court because he simply shut the door and stood there.

A muzzled, inhibited silence vibrated in the air.

Then they both began to speak, stopped, went mute.

And another inarticulate hush ensued.

"I shouldn't be here," Nick finally said, half under his breath.

"I didn't think you were coming." She shouldn't have been so honest. She should have said something bland and innocuous. After all, he had just pointed out that he shouldn't be here.

"I tried not to." He was resting against the door, seemingly at ease, in spite of his brusque comment.

Her temper spiked. *Rude prick.* "Should I be honored you decided to show up or offended by your rudeness?"

"Suit yourself." Edgy, restive words. But he didn't move.

"I'll think about it," she said, cool and cheeky.

"Take your time," he drawled, abruptly pushing away from the door and moving toward the bed. "It's still early."

"No it isn't. It's late. You woke me up." For starters, he'd better apologize.

"Sorry, I couldn't sleep."

Okay, so he *had* apologized. Somehow it wasn't enough. "That's no reason to wake me," she peevishly retorted. This whole dance was too easy for him, too familiar, the payoff too certain.

"I'm sorry about that, too."

Oh, crap. Is this where a diplomat would say to the other side—it seems we are nearing detente?

It didn't help either that moonlight bathed the room in a silvery glow, inviting one to feel the bewitchment, exciting desire. The luminous chiaroscuro shadows also added potent dimension to Nick's powerful form as he advanced on her— intensifying his brute virility.

My God, he was *large*!

She took a small breath, pulled the covers up to her chin like some nineteenth-century virgin, and stared at him wide-eyed.

Nick abruptly stopped at the unexpected image of innocence. Then he recalled Zoe's ravenous appetite for sex and he moved forward again.

"You just said you didn't think you should be here. I'm thinking maybe you were right."

"If I hadn't just finished a bottle of whiskey trying to forget you, maybe . . ." He shook his head, as if to get his bearings. "I'm going out of my mind," he murmured, taut and low.

"Why?" She shouldn't have asked, but she was a woman.

He blew out a breath. "Because I want you more than I should, I guess. Because I want you every waking minute and in my dreams, too. You've taken up all the space in my brain, swamping reason, making me crazy"—he grinned—"in a good way. So do me a favor or have pity on me. Think of it as an act of charity if you like."

It was a staggering concept that she might be having sex with Nick Mirovic out of kindness. *He really must be drunk.* Most women would be willing to do just about anything to have him climb into their beds. "How drunk are you?" Zoe asked.

"I don't get drunk." He held out one hand. "Look, steady as a rock."

He probably shouldn't have used the word *rock*, because it instantly suggested other rock-hard images that effectively shut down the rational part of her brain. "I suppose I could do you a favor," she said with a faint smile.

"Bitch," he said, with a grin, jerking his T-shirt over his head. "And I mean it in the nicest way." He reached for his zipper.

A second later, he was standing nude and gloriously aroused only inches away and there wasn't a female on earth who could have resisted. Moral issues and equivocal doubts disappeared like the shoreline in a hurricane.

God's gift to women was close enough to touch, tonight might be her last chance at the full realization of her orgasmic potential, and whatever Nick's reason for being here . . . she was in full agreement.

"Lift up your arms," he softly said.

She did.

He pulled off her nightgown and dropped it on the floor. Then he lifted the covers and climbed in.

"I'm going crazy for wanting you. I don't know how else to say it." He blew out a disgruntled breath. "And at the risk of offending you, I wish I didn't feel this way. It's not a good time for me, but there it is and it's freaking me out."

She smiled. "That's sorta sweet."

Coming up on one elbow, he gave her a grumpy look from under his long lashes. "It isn't anywhere near sweet for me, babe. It's a real head trip."

"Just for the record, I wasn't sleeping. I was thinking about you."

His smile was instant and heart-stopping. "Is that a fact?"

"I was also thinking about eating you alive."

"Welcome to my world, babe." He grinned. "We'll take turns."

Zoe grinned back. "Now that I'm off your hit list, you figure I won't make mincemeat out of your dick anymore—right?"

"You can't blame me for being cautious."

"I might need some makeup time tonight," she murmured, her gaze on his erection.

"You got it."

He was going to be a perfectly lovely first course, she decided, pushing him onto his back.

"Hey, don't be so rough," he teased, although she'd barely touched him.

"Brace yourself"—she grinned—"it's my turn tonight."

"Apparently one of us likes it rough," he drolly noted, glancing down at his surging erection.

"Why am I not surprised? He likes it every which way."

"I know something else that likes it every which way," he softly murmured.

"Don't start," she said. "I want to make this last."

He was well-mannered. He didn't say what he was thinking: *Lasting for you could be measured in seconds.* Spreading his arms wide, he smiled and said instead, "I happen to be available all night. No extra charge after midnight."

"Good," she said in a sort of faraway voice, like her mind was somewhere else as she gazed at him. She was imprinting him in her memory as he lay waiting for her, intent on taking home a souvenir album of memories that recorded the passion, tenderness, covetous lust, and now the taste and feel of him as well.

She started at the top, gently kissing his silky brows, his eyelids, his fine, straight nose, his sensual mouth that tasted of whiskey tonight, not peppermints. And he welcomed her kisses like a fond lover would—with tenderness and affection, with winsome restraint.

As she stroked and caressed him, he kept his hands clenched at his sides, knowing if he touched her he was lost.

He half raised his hands as her mouth trailed soft kisses down his chest, almost tempted beyond reason to cut to the chase. It had been a long, long evening of horniness suppressed; he couldn't remember when he'd last denied himself sex. But somehow he fought the urge to roll her on her back, mount her, and screw her till he dropped.

Although when her mouth closed around the head of his penis a few moments later, he drew in a breath of apprehension first and then restraint. He quickly started counting backwards from a hundred in threes so he really had to concentrate. But as she drew his rigid length deep into her mouth, when he felt his cock hit the back of her throat, he forgot about counting, he forgot about everything on the face of the earth except raw, agonizing, unbelievably awesome pleasure.

Why her mouth should feel any different from any other woman's baffled him in some distant corner of his mind. But damned if it didn't, Nick decided. It not only felt different, but better in the way a million dollars was better than a buck. He wasn't going to last much longer.

She never swallowed, Zoe reflected, recognizing his climax was fast approaching. She just didn't for any number of reasons—all selfish. Tonight however, she knew she was going to break precedence. She had no idea why.

It was probably a collective, arcane, incoherent teeming

mass of willingness, weakness, prodigal sensation, Robert Herrick's love poems—*where did that come from*—and heart and soul desire.

She could feel his hands on her head, the constrained pressure like that in his abs and quads. He was too large for her to completely swallow—no more than half his length fit in her mouth. When she'd attempted more, she choked, he'd winced, and they'd both been more careful after that.

The sight of his cock sliding back and forth over her lush, pink lips, the feel of his dick bottoming out in her throat, the way her ripe boobs brushed his thighs as her head rose and fell over his cock, all contributed to one of the more cataclysmic highs in his life. Okay, *the* most cataclysmic high.

"That's it," he said through clenched teeth. It was politesse, a courtesy call, and whether she took him up on it or not wouldn't impair his fast-approaching orgasm.

But she didn't move.

His climax exploded like that of a man who had been living as a monk in the wilderness and celibate for a decade.

He came and came and came.

Like a man possessed.

And she swallowed, and swallowed, and swallowed.

When she never did.

It was a rash, rapturous, headlong, and hot-headed collaboration that finally ended when Nick touched her cheek and whispered, "That was fucking heaven."

Sitting up, Zoe smiled. "You have a rather talented mouth as well."

"Speaking of mouths." Grabbing the sheet, he reached up

and wiped her mouth and chin. "My come dripping down your face, babe—it's a real turn-on . . ."

"Everything's a turn-on for you," she murmured, taking note of his rising erection.

"Only when you're around."

"I doubt it, but thanks. In terms of truth and full disclosure, if it's okay with you, I'm going to take a rain check on the tasting menu. I want the real thing . . . as usual I know—you don't have to grin like that. I'm addicted to your beautiful cock."

"He might need a short intermission."

"It doesn't look like it."

"Give me a few minutes and I'll last longer. You want it to last don't you?"

"Not really."

"I forgot. You're the babe who wants to come ten times in ten minutes."

"Is that a problem?"

Nick rolled up into a sitting position, and swung his legs over the side of the bed. "It's definitely not a problem." He rose to his feet.

"Then where are you going?"

"I have a little present for you." He walked across the room.

"Give it to me later." She fell back into a sprawl and watched him.

He turned from the dresser. "You'll like this one." He pulled open the top drawer and lifted something out. "Here." Sitting on the edge of the bed, he held out a black lacquer box.

Zoe pushed herself up on the pillows, took the box, and

lifted the lid. Two gold Ben Wa balls rested on a cushion of red silk. "You brought these here?" She shouldn't have asked. Why did it matter anyway whether he had or not?

"Not exactly. I found them in the plane in my flight bag."

"So these are some other woman's?"

"No. They were given to me a long time ago. I forgot about them."

"They're not used?"

"Brand-new, babe—look, you broke the seal. And if it'll bring a smile to your face, Alan brought them back from Japan for me." *Or they were left behind by some woman whose name I can't remember.* "How's that?"

"You could be lying."

"But I'm not." *When it's about sex, it's never a lie.*

She smiled then. "I have no idea why I'm pressing you. It's really stupid. I apologize."

"I'm not offended, okay? Press all you want." This from a man who normally said he didn't have a phone when a woman asked for his phone number.

"I'm thinking it must be all the recent turmoil—that's a euphemism," she said with a grin. "Anyway, I'm addicted to sex when you're around."

"It must be something in the air. I've got a hard-on that won't go away." Taking one of the gold balls from the box, he deftly slid it up her vagina. "How's that feel?"

She couldn't answer him right away; she was trying to catch her breath. "Not bad," she whispered a few moments later.

He smiled at her skittish understatement. "Ready for more?"

She took a small breath because a deep one would have restarted the wild strumming deep inside her. "I'm not sure."

"Yeah you are," Nick said, slipping the second little globe up against the first.

If she wasn't trying to keep from coming, she might have taken issue with his cool assurance.

He jammed his hand against her swollen vulva and pressed upward.

With a brief shudder and a breathy cry, she immediately climaxed.

Maybe he'd drunk too much tonight, or did he prefer that defense to facing the truth?

She had begun to matter to him—beyond the obvious sexual attraction. And not only was this the worst possible time to consider anything other than transient sex, he didn't want to get involved with a woman who treated fucking as casually as he did.

It didn't have anything to do with Zoe. It was just that after Trish and all the nastiness and revelations of their divorce, he was more wary than usual. It was only sensible to move on. He wasn't ready for more than casual sex anyway. Maybe he never would be.

Having talked himself down off the cliff in terms of pissed-off indignation at something he shouldn't give a rat's ass about, he returned to what he did so well.

Exerting a delicate pressure on the snugly ensconced little gold balls, he transported Zoe into the land of Nirvana and orgasmic bliss five times in rapid succession.

He finally stopped when her screams grew faint.

He deftly slipped out the small globes. As she involuntarily twitched under his touch and softly groaned, he understood he probably should have stopped a couple of orgasms ago.

Bending low, he gently kissed her cheek. "I'm sorry," he whispered. When she didn't reply, nor open her eyes, he questioned both his sanity and sobriety. *Christ, what came over me? Why did he feel the need to retaliate because she was so fucking hot?*

When her eyes fluttered open, he suddenly felt strangely whole again, as if her well-being colored and illuminated his world, gave it meaning. "You're amazing," she whispered, "*this* is amazing; my wanting you with such urgency on the other hand—is scary."

"No, it's charming and awesome." He smiled. "I'm counting my blessings."

"How much time do we have?" Even while basking in pleasure, she felt as though the *Titanic* was going down.

"Plenty of time. We don't have to leave early." Sitting up, he lifted her onto his lap. He held her close, gently kissed her, and whispered all the sweet, seductive words, the disarming, captivating words about sexual desire and longing. About his fascination for her.

And soon, she wrapped her arms around his neck and kissed him back, not gently but with her familiar impatience.

He smiled against her mouth. "I've never felt this good," he said.

They made love more leisurely as the night progressed, savoring every sensation and pleasure, knowing full well that time was running out.

When at last sunlight filled the room, Zoe looked at Nick and said, "Thank you for everything"—she smiled—"for saving my life and giving me pleasure. And now we have to go," she added, pretending she was a responsible grown-up.

"We probably should." He'd been up for an hour, waiting for her to wake. Although, if taking out Harry wasn't urgent, he would have willingly stayed.

"Do I have time to take a shower?"

"Absolutely. I'll go make us some lattes." Throwing the covers aside, he quickly rose from the bed before he was tempted to follow her into the shower. If he did, they wouldn't be going anywhere today.

Thirty-four

When Nick walked Zoe into the airport that afternoon, he surreptitiously scanned the small concourse for anything that looked suspicious. Willerby's people weren't likely to be here, but Harry could have been thorough enough to have watchers at all the local airports.

However, no one looked out of place in the throng of summer tourists with their camping gear. Even the occasional business type catching a flight to the Cities or Chicago didn't have an earpiece that shouldn't be there or the wrong kind of shoes with his suit or a briefcase with nothing in it.

He'd learned the hard way how to spot the smallest irregularity. After seeing people blown up in Kosovo by some lunatic who looked as ordinary as the next guy, or by sniper fire from a window with lace curtains you learned to never take anything for granted.

It looked like they were in luck today though.

There didn't seem to be any sign of Harry's people.

After checking Zoe's luggage, Nick suggested a coffee while they waited for her flight. For the next half hour they drank bad coffee and politely talked of generalities like strangers might, a continuation of their unexceptional conversation on the car trip from Ely.

But they were both struggling by the end to dredge up innocuous subjects. Finally it came time for Zoe to go to her gate and board.

In the absence of any talk of the future, both understood today was a polite adios. They were grown-ups; great sex did not necessarily equate with anything enduring. It was the pink cotton candy of life—delectable but quick to melt away in your mouth and disappear.

They carefully kept their distance on the short walk from the café to the entrance accessing the gates.

"Thanks very much for rescuing me from Willerby's cheesy stooges," Zoe said, as they reached the security line. "I really appreciate all your help."

"You're more than welcome. I enjoyed your company."

"And I yours."

Both were careful not to allude to the outpost camp, the attack, or the amazing sex.

"You're an excellent cook, too," Zoe said, cordial and bland, like one would be to a neighbor who brought over a basket of muffins. "The food was great." *You clean up real good, too,* she reflected in a less casual assessment, his white linen shirt and black slacks elegant, tasteful, and beaucoup sexy.

"Thanks." He was trying to keep it together. *She looks good enough to eat even though she's covered up in a green silk turtleneck and tan gabardine slacks.*

They both went silent for an awkward moment.

Then Nick quickly dipped his head, brushed Zoe's cheek with a polite kiss, and taking a step back, said with a smile, "Call me and let me know you arrived safely."

"Will do." With a wave, Zoe turned and swiftly walked away before she totally embarrassed herself and babbled out something completely ridiculous.

She showed her driver's license and ticket to the TSA agent without really paying attention, her thoughts on the fact that she'd never see Nick again. *It's over*, she reflected, as she had last night and a hundred times since then. His silence had made that pretty clear. No talk of the future, not so much as an passing allusion.

But thanks for the memories, she thought, setting her backpack on the X-ray machine conveyor belt. She had scrapbook-worthy memories for a lifetime.

A shame it had to end, Nick reflected as he exited the small passenger concourse. The sex had been incredible, fantastic, and every other superlative known to man.

But sex was way down his list of priorities right now. He had more pressing concerns—life-threatening ones. First, track down Harry and hopefully make the world a better place by zapping him. After that, maybe he could consider his own pleasures again. In particular, Zoe.

Although, he wasn't really in the market for a permanent arrangement—so what the hell was the point? He wasn't sure he wished to mess with his relatively peaceful existence.

Dostoevski had said, "If everything on earth were rational, nothing would happen." But at the moment he was inclined to favor the rational over self-indulgence.

He was laser focused on the hunt for Harry.

He'd head back to Ely for a day or so, square up his affairs, give Tony the lowdown on the firefight and his coming hunt for Harry; Tony had power of attorney for him should anything happen. Then, he'd drive down to the Cities and make sure the plane was ready on Thursday.

When Zoe called, he'd already been home for a couple of hours and was watching the evening news with a beer in his hand.

Singularly elated on seeing her name come up on his caller ID, he wrote it off as simply recall of all the mind-blowing sex. "Hi. How'd it go?"

"I'm safe and sound in my undisclosed location," Zoe replied.

"Good. You had an uneventful journey?"

"Smooth as silk. Rosie says hi."

"Hi back. I'll give you a call when all our outstanding issues are resolved. Stay put until then."

"Yes, sir," Zoe teasingly replied. "And thanks again," she softly added. "I'm in your debt."

The softness of her voice sent a little warm buzz up his spine, but he said, cool and collected, "Better wait on your thanks, babe, until you hear the final report."

"Well, a thank-you for everything up to now, then."

"Back at you. Expect a call in a week or two." Temperate and crisp—all business.

"Okay. Bye."

"Yeah," he murmured.

Afterward, he sat with the phone in his hand until the beeping dial tone caught his attention. Setting down the phone, he shook away the tantalizing but inconvenient memories and, rising to his feet, walked toward his study. A few moments later he was online with Alan, concentrating on what he should be concentrating on—firming up the details of their operation.

On the Near North Side of Chicago, Rosie MacNamara gazed at Zoe over her martini glass and said with a lift of her brows, "He must be something special."

Zoe had flipped her phone shut and was studying the olive in her martini. Looking up, she met her friend's blue-eyed gaze. "Oh, yeah—definitely special. Unfortunately I'm not the only woman who thinks so."

"But you're still in contact, right? He's taking care of business for you. Some guy who doesn't give a shit wouldn't have done what he's done or be doing what he's doing now."

Zoe had given Rosie a severely edited version of her time with Nick. She'd explained Nick's help with Willerby's men, of him possibly assisting her some more, but she hadn't mentioned any artillery battles or attack helicopters. Rosie wouldn't have believed it anyway. Who the hell would? Anyone who heard the whole outlandish tale would most likely suggest she find herself a good psychiatrist, get some Prozac, and stop reading spy novels.

"We'll see what happens," Zoe said, neutrally. "I'm pretty much in the dark about the eventual outcome of my problems or his. But, hey, I'm not complaining about all that's transpired. It was really nice knowing him, and if nothing else comes of it, I'll at least have some world-class memories."

"Define *world-class*," Rosie said with a grin.

Rosie had naturally curly red hair, a can-do attitude, and a smile that could charm the birds from the trees. Plus she didn't take *no* for an answer.

"Let's just say, better than average memories," Zoe replied, keeping it simple.

Rosie fluttered her fingers in a give-it-up gesture. "You don't seriously think I'm gonna be satisfied with that tame answer. You gotta share, sweetie. Remember, I tell you *everything*."

Rosie's blow-by-blow accounts of her sex life were definitely graphic and admittedly titillating. Zoe could likely recognize Rosie's dates without looking at their faces. "Okay, okay," she relented. "Nick's the best I've ever had. Bar none, and that includes Jonathan Fuller, who you know very well is a ten when it comes to hot sex."

"Oh, *baby*," Rosie murmured, lifting her brows in a dramatic leer, "for sure I want details now. Tell me *every* little thing"—she grinned—"or better yet, every big thing—which I presume is the case."

Zoe blushed.

"Wow. I haven't seen you blush since Joey Castlemaine asked you to marry him at Ziggy's Bar."

"I'm not blushing."

"Yeah, you are. Are you in *luv*? Is this Nick guy the *one*?"

"Jeez, Rosie, cut it out. He's just hot, that's all. No one's in love." She'd be incredibly stupid to even think about being in love with a man like Nick.

"You must like him anyway. That seems pretty obvious."

"He's very likeable. He even cooks—beautifully. And he builds canoes and is a linguist who used to teach Slavic languages at some college out East. He also makes the best espresso I've ever had."

"Not to mention he's apparently good in bed."

Zoe sighed. "*Good* doesn't even begin to describe it."

"So don't keep me in suspense. Start describing."

Zoe offered up a carefully redacted version of Nick's sexual skills, giving Rosie just enough information to satisfy her prurient interests. For the first time in her life she didn't feel like revealing the particulars of her relationship with a man.

It should have been a clue.

At the same time Zoe was politely fending off Rosie's need to know, Nick was not so politely fending off a visit from Lucy Chenko.

Lucy had walked into his house unannounced—although not unseen with his advance warning system—and while in the past Nick had accepted her flagrant behavior with equanimity, even warm hospitality on occasion, this time, he offered excuses.

"You're kidding," she petulantly muttered, as he held her at arm's length. "Since when are you too tired for sex?" With a toss of her short platinum curls, she stared at him pouty and sullen. "Donnie's out of town tonight and I don't have anything to do!" The large diamond studs in her ears sparkled as she lifted her chin defiantly and glared at him. "You can't be serious about sending me home."

"I just got back from my outpost camp and I'm tired as hell. Really," Nick added, slowly releasing his grip on her arms.

"You don't really mean it." She made a grab for his zipper again.

"Yeah, I do." His grip was harsh on her hands this time. "Give me a few days," he said, figuring he could buy some time, maybe change his mind in a few days. At least by the time he returned from DC maybe he'd be in the mood for Lucy's deviant version of sex.

"What do you mean by *a few days*?" she said with a pettish sniff, thrusting out her big boobs barely covered in a pink stretchy chemise.

"Three or four," he lied, ignoring her provocative pose, gingerly releasing her hands.

"For your information," she said, sourly, "men never turn me down." She ran her palms over her hips in case he hadn't

noticed her extremely short pink Versace skirt with an embroi-
dered rose conspicuously placed at crotch level. "What if I
don't come back to visit you?"

"Naturally, I'd be heartbroken," he smoothly replied.

"You'd better be." She scrutinized him for a moment, her
glossy pink lips pursed. "You *do* look tired. You've got dark circles under your eyes."

"I haven't had much sleep lately."

"Poor baby." She brushed a perfectly manicured finger
down his cheek. "I'll come back in a few days and make you
feel *all better*." She smiled, her quantum leap from anger to understanding typical. Lucy's short attention span and her affinity
for Ecstasy one in the same.

"That'd be just fine." He smiled, hoping she'd go.

"I don't suppose you have any X? I'm out." Narcissistic
self-interest, that was Lucy.

"Sorry. Try Chris at the Moose Lodge. He's usually got
some."

"Chris Dawkins?"

Nick nodded.

"Really?" Eyebrows beautifully arched, her voice soft as
silk.

"Yeah, really." It looked as though he was off the hook,
Nick decided, Lucy's purr indicating definite interest. He
should have mentioned Chris before. "Tell Chris hey if you see
him."

"Okeydokey, darling." She was all smiles now. "Make sure
you get plenty of rest."

It sure as hell wasn't his style—turning down sex—but he didn't give a shit. He was just glad she was gone. The last thing he wanted to do tonight was play rough with Lucy Chenko. Chris could have the pleasure of her S&M games.

He was gonna finish his beer, find something on the tube to watch, and zone out.

Time enough in the morning to pack for his trip east.

Thirty-five

It was a Friday night in the Virginia hunt country and traffic on the narrow, winding road had dwindled to an occasional car. By now, most of the DC weekenders escaping the sweltering temperatures in the city had reached their destinations.

The rain had begun an hour ago—lightly at first, then heavier as two weather fronts clashed in the sultry summer night. Cool air coming in off the Atlantic was meeting the steamy jet stream sailing out of the Ohio Valley. Lightning flashed continuously overhead, the rolling thunder in its wake serving as bass chorus to the fireworks show.

It was ten fifteen. To the two men waiting in a thicket of brush, 2215 military time. A familiar, instinctive reckoning now that they were on a mission—as familiar as their Kevlar vests, automatic weapons, and vigilance.

"I'd like this better if the asshole was shooting at us," Nick grumbled, struggling with the moral ambiguity of his role as executioner.

Self-defense was one thing—simple and sharply defined. This style of killing was nominally self-defense as well— still . . . it fucked with his head.

"Don't be having second thoughts," Alan muttered. "Harry deserved killing a long time ago."

"I know." Nick had already reminded himself a dozen times that Harry had tried to wack him twice, and innocent men had died because of Harry's interrogation methods. Unlike Alan though, he hadn't been trained to kill.

"This is no time for a conscience, bro," Alan gently noted. "Harry'll blow you away while you're debating right and wrong."

Alan was right. Harry wouldn't hesitate a second. And unless he wanted to look over his shoulder the rest of his life, he had a job to do.

They were waiting for their target west of a wide curve in the road, their operation planned for *this* particular evening *because* of the forecast. Slick roads, less traffic, overcast, and pitch-black—all pluses for them.

They'd had Harry Miller under surveillance for ten days, tracking his movements around the clock, noting what he did routinely, and what he did not—that in particular. It was the variables that could fuck them up. His visits to Abigail were in the routine category—Wednesday afternoons and Fridays— like clockwork, although he often stayed over on the weekend according to one of Alan's sources.

Unless Harry had a weekend meeting, but those were rare. Harry was not a hard-working bureaucrat. He was a lazy fucker. A direct quote from Mike Dunleavy—one of the better analysts who was still hanging in at Langley.

Mike had given them the heads-up about this particular meeting scheduled for eight o'clock Saturday morning. That meant Harry would be driving home Friday night.

In a rainstorm, according to the weather forecast.

And what his watchers had found most auspicious was the fact that Harry traveled to his little love nest sans bodyguards. They decided it had less to do with discretion than fear of competition. Harry's bodyguards were young men in their prime. He didn't want them anywhere near his twenty-something ex-Miss Alabama.

In addition to Harry traveling solo to Miss Alabama, they had been fortunate to have this storm coming in off the Atlantic just prior to Harry's Saturday meeting.

"Christ, I'm soaked," Nick muttered, rain streaming down his face. "What time is it?"

Alan glanced at his watch. "Coming on ten. I suppose Harry's reluctant to leave his hot babe. Maybe you should think about consoling the grief-stricken Miss Alabama afterward. I'm sure she'd prefer your hot bod to Harry's tub of lard."

"Not interested," Nick replied. "She might already be taken anyway." In the course of their surveillance, they'd seen a young, buff guy in jodhpurs come to visit on one of Harry's off days. The man hadn't stayed long, so Abigail Cathcart and her visitor had either gotten off in a hurry or she'd only given him a taste. But it definitely had the look of a blossoming friendship the men decided, watching the couple play footsie through their binoculars. When the two had disappeared into the back of the house, Nick and Alan had moved to a new position, but the bedroom curtains had been drawn so they couldn't tell whether everyone had been suitably pleasured.

Although the guy *had* been smiling when he'd left.

"Jeez—what if Harry decided to stay till morning with this rain." Alan checked his watch again.

"Nah. Remember—he doesn't like to get up early. Asshole could never drag himself out of his palatial hotel room until ten or eleven." Harry had always commandeered the best hotel room in whatever Kosovar town they were in.

"I still don't understand why he isn't armed to the teeth and guarded twenty-four seven after his crew disappeared."

"Hubris. Vanity. Stupidity. Who knows? For one thing, he's a crazy man, although we probably have his babe to thank for the absence of guards. Hey, hey, hey," Nick murmured, "speak of the devil."

A black Mercedes SUV sailed over a distant hill, coming at them like a bat out of hell.

"Jesus, that's one heavy foot on these slick roads."

"I can see the headline now," Nick murmured, pulling out one of the disposable phones he'd picked up at a gas station on his way to the Cities. 'CIA Chief Skids off Road and Dies.'"

Yesterday, with Alan standing watch, Nick had planted the guts of another disposal phone with a small C-4 device on the front axle of Harry's car.

It had taken less than two minutes.

Harry was in the habit of stopping at a small liquor store in a strip mall outside DC and picking up a pint of Wild Turkey on his visits to his mistress. He'd drink the whiskey on his drive and pitch the bottle before he reached the cottage.

Harry never came out of his love nest once he arrived, nor did he check his car before he returned to DC, so the explosive was safe. Apparently, he felt secure behind the cottage's security perimeter.

Harry trusted electronic surveillance.

Lucky for them electronic surveillance could be jammed or bypassed with the right equipment.

"What's chances Harry found the C-4?" Nick murmured, watching the SUV speeding toward them. He was thinking out loud, worried. Wanting to be certain.

"Pretty much nil."

"I'd be happier with 100 percent."

"If only. He's not a complete moron, although his survival this long has more to do with treachery than intellect."

The rain was falling in sheets now, the wind blowing hard from the east, compromising visibility.

But the gleam of headlights winked at them through the rain and dark.

"Come on, baby . . . just a little closer . . . come on, come on." Suddenly all the ambiguities were wiped away: Harry's crimes against humanity rose up in Nick's mind in all their horror and he knew why he was here. And as soon as the SUV reached the point where the road curved tight to the left, where Harry would have to slow down, justice would be served.

But Harry didn't slow down.

"He must be testing his fucking suspension," Alan said half under his breath.

Nick was furiously punching in phone numbers. Hitting the Send key, he glanced up, and started counting. "One-one thousand, two-one thousand, three—"

The C-4 detonated, lighting up the night, and the speeding black Mercedes careened off the road, trailing flames.

The men were already sprinting through the underbrush, racing toward the crash site.

Alan scanned the highway as they crossed it. "Are you good now?" They'd planned this minute by minute. He was to stand guard.

"Yup," Nick grunted, his adrenalin pumping, the outside world eclipsed, his mind laser focused on what he had to do.

Running headlong toward the burning car, he screwed on his silencer with a few quick twists of the wrist, slid down the slick shoulder of the road, splashed through the puddles in the ditch, and skidded to a sudden stop, his boot heels sinking into the soft muck.

Shit. The driver's door was open. It could have blown out in the crash. Or more likely, Harry had bolted. *Fuck.*

Crouching low, his finger on the trigger of his Beretta, he swiftly crossed the patch of ground that had been flattened by the heavy, hurtling SUV, coming up on the car from behind. Cautiously moving forward to the passenger door, he eased upward enough to peer in through the fire and smoke.

Empty.

Crap. So much for plans.

Already pressed for time, now he had to *find* the bastard before he could kill him. The fire was sure to attract attention, particularly once it hit the gas tank and the explosion lit up the sky. Not to mention, every passing second, Harry could be putting distance between them.

Although he might *not* be moving too fast, Nick decided after another glance at the driver's side. The front of the car was wrapped around a tree, the air bag splattered with blood— another dark smear streaked the pale grey leather of the driver's seat. Harry might have more than scratches.

Backing away into the shadows, Nick scanned the area, hoping to find a corpse. Or tracks. But the heavy rain and darkness beyond the flickering light from the burning car limited visibility.

A teeth-rattling crack of lightning, phosphorescent and blue, streaked across the night sky.

In that fateful pause between the lightning flash and the inevitable roll of thunder, Nick heard the sound of heavy breathing, the resonance so quickly obliterated by a thunderous boom he could have imagined it. But somehow, he knew he hadn't.

Turning to his right, he surveyed the dark tangle of brush and shrub pine beyond the burning car.

The sound had been close. That meant Harry wasn't moving fast. It could mean he was hurt—maybe badly hurt. Possibly drawing his last breath.

Wouldn't that be convenient?

Then to all appearances the newly nominated CIA chief simply would have died from an unfortunate *accident*. Other than the spooks, no one would be the wiser.

The first round hit Nick square in the chest, knocking the breath from his lungs even through the Kevlar and effectively destroying his rosy scenarios. As the second shot whined past him, he was already down and rolling, steadily pumping rounds in the direction of the muzzle flashes.

A high-pitched scream echoed from the darkness.

Bull's-eye, he thought, scrambling for cover.

Harry should have aimed for the face or neck—the only safe target in the era of Kevlar. Although maybe he had; his marksmanship was shit.

"Whoever you are, you're dead meat!" Harry shouted. "I've called in backup!"

Bluster and threaten. Vintage Harry. "They won't get here in time!"

"Fucking *Mirovic*! You're fucking hard to kill!"

A couple tracers followed by a barrage of large-caliber rounds shredded the brush over Nick's head.

"You still shoot like a girl, Harry!" In the pause while Harry was obviously reloading, Nick glanced toward the road. Alan had taken cover, but he'd stay on guard. Neither of them wanted witnesses. Taking a deep breath, Nick came up off the ground, sprinted for the tree line in a low zigzag run, dove into the underbrush, and lay panting for a moment before he lifted his head and surveyed the distance to his target.

"Maybe I won't kill you. Maybe I'll have you thrown in a black hole where no one will ever find you!" Harry yelled. "I'll have you tortured till you *beg* to die!"

"Shut the fuck up, Harry. You got nothin'." Nick patted down his pockets, counting his clips.

Mirovic's voice was closer—*Too close*, Harry thought. *Damned fucker has ice water in his veins, too.* How many times had he seen him walk into what could have been a trap in Kosovo without so much as a backward glance? A change in strategy might be called for. "Let's parlay, Mirovic! I'll give you ten million to walk away! That's a lotta money; you can live large anywhere in the world!"

"As if I fucking trust you, Harry." Nick wasn't shouting; he didn't have to. He was just waiting to go in for the kill.

"Twenty–thirty million!" Harry called out, raising the ante, equally aware of the small distance between them, but shouting as if to better press his point home. Or perhaps out of fear. "I can get you more if you want! Untraceable money! To any account, anywhere! Name your price!"

"Your head on a pike, Harry. How's that sound?"

In answer, Harry fired a full automatic burst—six hundred rounds per minute.

All of which sailed over Nick's head, although the bursts were a little too close for comfort. Concerned a rescue squad might be on the way, Nick swiftly pulled up stakes and moved to outflank Harry.

He traveled noiselessly through the brush and timber and came up behind Harry and his makeshift barricade. He couldn't shoot a man in the back though, so standing ten yards away, Nick quietly said, "It's payback time, Harry."

Harry spun around and opened fire.

A Heckler & Koch G 11, Nick weirdly reflected, admiring the state-of-the-art weapon Harry didn't know how to handle when he should be keeping his mind on business. A baby like that needed a sure trigger finger, a strong grip, and someone who could qualify on the firing range. And that wasn't Harry.

Nick's thoughts were going off on a tangent, but fortunately his brain was good at multitasking, because he had already dropped, rolled, and pumped two carefully placed rounds in the center of Harry's forehead.

Instinctive aim and shoot.

Instinctive self-preservation.

Or maybe at some level, he was tired of fucking around; he just wanted it over.

How many years had it been that he'd had to be on guard, wondering where Harry might be, waiting for the fucker to make a move.

Too many fucking years.

Over a worthless shit like Harry.

Coming to his feet, he walked toward the man who had seriously impacted his life. "Judgment day, Harry," Nick said under his breath, staring at the crumpled, lifeless form.

Harry had tumbled back against the rough barricade of fallen trees and brush he'd thrown up. His head was listing downward, his lower body in a sprawl, a hole visible in the arm of his leather jacket—precipitating the scream Nick figured—and another hole from a round in his chest—the Kevlar beneath intact.

The two forehead wounds were the fatal ones.

He's bleeding out.

Like so many of his own victims, Nick dimly thought, nebulous images of violent death suddenly looming in his brain. He unconsciously shook himself, as though to ward off the repellent memories.

But those nightmares had held him hostage too long.

What if Harry wasn't dead?

What if he came back from the dead like some diabolical demon?

Nick needed certainty—a-stake-through-the-heart-for-vampires kind of certainty.

Taking aim at Harry's head, he shot twice.

"That's for the farmer in Pristina," he muttered, unscrewing the silencer. *And for all the others*, he said to himself. Shoving the Beretta and silencer into his jacket pocket, he swung around and strode toward the road, thinking he should be feeling some elation. Or relief. But not feeling much of anything at all.

Making the concept of *closure* wildly overrated.

Like most of the psychobabble.

He blew out a breath. One foot in front of the other, keep moving, and maybe someday he'd feel good about this.

Walking away from the body, he reached Alan a few moments later. "We're outta here."

"Harry's smoked?"

"Yup. On his way to hell."

"There was a lot of gunfire. I was hoping you didn't need help."

"Nah." Nick turned to his friend. "I was on a mission from God."

Alan laughed. "Nice backup."

"That's what I thought."

"So the world's a better place now?"

"I'm guessing. Satan's shaking Harry's hand about now."

"That means everyone can get on with their lives."

Nick smiled faintly. "Here's hoping."

The men took the long way around to their car, staying well clear of the highway, following the route they'd previously reconnoitered. They heard the explosion and saw the sky light up behind them three minutes later.

"Good timing. There goes the evidence," Alan said.

"Not that it matters. Everything's untraceable."

"But then, we're not novices."

"No shit." Although there were times Nick wished he was. He'd lost his innocence about the decency of man long ago.

They soon reached the car that Alan had borrowed from a friend. Stripping off their Kevlar vests, they tossed them in the trunk and drove to a landfill two hours away.

There, they disposed of their jackets, pants, vests, and boots, digging them separately, well distant and deep into the acres of waterlogged trash. After burying their gear, they dressed in clean clothes, drove to a small unmanned airport three hours away where they left the car as arranged, taxied their small cargo plane to the end of the lone runway, and took off into the rain.

They were back in Minneapolis by morning, landing with their fictitious cargo at the cargo airfield and leaving the plane in its hangar.

They had a drink to celebrate before Alan caught a flight west.

Raising his glass, Alan murmured, "To good times and the wisdom to appreciate them."

"Amen. To freedom from the past."

"Except for the good stuff."

"Yeah, except for that." At which point, thoughts of Zoe immediately came to mind.

"You should go see her," Alan suggested.

Nick shot him a look.

"I don't have to be a mind reader, dude. It's clear as day. Zoe rings all your bells."

"Maybe I will." Nick didn't want to argue.

"Seriously, she'll help you forget all your demons better than anyone else. If I didn't have Ginny, I'd have gone over the edge more than once. Who wouldn't, with all the shit we've been through? So consider it."

"Okay, I'll consider it."

Alan smiled. "You're wound tight as a drum. You know that don't you?"

Nick smiled back. "Hey, things are on the upturn now. No more Harry—maybe no more nightmares."

Alan drained his glass and came to his feet. "Remember to invite me to the wedding."

Nick flashed him a grin. "You'll be the first to know, believe me."

After a quick hand shake, Alan left. Nick drove to the Airport Hilton and slept straight through until the following day.

Then he bought a plane ticket for New York.

He had one more mission to complete before returning home.

Thirty-six

 Zoe had been working hard since she'd arrived in Chicago, her first draft in the final stages.

Two days ago, Joe had stopped for a short visit en route to San Francisco. He'd brought all the pertinent manifests and invoices discovered in Trieste. He'd also threatened to put out a hit on Willerby.

Joe was generally more bluster than action, but Zoe wasn't entirely sure he wasn't serious this time, so she did her best to calm him down. She gave him a quick report on the chopper attack in Canada as preface to her suggesting they wait until they heard from Nick.

"He said he might be able to resolve our problem with Willerby. I'm not certain what that means, but why not wait and see? If we don't hear anything after another week or so, you can go to plan B." Although the idea of a hit on Willerby was way the hell outside her comfort zone. "Law enforcement is an option as well," she added. "We could always hire a lawyer to protect our rights."

"He threatened my daughter."

Joe had spoken quietly, through clenched teeth, which gave Zoe the impression a lawyer might not be on his agenda. "Give me another week, okay? Then if we don't hear from Nick, do whatever you want."

"I don't need your permission."

"I didn't mean that. And I understand your anger. Mandy's fine though. She's been protected all along by some people Nick knows."

Joe slid down on his spine in one of Rosie's Mies chairs and softly exhaled. "I shoulda come back sooner. I'm feeling guilty and taking it out on you. Sorry."

"You needn't apologize. Willerby is way out of line. Neither you nor I should have to deal with his shit."

"Yeah, in a perfect world, maybe. Look, I need a drink." He surveyed Rosie's ultramodern living room, leather, stainless steel, and glass the basic decorating components. "Whadda you have here?"

"Pretty much anything." Zoe came to her feet and moved toward a small bar concealed behind frosted glass doors. "Name your poison."

Over two gin and tonics, Joe calmed down, Zoe heard more details about the excavation site, and further talk of hits evaporated. Zoe said she'd call Joe the minute her manuscript was completed and on its way to her publisher.

Joe said, "Good. And make sure you call me when you hear from this Nick guy."

"You'll be the first to know. I promise."

They were on their third drink when Rosie came home from work, and after introductions, Joe had a quick one for the road and took his leave.

"He has a flight to catch," Zoe said as the door closed on him.

Rosie smiled. "I thought it might have been something I said."

Zoe laughed. "It could have been that, too. I'm not sure he's often asked whether he misses being married. And whose fault the divorce was."

"You told me he was divorced and had a daughter. Those were natural questions. You don't know how many people at work talk about their divorces. I swear it's the number one topic of conversation: who was the bad ass, or the baddest ass, and then all the tedious whys and wherefores. Personally, I don't understand it. If you like your spouse, stay and if you don't, leave. What the hell is all this useless recapitulation?"

"I guess everyone can't be as decisive as you."

"Perhaps everyone didn't walk in on their husband fucking one of their best friends."

"Ex-best friend."

"No shit. The bitch. Speaking of slutty women and faithless husbands, what say we go and check out the merchandise in our local bar scene?"

"Nah. I told you I'm not in the mood."

"'Cuz you're in luuuuuvvv," Rosie said with a grin.

"Am not."

"Are, too."

"Since we're not eight, I'm changing the subject. Do you like shrimp? I saw the most beautiful shrimp at Whole Foods when I got my morning latte. I bought a bunch."

"I didn't know you cooked." They'd been eating takeout.

"Of course I cook."

"Since when?"

Zoe smiled. "Okay, since I saw those lovely shrimp this morning."

"And now you're gonna experiment on me."

"How hard can it be? The fish guy at Whole Foods said you boil them for four minutes in beer and spices if you want. And for your information, if I have a cookbook I can cook anything. It's just a matter of following directions."

"Okay," Rosie said with a small sigh. "But let me have a couple of martinis first. We can always call for a pizza if the shrimp doesn't work out."

"I appreciate your vote of confidence."

"I'd appreciate it if you'd go out with me, if not tonight, tomorrow." She lifted her brows. "I'm promising to eat your shrimp . . ."

"Okay, okay . . . tomorrow."

Thirty-seven

The next day, Nick landed at Kennedy, rented a car, and drove out to the Hamptons.

According to his car radio, a new director for the CIA had been announced, subject to congressional confirmation, of course. Harry's death had dominated the news cycle yesterday, but apparently, the CIA was quickly moving on.

News reports had Harry driving off the road in a rainstorm and dying in a crash. The CIA was quoted as saying Harry's death was an *unfortunate accident.*

As if they hadn't seen the bullet holes in Harry or found the C-4 residue. But what the hell, if they told the truth, they wouldn't be the CIA.

By ten, Nick had rented a motel room in East Hampton, paying cash. After carrying in his overnight bag, he walked downtown, bought a local map, found an Internet coffee shop, and Googled Bill Willerby.

He needed Willerby's address.

There's no privacy left in the world. Nick pulled up an aerial view of the property, Willerby's phone numbers, his addresses in Manhattan, both home and office, and even the names of his doctors, accountants, and lawyers. Quickly perusing the roster of the law firm, he found photos of Zoe's two visitors. Which then required further Googling of those two. Two hours and three espressos later, he drove back into Manhattan to pick up some weapons at a pawnshop known to him through Alan.

Alan's contacts were all ex-military, as were his customers. Many former special ops were fighting other peoples' war around the world and if they needed the best in personal protection, they could count on Alan getting it to them quickly.

The owner remembered Nick, offered his warm regards to Alan, and sold him what he needed. From there, Nick made additional purchases at a hardware store, and one of those spy shops where people bought hidden cameras to watch their nannies or servants or spouses.

By the time Nick had made all his buys and returned to East Hampton it was nearing eight. Perfect timing. A quick drive by Willerby's property while it was still light and then he'd spend tomorrow reconnoitering the terrain.

It was a small town, and people liked to gossip. Or maybe they liked to chat up a good-looking guy with a winning smile. By the end of the day, he pretty much knew the down and dirty on the Willerbys, along with their favorite wines—Italian

reds—most frequented winter homes—St.Barts and Antibes—
and nail polish color—peony pink for her, clear for him.

It was midnight when he dropped over the eight-foot-high
brick wall and surveyed the back of a turn-of-the-century
thirty-five-thousand-square-foot colonial.

He entered the house through the garage, using a universal
Genie garage door opener he'd purchased in the city. Raising
the door barely a foot to minimize noise, he slid under it and
found his way down to the basement. Security system control
panels were invariably there. He quickly bypassed the power to
the alarm with some number eighteen wire and alligator
clamps, disengaged the telephone lines, then double-checked
all the circuitry in case he'd missed something.

Nope.

Either Willerby had pissed off the installer or he'd paid for
the discount package, because there were enough holes in his
security to drive a semi through, including the gaps in the outside cameras that missed a couple straight shots to the house.

In less than twenty minutes, he was climbing the stairs to
the second floor, following the sound of snoring to his target
audience.

Or audiences, as it turned out.

Mr. and Mrs. Willerby slept in separate bedrooms. Like no-
bility, royalty, and apparently very rich people.

In a way, it made his pitch easier. The young Mrs.
Willerby would likely freak out. He doubted a cutthroat like
Willerby would. Anyone who could take over a record num-
ber of firms, gut them of their assets, and leave debt and

massive job cuts behind wasn't by definition an oversensitive, impressionable human being.

It turned out he was right on.

When he woke Bill Willerby a few minutes later, gently prodding his shoulder with the muzzle of his handgun, Willerby simply sat up, peered at him in the dim light, and said calmly, "Who the hell are you?"

"Your worst nightmare." Nick was dressed in black, including the knit mask pulled down over his face.

"I doubt it." Willerby leaned back on his pillows. "You're too big to be my first wife."

"A comedian," Nick murmured.

"Look, wise guy, I can hurt you more than you can hurt me." Curt, cold, an unblinking stare.

Nick raised his Walther PPK marginally so the blunt barrel pointed at Willerby's gut. "And I could kill you if I want."

"Then you would have already."

Nick's teeth flashed white in a smile. "You have a point. So, here's the deal," he murmured, figuring there was no sense in wasting time. "I want you to leave Zoe Chandler alone. Call off your lawyers—permanently."

"And if I don't?" Willerby gave no indication of alarm.

"You're a cool motherfucker, aren't you? Okay, listen up. This is a onetime offer. No second chances, no refunds. If you don't leave Miss Chandler alone, first your wife will disappear. Her body will never be found. Then your son will disappear. He doesn't matter to you according to local gossip, but he'll be gone anyway and his body will never be found. Next, your grandson, who does matter to you, I'm told. You get the idea? You'll be last. And I don't care how many bodyguards you have—fuck with me and you'll die. By the way, your wife is going into hysterics next door. She's trussed up with duct tape. Be careful when you rip the tape off her mouth. Sometimes it takes the skin with it."

"What if I don't believe you?"

Nothing about his wife or grandson. Maybe the guy doesn't give a shit about anyone. "Then go for it, but you'll be having a lot of funerals in the family."

"You could be bluffing." But Willerby's former insouciance was shaken and a thin beading of sweat stood out on his forehead.

Duly noted. "Suit yourself. But I'm standing in your bedroom in case you haven't noticed, and no alarms are going off. So you should think about your future—however short it might be. And you might want to advise your wife not have her hair done anymore at Gloriosa's or lunch at her favorite restaurants—Pierre's or Cittanuova—or buy those Italian olives and marzipan cakes she likes at the Barefoot Contessa. Then there's Jesus who runs your yard crew. Great guy, although you don't treat him real well I hear. He said I could come work for him anytime I wanted. So here's the way I look at it. You can be more or less imprisoned inside your residences until I come for you, always looking over your shoulder, or you can call off your pissing contest over this book."

Willerby had gone pale by now, his ashen color visible even in the darkness.

"If you understand, you can just nod." The man looked like he might be getting sick.

Willerby opened his mouth, tried to speak, shut it again, and nodded.

"Great. We're both on the same page, then. One added suggestion," Nick pleasantly noted. "You might think about offering to return your hot property. Why not give back all those stolen antiquities as a magnanimous gesture to the art world? You wouldn't look like such a prick then, although I doubt that's an issue for you. But I understand your current wife is concerned with her image. Think of all the good publicity you'd get. It's just an idea, but I'd think about it if I were you.

"Now you have yourself a nice night. And don't bother trying to call the police. Your phone lines are down." Nick patted his jacket pocket. "I've got your and your wife's cell phones— including the one in your desk downstairs. But if you have others, go for it. I'll be long gone."

Three minutes later, he'd scaled the wall and was driving his rental back to Manhattan where he boarded an early-morning flight back to Minneapolis. He was home in Ely by suppertime.

He had a good feeling about his little talk with Willerby.

He figured when even a corporate hoodlum like Willerby went all white and pasty like that, he'd gotten the message loud and clear.

Thirty-eight

Nick had checked his security first on his return. Not that he was expecting any further incursions now that Harry was dead, but old habits died hard.

Nothing was out of place. Tony had kept a good eye on things.

He found a note from Chris in the workshop: *Call me when you get back. I'm stuck on the inwales*. But he'd been working on other things, Nick noted, taking in the fresh green paint on one of his old canoes.

Returning to the house, Nick opened a beer and sat down to call Zoe. He wanted to let her know that Willerby was no longer a threat. He'd thought about calling her from New York, but his libido had been whispering, *Stop and see her in Chicago on your way home* and he wasn't sure the sound of her voice might not have pushed him over the edge.

Zoe picked up on the second ring. "Hi. Where are you?"

"Back home. I just got here and wanted to let you know that Willerby shouldn't bother you again."

"For real? How do you know? Did you actually see Willerby or did someone else talk to him?" *Someone like Alan who flew in with serious weapons.*

"I saw him for a few minutes," Nick said, mildly. "He seemed willing to listen." *A measured understatement.* "He might even return his antiquities to Italy, although I'm not sure about that. I hope that doesn't screw up your book sales if he does."

"Not at all. I'm writing about the market for stolen antiquities. He happens to be a prime subject, but hey, I'm thrilled if he's out of my life. I can't thank you enough! It's wonderful news! Absolutely wonderful! Thanks about ten million times."

"Zoe! Get a move on! We have hot men waiting for us!" Rosie yelled. Rosie wasn't taking no for an answer tonight. Zoe had been putting her off for too long. "And I need a drink *now, now, now!*"

"Sounds like you're busy," Nick murmured, Rosie's voice coming through loud and clear. "I'll let you go." *What the hell did you expect? A woman who likes to fuck isn't gonna be sitting home.*

"No, I'm really not busy . . . not at all," Zoe quickly said, not wanting their conversation to end. "Rosie's just agitating for a drink. Say, I heard that CIA guy died in a car accident. Lucky for you."

"Yeah, real lucky." He found himself getting pissed for no good reason.

"Zoe, *hurry*!" Rosie hollered. "I'm in the mood for some hot sex and pretty soon all the good ones are going to be taken!"

"Look, I gotta go," Nick said. "See ya."

The phone went dead, and when Rosie appeared in Zoe's bedroom doorway a second later, she took a step back. "What?"

"Thanks for screwing up my life big-time," Zoe muttered, glaring at her friend.

"What'd I do?"

"I was talking to Nick until you started yelling about getting some sex tonight. He said he had to go and hung up."

"That could be good. Maybe he's jealous."

"Or maybe he didn't want to talk over your screams about getting some."

"Call him back. I'll apologize."

"It's too late. That train's already left the station."

Rosie shrugged. "Whatever. He could call back, too."

"Well, he's not going to."

"Jeez, don't go all pouty on me. I said I'd apologize to your Nick guy."

"He's not my Nick guy."

"It sounds like you'd like him to be."

"Look, it doesn't matter, okay?" She could still hear the change in his voice after Rosie's shouts. But what would she say if she called back anyway? *I don't want to see other guys. I just want to see you.* Yeah, as if that wouldn't bring a dead silence. While the sex had been awesome, she didn't think that counted when it came to a real relationship. And let's face it, she'd known him a grand total of six days, which was probably par for the course for him.

"Hey, I really am sorry. Tell me what to do to make it better," Rosie softly said, leaning against the door, looking penitent. Or as penitent as you could look in chartreuse fuck-me shoes and a color-coordinated little club dress that barely covered her boobs.

"Oh, hell, never mind," Zoe murmured, picking up her purse from the dresser and putting her phone back inside. "It's not your fault. I overreacted." She forced herself to smile. "So where are you taking me? I could use a drink right now."

"Yesss . . . that's more like it. We can't let a man fuck up our world—right?"

Another fake smile. "Absolutely." Zoe moved toward the doorway. "I don't need a jacket do I?"

Rosie wanted to say, *Are you going in those shorts and that T-shirt?* but having screwed up once already tonight, she said instead, "God, no. Not in the summer in Chicago. It's probably still ninety out."

Zoe found that after two drinks, she was able to smile with less effort. Unfortunately, she also found that the men in the bar Rosie favored didn't interest her in the least. It appeared as though no amount of liquor was going to change that. It wasn't as though she didn't try. She went through a good number of fruity summer drinks in an effort to gin up some interest in the various men hitting on her and Rosie.

The problem was none of them looked like Nick.

Which depressing thought required another drink; rebuking harsh reality couldn't be accomplished sober.

Shortly after, Rosie went off to dance to one her *favorite* songs and Zoe found herself cornered by a handsome, blond, intense man called Chuck, who would have been a stalker in any other venue but a bar. He'd managed to temporarily edge out the competition by waiting for her to come out of the bathroom.

Stepping in front of her in the narrow hall, he tipped his perfectly gelled hair in the direction of the minuscule dance floor and murmured, "Wanna dance?"

"Thank you, no." She tried to walk around him.

He shifted his stance and stopped her. "We could go somewhere quiet instead and have a drink. I know a nice bar down the street."

"I'm sorry, but I'm just getting out of a relationship," Zoe said, wanting to get rid of him politely. "And I'm just not ready yet. But thanks."

"I could make you forget—real easy," he whispered, bending close for a moment so his voice vibrated against her cheek.

Instead of saying, *Get the fuck out of my way*, Zoe said, with more civility than she was feeling, "I'm just visiting for a few days. I'm leaving soon. Maybe some other time."

His eyes almost literally lit up. "Better yet. Two ships passing in the night . . ."

Obviously, subtlety wasn't working. "You know . . . I was just thinking. Are you the Chuck I've been talking to in the herpes chat room on Yahoo?"

"Christ—there's my friend Dave." He did a fake wave toward the bar. "Gotta go. Nice meetin' you."

Zoe actually smiled a real smile for the first time that night. Then she threaded her way through the crowd, walked onto the dance floor, and tapped Rosie on the shoulder. "I'm going back to your place," she shouted over the deafening music. "I'll see you later."

Rosie was clearly enjoying herself. She didn't argue. She gave Zoe a thumbs-up. And then she went back to rubbing her body against a football player-looking guy who had smiling eyes and an even nicer smile.

Really nice, Zoe thought, pushing her way through the drunken mob to the door.

In another lifetime, she might have cared.

But it wasn't Nick's smile.

Jeez, of all the rotten luck. You run into a super guy who does everything right in all the right departments and he's not really interested.

She felt like writing sloppy, sentimental poetry about mountains high and oceans deep, about love and loss.

As if, she snorted.

Love and Nick. That'll be the day.

But she couldn't sleep that night and whatever it was she was feeling for Nick Mirovic, it was sad and bittersweet and painful as hell.

Damn. Who would have thought it could happen to her.

Thirty-nine

Zoe wasn't the only one who wasn't sleeping that night.

It got so bad, Nick seriously thought about calling Lucy.

And then it got worse and he *did* call her.

The minute he opened the door and saw her standing there he knew he'd made a mistake.

"Darling, I've missed you!" Throwing her arms around his neck, Lucy nibbled on his ear. "And I missed your gorgeous dick the most."

He unwrapped her arms from around his neck and took a step back. "Would you like a drink?" *Can I get her drunk enough to pass out?*

"You know what I want, babykins," she purred, moving toward him again.

"I'm gonna have a drink," he said, sidestepping her. "I've been traveling all day. I could use a little relaxation."

"I thought that's why you called *me*," she said with a dazzling smile.

Crap. Am I up for a courtesy fuck? "Sit." He waved her to a chair. "Tell me what you've been doing while I mix a drink."

"Nothing I'm going to tell you about," she slyly murmured, slipping off her jacket as she moved to the chair. "Life is *sooo* boring, darling."

"You need a hobby."

"Would *you* like to be my hobby?" Dropping into a chair, she slowly crossed her legs so it was obvious she wasn't wearing panties. "I think I'd like that a whole big bunch."

Jesus, not me—not even a little bunch. Although, what the hell, Zoe is out fucking someone. Why shouldn't I? He tossed down the three fingers of malt liquor he'd poured into his glass, poured three fingers more, and finished that off before turning back to Lucy. *Maybe it isn't gonna be a courtesy fuck. Maybe it's gonna be a get-even fuck.*

It turned out to be a dutiful, teeth-grinding, when-will-this-be-over fuck. And he felt like shit afterward. As soon as he decently could, he sent Lucy home. He even promised to take her swimming the next night to help speed her on her way.

Returning to the bedroom, he stripped the sheets from the bed as if he'd engaged in some shameful depravity and had to dispose of the evidence. Carrying the sheets and some soiled towels out in the hall, he shoved everything down the laundry chute, then grabbed some fresh linens from the hall closet.

Quickly remaking the bed, he picked up the handcuffs from

the floor, tossed them back in a drawer, and suddenly came to a standstill, struck by the graphic memory of the time before last when he'd used them.

He'd cuffed Zoe to the bed that night and fucked her so hard he thought he was gonna blow his brains out. Her orgasmic screams had kept his cock in top gun form for God knows how long.

Shit. I need a drink. Or ten.

Striding to the kitchen, he opened the freezer and pulled out his old standby. No way he was gonna get through the night sober. He lifted the bottle to his mouth.

By the time the vodka was half gone, he was finding it increasingly difficult to resist picking up the phone and calling Zoe. The only thing that stopped him was the bitter thought that she was probably fucking some other guy about now. *If that's the case*, he pissily thought, *I hope she's having as good a time as I had with Lucy.*

Christ, he was talking to himself now. Lifting the bottle, he eyed the diminishing contents, as if searching for an explanation for his outburst. He was going with the drunkenness defense instead of insanity.

Although, let's face it, he wasn't out of the woods on that front either.

Maybe it was time for his usual mental therapy remedy.

He'd head up north.

The wilderness had always been his refuge and salvation.

He set down the bottle and got to work. Just as dawn was breaking, he gave Tony a call. "Sorry to call so early."

"Don't worry about it. Everything go okay?" Tony had gotten a sketchy overview of Nick's plans before he left.

"Everything's great."

"Because you're loaded."

"Just sorta. Anyway, I'm heading up to my outpost camp on Trygge. Thought I'd let someone know. And if you'd give Chris a call and tell him I'll be back in awhile, I'd appreciate it."

"Not a problem. You saw your plane? I brought it back."

"Yeah. Thanks. I already packed it up."

"Well, listen to the radio reports. If I need to get hold of you, I'll leave a message."

"Will do."

"You're okay now, right?"

"I'm good. I just need a little space." *From memories of Zoe, mostly.* Although, after last night, he was also on the run from Lucy.

Since Nick had needed space more than once since he'd come back, Tony didn't ask any prying questions. He just said, "Keep in touch."

"Yeah."

Five minutes later, Nick took off into the morning sun and as the plane lifted from the water, he felt what he always did when he was on his way north. A demonstrable tranquility, a sense of regeneration, a common accord with nature. Like a modern-day Thoreau.

He smiled at the mawkish sentiment.

Then he smiled again.

It didn't really matter the reasons why.

He was feeling better . . . good in fact.

And the fishing at Trygge was always fantastic.

Forty

Zoe left Chicago a few hours after Nick flew north. Since Willerby was no longer a threat, she was able to return home and so she explained to Rosie, who was so infatuated with her football player she only nodded yes or no or smiled as Zoe talked; she wasn't really listening.

Later that afternoon, when Zoe arrived at the house she'd adored from the first moment she'd seen it five years ago, the familiar, heartwarming sense of safe haven failed to materialize. The modern rendition of a Cape Cod saltbox in a lovely weathered grey seemed inexpressibly empty as she walked from the garage to the back door. Even the grass was slightly yellowed, as though the summer was already waning. It turned out to be the result of a watering ban in effect she discovered after talking to the boy who took care of her yard. But her heavy heart preferred the more melancholy pathos of the passing of summer.

Liberated, independent woman that she was, however, she soon talked herself out of her *Woe is me* gloom. She gave her parents a call, in a position now to tell them everything was going well in her life. And through a scratchy, on-again, off-again signal, everyone was brought up-to-date.

Next, she unpacked, and afterward, she turned on her computer and reviewed her manuscript. As she scrolled through the pages, images and thoughts of Nick kept popping into her mind, and she had to sensibly remind herself that mooning over a guy who probably couldn't even remember her name was completely useless. She had to put the entire episode into perspective.

Or at least that was what mature adults were supposed to do.

What that really meant was living without something you wanted.

But wasn't that what adulthood was all about? Intelligent judgment instead of two-year-old tantrums over a lollipop?

So she put her nose to the grindstone, her shoulder to the wheel, and worked like crazy for the next two weeks. She compared notes with Joe at least ten times a day; he was back in Brooklyn after visiting Mandy. She'd also spoken to Roberto at the TPC and told him that the Willerbys might be interested in negotiations, so he was in touch with her, getting photos from time to time. But interruptions aside, on day fourteen at two a.m., she crossed the last T and dotted the last I on her manuscript.

The first week of July, her work on stolen antiquities was sent off to her publisher and instead of feeling her usual delirious relief at finishing a book, the moment after she closed the door on the FedEx man, she burst into tears. Rattled by her outburst—she was not one to cry for no reason—she stood in her small foyer and tried some calm breathing. But she could never remember if you counted to eight on the inhale and nine on the exhale or the other way around, or maybe it was four in and eight out or, Hell's bells, why not an all-purpose espresso for whatever ails you?

Moving toward her kitchen, she rubbed the tears from her cheeks and speedily shifted into full-fledged rationalization. She reminded herself that this book had been especially fraught with peril—a rare and unwelcome circumstance in her life. She told herself she would feel more serene in a day or so, once she resumed her normal routine. Finishing a book often turned into an arduous marathon with too little sleep and too much coffee.

Maybe she *should* think about reducing her caffeine intake.

Mildly chastened by her strange fit of weeping, she actually tried to cut back on coffee. Instead of an espresso, she took a bottled water out of the fridge and went out on the back porch to drink it. She sat—or more accurately lounged—on her chaise, which was not cushioned in an Hawaiian print fabric her brain improbably noted, and drank her bottled water.

But it tasted like bottled water—not espresso. Wouldn't you know.

Several bland, stimulant-free sips later, she decided that giving up coffee after years of overindulgence was unnecessary and counterproductive to a person as busy as her. Also, her withdrawal symptoms were becoming increasingly manifest and, in terms of her headache, painful. She screwed the cap back on the bottle of water and dashed into the kitchen to make herself an espresso.

Within minutes, she was infinitely calmer—physically and mentally.

Of course, coffee consumption impacts sleep, she told herself, as she tossed and turned in bed that night. The fact that she drank coffee every day and normally slept like a baby was dismissed, as was the possible but unwanted reason why she was all atwitter. *Do not even think the name Nick Mirovic!*

Why not watch one of the many movies there'd been no time to watch? She congratulated herself for hewing to the mature adult construct and directing her agitated senses toward a course of measured self-restraint. One devoid of impractical, fruitless tilting at windmill wishes. Lying back on her pillows, she clicked on the cable guide and selected an Italian film that had garnered fantastic reviews. Unfortunately, no more than ten minutes into the movie she witnessed the most cinematically gorgeous sex scene set in the lush, colorful garden of a Medici palace. She immediately hit the Guide button on the remote and searched for something less viscerally erotic.

Settling on an Irish film that had been touted as a witty, delightful comedy, she lay back once again and pressed the Play button. No one had mentioned that the secondary character of the young priest was not only an Adonis but was also dispensing his handsome favors among the parish ladies. In fact, he was so arrestingly beautiful, she ended up watching the movie for much too long and finally had to put the film on pause and go find her vibrator.

Afterward, nominally orgasmic, but still horny as hell, her

mature adult resolve began to seriously erode. Actually, it disappeared into some black hole with such incredible speed, she literally whispered, *Holy shit*.

Having been raised distant from organized religion—the Amazon tribes preferring nature gods—Zoe accepted such "lo and behold" moments with relative ease—perhaps even a pagan naivete.

Tossing aside her vibrator, she flicked off the TV, rushed to her computer, and pulled up Travelocity. Moments later, she had bought herself a ticket to Ely.

In addition to the obvious bolt from above, she appropriately noted that she'd rented the Skubic place for the entire summer and it was only July. Why shouldn't she take advantage of the remainder of the season in what was lauded as Minnesota's summer paradise by the local chamber of commerce and various and sundry travel sites?

Really, it was silly to deprive oneself of an idyllic summer respite for no good reason.

She was rapidly coming to the conclusion that mature, adult behavior was much, *much* overrated.

The concept was based on obsolete Puritanical notions of duty and virtue. Or was it Methodist or Presbyterian, Catholic perhaps? Hadn't witches been burned at the stake for infringements of such protocols or people punished for dancing or playing cards on Sundays? Not to mention the Inquisition. Really, it seemed that rules of right-minded morality often defied not only logic, but good taste if stretching someone on the rack was the result.

She could choose to be a slave to other people's sense of

propriety or she could set her own standards for personal conduct.

Her philosophical rationalization quickly concluded, she dressed, packed, and drove to Newark airport, the easiest commute. Arriving three hours before her flight gave her the opportunity to have two Starbucks iced lattes, which put her in an even better mood. She didn't even care that the last-minute reservation had cost her an arm and a leg. Nor did she mind that the TSA agents went through her luggage with a fine-tooth comb and frisked her because of her spontaneous travel plans.

Since she had jettisoned all that mature adult crap, she was in a lovely Zen mood—all mellowness and live-for-the-moment bliss. Armed with the *New York Times* and three fashion magazines, she intended to wallow in life's simple pleasures on her coming journey.

Once she reached Ely, she might find some other more definitive pleasures in the form of Nick Mirovic.

Forty-one

Zoe rented a car at the airport in Duluth. In all the recent turmoil and upheavals, she'd not given much consideration to her car, which she'd left behind at Skubic's. She hoped it was still there. She hoped even more that Nick was next door. Her car was insured, after all, while there was no substitute for Nick Mirovic's many charms.

It was yes on her car, she discovered on driving up to the Skubic cabin. And no on Nick being next door, she found out a short time later. No one was in the workshop either. So she drove her rental car to the Enterprise dealer in Ely, told them she'd come back when she needed a ride home, and walked to the Front Porch Coffee Company. Janie would know whatever there was to know in town, including Nick's whereabouts.

But Janie wasn't any help other than knowing that Nick had

gone up the lake. "Tony knows, but he's not saying, which is slightly unusual"—she shrugged—"but not without precedent. Nick and Tony are joined at the hip. They grew up together; Nick and Tony's dads are cousins. Are you staying long?" Janie was already making Zoe's iced triple espresso without asking.

"For a while." Zoe wasn't about to spread out her hopes and dreams on Janie's counter. "I thought the dads might have been brothers," she said, changing the subject, "with Nick and Tony having the same last name."

"Uh-uh. Nick's dad was an only child."

"Tell me about Nick's family. He's not real communicative." Nick had told her about his parents' and grandparents' deaths, but he'd mentioned very little else about his family.

"It looks like he's gotten to you. Not that I'm surprised. He has that effect on most women."

Zoe grimaced. "I don't care to hear about *most women* if you don't mind."

"Gotcha. Did he tell you his parents died in a bizarre snow-mobile accident when he was twelve?" Janie slid the espresso toward Zoe.

"He mentioned it in passing."

"They never found the bodies, but Knife Lake is five hundred feet deep so it's no wonder. Anyway, he lived with his grandparents after that. He learned most of his wilderness skills from his dad or grandpa; as a forester for the Department of Natural Resources, his father spent a lot of time in the back country. Nick lettered in four sports in high school, was president of his senior class, homecoming king, on the honor roll." Janie ticked off his achievements. "But he never had a big head; he was always a nice kid."

It was late afternoon and even at the height of the tourist season, the coffee shop wasn't too busy. Janie waved to her helper to pick up the slack and she sat down to talk about Zoe's favorite subject. Afterward, when she'd run out of factoids, Janie said with a smile, "You'd be a whole lot better for him than Lucy." She wrinkled her nose. "She's a real piece of work. Not that it's any of my business who sleeps with whom."

Reading between the lines, Zoe grimaced faintly. "Nick must have seen Lucy then when he came back."

"Just once. That's all," Janie said, apologetically, in an attempt to partially negate her slip of the tongue. "Lucy's been complaining ever since that he left her in the lurch. As if Nick took her seriously anyway."

"I doubt he takes anyone seriously."

"It might have been his nasty divorce," Janie said, still trying to smooth over her faux pas.

"Or maybe he's just not likely to settle for one woman."

Janie didn't quite meet Zoe's gaze. "I wouldn't say that exactly."

"What exactly would you call his lone wolf mentality?"

Janie shrugged. "He has issues."

"I'm probably as crazy as he is," Zoe muttered, "if I think that I can actually get to him."

"I'm not so sure about that," Janie murmured. "According

to Tony, Nick's never taken anyone up to his outpost camp before."

"He probably didn't have a choice." Zoe didn't know how much to say about the bizarre circumstances.

"Whatever. If I were you, I'd go talk to Tony. He knows where Nick is and if he wants to, he'll tell you."

But when Zoe went to the courthouse and found Tony in his office, he looked at her blankly from behind his desk and said, "I'm not sure where Nick went. He just told me he was going north. Sorry."

"Did he tell you about anything that went on at his Jackfish outpost?"

Another blank look. "Some."

"About Willerby and Harry Miller?"

Tony leaned back in his chair and hesitated for a fraction of a second before he said, "Nick mentioned them."

"Look," Zoe said with a sigh, "I'm not here to stalk him. I'd just like to know that he's all right."

"He sounded good last time I talked to him." Tony didn't say, "Good and drunk."

"Well . . . thanks." Zoe smiled. "I appreciate your time. And if you *should* talk to Nick, you might mention that I'm staying at the Skubic place for the rest of the summer."

Tony nodded.

Zoe lifted her hand. "See ya."

"Yeah, see ya."

Nick's cousin clearly wasn't going to give away anything, Zoe decided as she walked away. *Like Janie said though, it was worth a try.*

Tony wondered if he should send a radio message to Nick and tell him this woman was back in town?

But in the end he didn't.

Nick regarded women as a physical necessity lately, but not much else. Not that Miss Zoe Chandler wasn't easy on the eyes—he certainly understood Nick's wanting her company out in the bush.

But if Nick wanted to see her again, he would have mentioned it.

Forty-two

Nick had been spending his time at Trygge Lake, building a gazebo for reasons that weren't entirely clear. It was something to keep him busy, he told himself, and he didn't have any other use for the lumber stored in the rafters of his woodshed. With no electricity on site, he used only hand tools to construct a small rustic affair perched out on the rocks by the shore. He even hand-split shingles for the roof. There was always a nice breeze from the lake out on the point, but he screened in the gazebo to keep out the mosquitoes at night when the wind died down.

Once he'd put on the screened door with its carved wooden latch, he sat inside the gazebo on one of his handmade chairs and had a drink or two or ten.

He was drinking more than usual, again for reasons that weren't entirely clear.

Since his Trygge camp was devoid of amenities, he chopped his own wood, carried water from the lake, used kerosene for lights and cooking, and pretty much lived like a nineteenth-century settler. He had a battery radio he recharged by pedaling, but otherwise, he was remote from the civilized world.

He listened to the message hour each morning in the event Tony had some news. None came, nor had he expected any. Afterward, he'd resume his building project, go fishing so he had something for supper, swim across the lake, or paddle his canoe a few miles to burn off excess energy.

Just performing the routine chores each day required several hours. Chopping wood, carrying water, washing dishes and clothes by hand, cooking. Since the nights were cold this far north, he stoked the woodstove each night and the sauna stove every few days. He'd always liked saunas, ever since he was a kid—the smell of the pine fire, the soothing heat, the chill lake water that felt like silk on your skin when you dived in straight out of the sauna. He'd always have a beer afterward, lean back on the bench in the changing room, and drift for a time in a narcotic limbo.

At times like that, he might have even found a modicum of peace in his hermitage.

The operative word was *modicum*.

His brain was still in turmoil, haunted by some of the same old bad memories and others more recent and not bad at all— just difficult to absorb or absolve. He wasn't sure which.

So he was drinking a lot.

If he stayed here long enough, he might be reduced to cracking open that ancient bottle of gin brought up here long ago by a friend of his grandpa who drank martinis. But he'd checked his supply the other day, and he was still good for at least another month.

At the same time that Nick was contemplating having to eventually broach the bottle of Plymouth gin, Zoe was busy writing down what she characterized as a sales pitch for Tony Mirovic.

She was choosing her words carefully. She didn't want to come off as either a stalker or a pushy bitch. Her fundamental debate, however, was more about how to explain her motives to Tony and properly define her feelings about Nick. Not that she would be so gauche as to use the actual word *feelings* when talking to the sheriff. She understood that alluding to explicit, meaningful emotion was generally anathema to the male species—especially in this instance, when she and Tony were virtual strangers.

She was way out on a limb here; she and Nick had known each other for such a short time. And Tony knew it.

She certainly couldn't mention anything so bizarre as *love at first sight*. She didn't want to be laughed out of his office. Nor was she entirely sure that was precisely what she felt. But if it wasn't, it was definitely something in the same neighborhood. She couldn't eat or sleep lately—neither issues in the past. Even Janie said to her the other day, "Don't forget to eat, sweetie. You're beginning to look peaked."

If she had any chance of seeing Nick again, the last thing she wanted to look was *peaked*. She wanted to look *fabulous*! So she might have eaten a tad more than necessary once she returned home, but there was a shop in town that made organic ice cream, and she happened to have several pints in her freezer and one thing led to another.

She rather thought she didn't look peaked anymore.

Janie had agreed, telling her the next morning, "If I didn't know better, I'd say you just had sex. Your skin is glowing."

"What do you mean?" Zoe protested. "I *could* have had sex."

Janie gave her an arched brow look. "You and I both know you're waiting for your one and only." Since Zoe's return, Janie had read between the lines, not that it had been all that difficult with Zoe moping over her espresso practically every day.

"Not anymore," Zoe determinedly said, staring Janie straight in the eye. "I'm actually going to do something about it today. I'm going to see Tony and"—Zoe smiled—"give him my sales pitch. Don't laugh. I actually wrote it down last night and practiced."

"It's about time." Janie directed a mom look Zoe's way. "In my experience, the ones you want don't come riding up on a white horse and knocking on your door."

Zoe grinned. "I've reached the same conclusion, although living next door to Nick's empty house has been a huge incentive. I can't stop thinking about him."

"It's probably not just the empty house," Janie drily remarked. "So give me a clue. What are you gonna say?"

"Promise not to laugh."

"Hey—no way I'd laugh. I think you're perfect for Nick. Haven't I been saying that for a long time now?"

"Yeah, thanks . . . you've been great—listening to my whining, bucking up my spirits."

"My pleasure." Janie dipped her head toward the paper Zoe had unfolded.

Zoe shot a quick glance around to see if anyone was close enough to hear, but everyone was at the tables. The counter was empty. "Okay, it goes something like this . . ."

When Zoe finished, Janie was supportive as usual. "You go, girl," she asserted, giving Zoe a high five.

Zoe blushed. "This is still kind of embarrassing, but I'm tired of waiting around and just hoping something will happen."

"You're right. Why wait? Go talk to Tony. What do you have to lose?"

"Not a whole lot considering I've been spending every night watching TV."

"Exactly." Janie glanced at the clock over the door. "You might catch Tony now. He sometimes works on reports in the morning."

The minute Zoe left the coffee shop, Janie reached for the phone. "Just listen, Tony," she said when he answered, "and don't give me any crap. Zoe Chandler's coming over to give you a heartfelt little speech. So do your cousin a favor and tell her where he's holed up. You know as well as I do that Nick's never taken a woman with him up north. So it's not business as usual for him."

"There were extenuating circumstances," Tony gruffly said.

"More reason for him to leave her behind with trouble on his tail. *Capiche?*" Janie knew everything: NASA could only hope to have her access to information.

"I'll think about it."

"What you can think about is Nick killing himself with alcohol somewhere down the line. And it'll be on your head."

"Christ, don't lay that on me."

"It's the freakin' truth. Look, I'll bet you five hundred bucks I can't afford that you and I will be invited to their wedding if you do the right thing."

"Crap."

She knew that meant he was thinking. She knew he was thinking she was right. "Just tell her, okay?"

Caught between a rock and a hard place, Tony was slumped down in his chair, grumpy and out of sorts, when Zoe walked in.

He looked up, saw her sweet smile that went with all the rest of her sweet, blonde, beautiful self, and said, "You know, I was thinking maybe Nick wouldn't mind if I told you where he was."

Her thanks were on-top-of-the-world effusive and so damned enchanting that Tony thought if Nick didn't give this babe a chance, he might be tempted.

"I'll give Jerry Dolan a call," he said, reaching for his phone. "He can fly you up there. I would, but I have to testify in court this afternoon."

Forty-three

At first Nick ignored the sound of a bush plane approaching. This was fishing country; resorts frequently flew their clients north for choice sport. But he took notice when the plane began its descent.

He ran to the cabin to get his binoculars and a rifle.

As the seaplane pulled up to his dock, he watched from his porch. The plane was from Burntside Resort, but that didn't mean anything. Friend or foe could hire a plane, although he didn't think he had enemies left. Even if he did, they wouldn't have come in so boldly.

"Hey, Nick!" Jerry Dolan waved from the dock. "I brought you some company!"

Nick waved back, but he didn't move and his rifle stayed in his hand.

When Zoe stepped out onto the pontoon, he blinked. How many drinks had he had today? Then she smiled and he knew she was for real. Dropping his rifle, he took the porch stairs in a flying leap.

She started running when she saw him.

They met halfway up the mossy grade and came to a stop—both hesitant and uncertain. Neither sure of their welcome.

"Nice company," Nick murmured, speaking first.

"You're a hard man to find. I finally convinced your cousin Tony I'm harmless."

"Not exactly." Nick grinned. "You're the cause of all my discontent."

She smiled. "Maybe I could fix that."

"No doubt."

He opened his arms, she walked into them, and the world disappeared.

Jerry Dolan didn't stick around; he was a polite man. After unloading Zoe's luggage, he shouted good-bye and took off.

"How long can you stay?" Nick murmured, as the plane disappeared into the sun.

"As long as you can stand to have me."

His smile was slow and easy. "That long."

"Yup. So what should we do first?"

"Silly question." His erection was jammed against her stomach.

Her brows rose faintly. "Here or somewhere else?"

"Not here. I must be gettin' old," he wisecracked. "Let me get your luggage and I'll show you my bed."

She followed him to the dock, and helped him carry her bags up the hill. "I hear there's no TV, no lights, no nothing up here. Is this like the last frontier?"

"Depends. I like to think of it as a little bit of heaven"—he shot her a look—"especially now that you're here. And don't worry about the no TV. I'll keep you busy at night."

"Oh, good; I forgot batteries for my vibrator."

He gave her the once-over, jungle fever in his gaze. "You won't be needin' that, babe."

"Perfect." She gave him a sideways glance. "And just in case, I brought condoms."

"I hope you brought a lot. I've been missing you like crazy— not that kind of crazy. Actually, I'm pretty laid-back up here."

He looked it, he sounded like he was, he even smiled differently—less smart aleck, more boyish charm. Although the moment she'd seen him, dressed in his usual cargo shorts and T-shirt with cutoff sleeves—all power and brawn and swarthy beauty—she was a goner, wiseass or not.

He'd let his hair grow; it was longer, his dark, ruffled curls pulled back behind his ears.

"You let your hair grow," she said. Her frontal lobes weren't working and everything she thought, she said.

"I've been lazy. Cut it if you like."

Samson and Delilah, she thought, but thank god she had brains enough not to say it this time. Still, it was sweet of him to make the offer. "It looks good long," she politely said—all civilized constraint—like she hadn't been thinking about his sexy, virile, muscled strength. And how Caravaggio would have really done him justice.

"A gazebo," she murmured, pointing at the new addition to his property as they moved up the path to the cabin. "You've been building." It was obviously new, the smell of cut lumber still in the air.

"I knew you liked the one at Jackfish. Not that you were here—although sometimes it seemed like you were." He shrugged as they moved up the porch stairs. "It doesn't make much sense."

"Ta-da!" she said with a flourish. "Here I am."

He smiled. "Maybe dreams do come true." Reaching out, he opened the cabin door and held it open for her.

The instant she walked in, she smelled the pinks. She scanned the room: there, in a vase on the kitchen table. "I *love* that smell," she breathed, inhaling deeply.

"I know. I was trying to forget you and not wanting to forget you at the same time," he said, setting down her bags. "The flowers reminded me of you."

Dropping her duffle bag, she closed the distance between them in two quick steps and wrapped her arms around his waist. Holding on tight—being where she most wanted to be she decided in a flash of naked instinct—she rested her chin on his chest and looked up. "I probably shouldn't say this, but you're going to have a real hard time getting rid of me." She smiled. "Just a warning." It had taken courage to face Tony and even more to come here uninvited. Now that she was here, she didn't feel like quibbling over her feelings.

"Music to my ears, babe. I was thinking about keeping you prisoner anyway."

Maybe there really are soul mates. "So we're both in a possessive mood," she said, knowing better than to mention the word *soul mates*.

He grinned. "That's a nice way of putting it." His mood was slightly more feudal and proprietary.

This was a case of two people sailing without a compass—going slow and easy when it came to exposing their susceptibility.

"Then you should be nice back to me," she softly said.

Unwrapping her arms from around his waist, he took her hand and pulled her along. "Come on. I'll show you nice."

His outpost camp at Trygge Lake was small, consisting of a single room that served as kitchen and living room, to which was attached a smaller bedroom and a minuscule washroom.

"No plumbing," Zoe murmured, standing beside Nick and surveying the bedroom. "Just like my Amazon days."

"I hope that's not a deal breaker."

"You don't understand, darling," she said, looking up and directing a pointed look his way. "I'm here for the duration."

In the past, he would have run or completely shut down at those words, but instead, her comment warmed his heart, beguiled his romantic sensibilities—long defunct—and induced him to say something he never thought he'd say again, "We should maybe talk about getting married somewhere down the road."

Talk about—somewhere down the road? Against the advice of the little voice inside her head screaming at her to shut up, Zoe put all her cards on the table. "What do you mean—talk about?"

He pulled her around and held her lightly in his arms. "How many languages would you like it explained in?"

"Show-off."

"Okay, marry me."

"Okay."

He grinned. "I love your warm, fuzzy, romantic side."

She smiled. "While I like your really hard . . . just teasing. Look, if you have a couple hours, I'd be happy to tell you every last thing I love about you." Her eyes flared wide for a moment. "Wow. Love." She'd never actually used the word with Nick, thinking more in terms of can't-live-without-him hot sex and feeling *good*. "Are you sure about this getting married stuff?" It was a shockingly lovely idea, but she wasn't altogether certain he hadn't been teasing.

"I'm pretty sure. Unless you dye your hair black and start teaching Slavic languages. That might be a no-go."

"Bad marriage, hey?"

"Turned out that way. I got my divorce papers when I was lying half dead in a hospital bed in Germany."

"Tell me about it," she muttered.

"You're divorced, too? Along with 16.7 percent of the country." He grinned. "I just read that statistic last week."

"In my case, it was good riddance. Max couldn't keep it in his pants. He's on his third marriage and I expect there'll be more."

Nick's brows rose. "Trish is on her third, too. Maybe they know each other."

"Maybe they're married to each other. Wouldn't that be poetic justice?" She had a moment of panic. "How many times have you been married?"

"Calm down, babe." He recognized panic better than most

after his hellish months with Harry. "I've only been married once. How about you?" He was guessing from her recent panicked query she wasn't on number five, but full disclosure never hurt.

"Just once. I don't share well."

"Glad to hear it. Neither do I. In fact, I'm thinking maybe I'll handcuff you to my wrist and keep you close."

"Ummm . . . you sure know how to sweet talk a woman," she murmured in a low, sexy undertone, leaning into his strong, hard body.

He looked at her from under his lashes. "Maybe I mean it."

She grinned. "I should be so lucky."

"It's not as though I haven't had plenty of time to fantasize about you up here. And think about other stuff, too. Maybe that's where the marriage talk came from."

It wasn't to her advantage to be overly inquisitive, but she couldn't help it. "You have to be sure. Not just sort of sure if you're talking marriage."

"I'm sure, babe. You can take it to the bank."

"Speaking of warm fuzzies," she sardonically murmured.

He grinned. "Okay, roses are red, violets are—"

She stood on tiptoe and kissed him, because bottom line, she didn't care about tomorrow or next week or warm fuzzies right now. He was holding her close and that was about as good as it got.

"I'll do warm fuzzies later," he whispered as his mouth lifted from hers, already pulling her T-shirt over her head. "Right after I show you how much I love you."

He was really good at warm fuzzies, too. He actually knew a Robert Herrick poem, and while she was real tempted to ask him *why* he'd happened to memorize those lines, she had sense enough to keep her mouth shut. She would pretend he'd never, ever uttered those words to another woman and continue floating on her soft, pink cloud.

But she was *convinced* he was a master of the warm fuzzies when he undressed her slowly, like he was opening a special Christmas present and had to be careful not to tear the paper or ribbon because he was gonna save them. And afterward, gazing at her lying nude on his bed, he said softly, "I just have to look for a second. I'm still not sure you're for real. Say something."

Then what was even sweeter was when he was lying atop her, resting his weight on his arms like he did so his body was barely touching hers, and he whispered, "If we're going to get married, let's not worry about condoms—okay?"

Wow. That's even more of a commitment than a marriage proposal. "Are you sure?" she whispered back like a complete idiot when the man of her dreams, her Prince Charming, maybe even the most beautiful man on the face of the earth, was asking her to have his child. *Okay, okay, so looks aren't everything, but still* . . . she began picturing a little boy with dark hair or a little girl or wouldn't twins be just perfect—actually a dream come true. She'd always wanted twins or at least a brother and sister. "I want two children," she said, half dizzy with love and half calculating, figuring why not find out now how he felt while the issue of condoms was still under debate.

"Me, too."

"Being an only child leaves a lot to be desired," she said with chagrin.

"What—are we soul mates?"

"Don't joke."

He smiled. "Sorry, I couldn't resist, but it's a great idea. You've got my endorsement. At least two kids."

"Hey, don't get carried away," she protested.

"You're really fun to tease," he said with a wide grin. Then his smile disappeared and he spoke with a solemn gravity she'd never heard before. "It's up to you, darling. One, two, none, whatever you decide. I just want you, that's all."

Tears came to her eyes, and if there really were heart-strings, it felt like hers were being tugged. He was so sweetly earnest in that calm, unruffled way of his that paradoxically only confirmed his intrinsic power and strength. Which also made her weak in the knees, flipped the switch on every one of her sexual receptors, and seriously shifted her focus from conversation to other amusements. "Let's decide afterward," she whispered.

"On?" He was being well-mannered. *Are we still talking about condoms?*

"On the number of children," she clarified.

He grinned. "Because you can't wait."

"You don't know how *long* I've been waiting."

"Oh, yeah, I do. Since May twenty-ninth."

"You remembered," she murmured, smiling sweetly.

"I've really missed you."

She pulled his head down and kissed him hard. "So what

are you waiting for?" she heatedly breathed a moment later. "Show me what you got."

He laughed at the words he'd spoken the first time they made love in his kitchen. And looking back on it now, it probably *was* love even then. Which went to show that *love at first sight* wasn't just fiction.

The consummation of their love that day and night and into the morning was definitely not fictitious. It was profoundly real, passionate, tempestuous, and so stubbornly insatiable that they finally found themselves lying side by side, panting for breath, yet ravenous still.

"What are . . . we . . . gonna do," Nick gasped.

"We . . . have to . . . stop."

"Can't."

"Make me breakfast. I'm starving."

"You gotta be kidding. I'm still burnin' up."

"Please?"

Taking a deep breath, then another, Nick exhaled and said, kind and gallant, "Sure. How about pancakes?"

"I would *adore* pancakes." *Along with you for the next thousand years.* But she didn't say that because any little thing might turn him on and she really was hungry.

Their summer at Trygge Lake was perfection. They lived simply like pioneers in the wilderness and in that purified life, they found a kind of happiness both deep-felt and joyous.

They didn't fly home until the ice started setting on the lake. By that time, they'd come to truly know what love was.

And while maybe it was impossible to completely escape one's past, in time, Nick's nightmares diminished and left him more whole. As for Zoe, her future research projects avoided those areas of the art world where exposés might prove dangerous.

Eventually, the man traps around Nick's cabin were dismantled.

It was the advent of a cloudless, unafflicted reality.

It was visible evidence of the healing power of love.

And two years later, when their twins were born, the young Mirovic family entered a new realm of well-being and contentment.

ML

8/
08